W9-AXT-279

NOBODY'S SWEETHEART NOW
The First Lady Adelaide Mystery

"I don't normally like ghost stories, but who could resist such a real and witty ghost who won't depart and leave his not-at-all grieving widow to get on with life without him. Poor Lady Addie—how is she to enjoy life with her husband's ghost appearing at will and a body at her house party. This 1920s romp is absolutely my favorite cup of tea!"

—Rhys Bowen, award-winning *New York Times* bestselling author

"A lively debut filled with local color, red herrings, both sprightly and spritely characters, a smidgen of social commentary, and a climactic surprise."

—*Kirkus Reviews*

"Set in England in 1924, this promising series launch...is...frothy fun."

—*Publishers Weekly*

"This was one of the most delightful mysteries I've read in quite some time. The mystery plot was well written and kept me guessing until the end. The story was witty and had just the right amount of romance sifted in to keep it interesting without being a romance novel. The characters were well developed and fit the story and setting perfectly. I hope to see more in this series in the future."

—*NetGalley Reviews*

LADY ANNE'S LOVER

"Robinson never fails to provide plenty of brio, banter, and interpersonal heat...Fans of humorous historicals will enjoy this delightful romp."

—Publishers Weekly

MISTRESS BY MARRIAGE

"A very talented debut author."

—Romance Junkies

IN THE ARMS OF THE HEIRESS

"This reviewer was in thrall from page one. Highly recommended."

—Library Journal (starred review)

Nobody's Sweetheart Now

Books by Maggie Robinson

The Lady Adelaide Mysteries

Nobody's Sweetheart Now

Historical Romance

Seducing Mr. Sykes
Redeeming Lord Ryder
Catalyst
Schooling the Viscount
Welcome to Serenity Harbor
Once Upon a Christmas
All Through the Night
The Unsuitable Secretary
The Reluctant Governess
Lady Anne's Lover
Captain Durant's Countess
In the Arms of the Heiress
In the Heart of the Highlander
Holiday for Two: A Duet of Christmas Novellas
Master of Sin
Lord Gray's List
Mistress by Marriage
Improper Gentlemen
Lords of Passion
Mistress by Midnight

Nobody's Sweetheart Now

A Lady Adelaide Mystery

Maggie Robinson

Poisoned Pen Press

Copyright © 2018 by Maggie Robinson

First Edition 2018

10 9 8 7 6 5 4 3 2 1

Library of Congress Control Number: 2018940948

ISBN: 9781464211119   Hardcover
ISBN: 9781464210723   Trade Paperback
ISBN: 9781464210730   Ebook

All rights reserved. No part of this publication may be reproduced, stored in, or introduced into a retrieval system, or transmitted in any form, or by any means (electronic, mechanical, photocopying, recording, or otherwise) without the prior written permission of both the copyright owner and the publisher of this book.

Poisoned Pen Press
4014 N. Goldwater Blvd., #201
Scottsdale, AZ 85251
www.poisonedpenpress.com
info@poisonedpenpress.com

Printed in the United States of America

Cast of Characters

**Residents of Compton Chase,
Compton Under-Wood, Gloucestershire**

Lady Adelaide Compton (Addie), widow of Major Rupert
  Compton, older daughter of the late Marquess of
  Broughton

Major Rupert Compton, ghost

Beckett, Addie's maid

Forbes, the butler

Mrs. Drum, the housekeeper

Mr. McGrath, head gardener

Cook, Mrs. Oxley

Jane, parlor maid

Jack Robertson, Mr. McGrath's grandson

The Weekend Guests

Constance, Dowager Marchioness of Broughton,
  Addie's mother

Lady Cecilia Merrill (Cee), Addie's younger sister

Lord Lucas Waring, viscount, Addie's childhood friend
  and Cotswold neighbor

Eloise Waring, Lucas' orphaned cousin raised at Waring Hall

Pandora Halliday (Pansy), Addie's classmate at Cheltenham Ladies College

George Halliday, Pansy's husband

Sir David Grant, divorced father of three young sons

Kathleen Grant, his ex-wife

Barbara Pryce, Addie's oldest friend and department store heiress

Gerald Dumont, Barbara's (fifth) fiancé

Angela Shipman, Addie's London neighbor on Mount Street

Ernest Shipman, financier, Angela's husband

Colonel Paul Mellard, Rupert's commanding officer and village neighbor

Village Residents

The Reverend Edward Rivers
Constable Frank Yardley
Felix Bergman, retired village doctor

Scotland Yard

Inspector Devenand Hunter
Sergeant Bob Wells
Harry Hunter, Dev's father
Chandani Hunter, Dev's mother

Chapter One

Compton Chase, Compton-Under-Wood,
Gloucestershire, a Saturday in late August 1924

Once upon a time, Lady Adelaide Mary Merrill, daughter of the Marquess of Broughton, was married to Major Rupert Charles Cressleigh Compton, hero of the Somme. It was not a happy union, and there was no one in Britain more relieved than Addie when Rupert smashed up his Hispano-Suiza on a quiet Cotswold country road with Mademoiselle Claudette Labelle in the passenger seat. If one could scream with a French accent, it was Claudette, and it was said her terrified shrieks as they hit the stone wall were still heard on occasion by superstitious farmers and their livestock near midnight when the moon was full.

Addie was just getting used to her widowhood when Rupert inconveniently turned up six months after she had him sealed in the Compton family vault in the village churchyard. The unentailed house was hers to do as she pleased, and she had decided to open it up to her family and a few convivial friends for the weekend now that she'd made some much-needed improvements. Rupert had always been stingy with her money, and with him gone on to his doubtful reward, she had employed most of the district's laborers in an attempt to bring Compton Chase into the twentieth century.

True, it was early in her mourning period to entertain, but she made the concession to wear black, even if there wasn't much of it in yardage, thank God, because it was so bloody hot. And her mother was there to chaperone.

When Rupert appeared, Addie was dressing for her house party, and dropped the diamond spray for her hair on the Aubusson.

"That dress is ridiculous, Addie," Rupert intoned from a dim corner. He was wearing the dark suit with the maroon foulard tie she'd had him laid out in, and apart from being rather pale, was still a handsome devil, emphasis on the devil. If he'd been in his uniform, she might even contemplate marrying him again.

Oh, she was going mad. Too much stressing over the seating arrangements in the dining room. Who was billeted next to who. Or was it whom? She'd tried to make it easy for those who wished to be naughty tonight to be successful. Then there was the bother over her sister turning vegetarian and ruining the menus at the last minute. Cook was cross and was apt to get crosser.

Addie was already sitting at her vanity table so she didn't collapse alongside the diamonds. She shut her eyes.

"I'll be here when you open them. And believe me, it's no picnic for me, either."

Addie did open them, and her mouth, but found herself incapable of uttering anything sensible.

"Yes, I'm back. But, one hopes, not to stay. Apparently, I have to perform a few good deeds before the Fellow Upstairs will let me into heaven. It will be a frightful bore for you, I'm sure."

She told the truth as she knew it, feeling absurd to even speak to someone who couldn't possibly be there. "You're *dead*."

"As a doornail. What does that mean, anyway? The expression dates from the fourteenth century. Langland, Shakespeare, and Dickens all used it. Dickens was of the opinion that a coffin nail is deader, but there you are."

Addie reached for her cup of cold tea and downed it in one

gulp, wishing it was gin, brandy, anything to make Rupert go away. But if she were drunk, more Ruperts, like those fabled pink elephants, might actually appear. It was a conundrum.

"I'll try to stay out of your hair as much as possible. Speaking of which, thank God you haven't cut it into one of those awful shingles. I always did like your hair."

Addie's hand went up involuntarily to the golden roll she'd so recently pinned up without her maid's assistance. Beckett was seeing to Addie's impulsive sister Cecilia, who, apart from her sudden conversion to vegetarianism, *had* cut her hair into a bob that was more or less untamable because of the stubborn Merrill curls. Beckett had her work cut out for her. Cee resembled someone who had stuck their finger in the newly rewired sockets of Compton Chase and lived to tell the tale.

"What's wrong with my dress?" Addie asked, peeved. Though she knew he wasn't truly there—that he was *dead*—he still had the ability to irritate her, even in her imagination.

"It's far too flimsy and sheer and short. I can practically see your nipples if I squint hard enough. I admit you do have lovely legs, but everyone and his brother doesn't have to see them. Your father would not be pleased."

"My father is dead." Panicked, she looked around her bedroom. "My God, he's not going to turn up too, is he?"

"Only one ghost at a time, I believe. I'm still not entirely conversant with the rules. It's been a confusing few months."

"It's the very latest style," Addie said to herself—and *only* to herself—tugging down the beaded skirt. It really could have been much shorter. She'd had it sent over from Paris after a flurry of letters and telegrams back and forth from Charles Frederick Worth's grandson Jacques, who had recently taken over the famous fashion house. Addie had sketched the initial design herself, not that she had any pretensions to become a couturier. A marquess' daughter was supposed to be decorative, and possibly witty and wise, but never *work*.

"I don't like it, but then so little appeals to me nowadays. *Ennui* is my middle name, but I hope this little visit changes things up. Who have you put in my room? That bounder Waring?"

"I understand it takes one to know one. Lucas is not a bounder, as *you* must know. Why am I talking? You are not here."

Lucas was, in fact, assigned a bedroom across the hall. Addie didn't trust a mere connecting door to stay shut all night long, and in her well-run household, servants were apt to be scurrying down the corridor at any moment at a guest's whim, discouraging all attempts of Addie's to be naughty herself. She was not ready to be a merry widow anyway, despite Lucas' tentative blandishments. Rupert wasn't cold in his grave.

Apparently, Rupert wasn't *in* his grave.

Rupert smiled ruefully. Could an apparition be rueful? Or was Addie really unconscious, perhaps on her deathbed, suffering from heat stroke or a regular stroke or some kind of tea-induced hallucination? Cook could easily have put poisonous leaves in the pot in retaliation for the menu adjustments. She was set in her ways, and had been at Compton Chase since the dawn of time.

Addie had only just turned thirty-one, much too young to die in the usual course of things. However, the past few months had been more than difficult for her too, even apart from Rupert's death.

"I admit I bounded in my time. Poor Addie. I wasn't much of a husband, was I?"

"Please go away. I haven't time for this." In ten minutes, there would be a dozen houseguests downstairs in the Great Hall admiring its two-story, multi-paned window and having cocktails without her, and Lord knows, she needed one. Or three. She bent over, picked up the pin and stuck it behind an ear.

"Tut. Let me help you with that." Before she could say a word, she felt his hands in her hair. Cold hands. Really quite icy. He moved the diamonds over a few inches, and she began to see spots dance the tarantella before her eyes.

Good. She was going to faint and stop all this. Addie knew how to faint like a champion—her mother, the Dowager Marchioness of Broughton, a short but formidable woman, had indoctrinated both her daughters in all the ladylike accomplishments. She slid with ease off her slipper chair to the thick carpet and waited to black out, knowing her limbs to be in perfect order, and the hem of her dress where it should be, not riding up to show Rupert her French silk knickers.

Not that he'd care.

"Dash it, Addie! You have more spine than this! I recognize the situation is hardly ideal, but you're stuck with me for the foreseeable future, so buck up, my girl. I'll leave you alone for now, but look for me before bedtime for a little chat. No finky-diddling with that Waring chap, no matter how much he bats those baby-blues in your direction. I know what he's up to—you're a rich and attractive widow, ripe for the fuc—um, plucking. Don't fall for his innocent act."

"I've known Lucas since I was six years old. He *is* innocent," Addie said from the floor. You couldn't find a nicer man than Lucas, not that she'd tried. No, she'd allowed herself to be lured away by Major Rupert Charles Cressleigh Compton of Compton Chase, an ancient Jacobean pile in dire need of restoration. The house, not Rupert. Rupert had been unbearably handsome and fit and had shone with good health and bonhomie. If he could live through the horrors of the Great War, he should have lived forever, were it not for too many French 75 cocktails, unnecessary speed, and that Cotswold stone wall.

"That's what he wants you to believe. All men are the same, perfect hounds."

"You're giving dogs a bad name." Idly, she wondered where her terrier Fitz was. Would he be able to see Rupert, or would he be barking at the shadows? Fitz had never met Rupert; he was Cee's crackpot idea of a mourning present and arrived with a big black bow around his scrawny neck a week after the funeral. The fleas in her bed had been an unforeseen complication.

Fitz's neck was thicker now, the fleas a distant memory. Addie supposed that since she had no children, the dog was the next best thing to distract her from her lonely state.

She wasn't lonely now. There were far too many people in her house for comfort, starting with the man who was disappearing right in front of her. Going, going…

Absolutely gone.

She swallowed back a little cry and struggled to sit up, the room still spinning a bit. That afternoon nap hadn't helped. It had been a long day, perhaps way too hot to play tennis. Far too much sun had roasted her cheeks and brought out her freckles. She was rubbish at tennis anyhow, being too vain to wear the glasses Dr. Bergman had prescribed before he retired two years ago. Maybe if she put those glasses on—

Addie leaped up and rummaged through the dressing table drawer. Wrapped in an embroidered lace handkerchief, the dratted tortoise shell spectacles were still as ugly as ever. But they would help her see clearly, wouldn't they? To *not* see things or dead husbands that really weren't there. The mirror came into focus and she noticed at once that the diamond pin was dangling from a strand of loosened hair. She'd have to start again, this time with no assistance from the man who'd made their five-year marriage a living hell.

Ha. So he thought he'd eventually wind up in heaven? It would take more than "a few good deeds" to send him to the front of the queue. If he hadn't died six months ago, Addie might have been tempted to shoot him herself. Her father had done his bit and taught her and Cecilia all the *un*ladylike accomplishments, and when she wore her glasses, she was a very fair shot.

Addie had been vastly tired of the faux sympathy she received from her so-called friends as she tried to hold her head up and pretend Rupert was a faithful husband. Despite the potential scandal, the exhortations of her mother, and reservations of her sister, she'd been close to demanding a divorce from Rupert when he'd skidded off the slippery road with that French wh—hussy.

She pulled out all the pins with a certain amount of vicious-ness, her hair tumbling down her bare shoulders and catching on the jet and sequins and cobwebby lace. Picking up the silver-backed brush, she tried to smooth the curls and her life back into some semblance of control.

By God, she was going to need something more than a hair-brush.

Chapter Two

"What on earth have you put on your face?"

If she had been wearing her own cheaters, Constance, the Dowager Marchioness of Broughton, wouldn't have to ask such a silly question. All the women in the family were plagued by poor eyesight, but Addie's father had forbidden them from visibly correcting their vision while he was alive—he liked his women to be pretty, posh, and perfect. If he couldn't have sons, then his exquisite blond daughters and enchanting blond wife must be the envy of his set. So what if they had the occasional bruise from bumping into things, or an inability to find a valuable dropped earring on the Oriental rug before it was hoovered up?

"My glasses, Mama. I was getting a headache." A tall one named Rupert, well over six feet, with dark hair and dark eyes and that stupid tickly mustache that made him look like a gigolo. Or Ramon Novarro, if one really reached for comparison. Addie wasn't much for the cinema, but her maid Beckett kept her abreast of the latest sensations and left her magazines all over the house. Even when the coal strike froze patrons in the theaters three years ago, Beckett borrowed Addie's second-best fur coat, attended loyally twice a week, and reported reel-by-reel. Addie knew who the current heartthrobs were, not that she'd ever fall in love with a handsome man again.

A plain one either.

"You'll never catch another husband looking like a frump," her mama complained.

"I don't want another husband." Addie was sure she meant it. If one marriage could make her lose her mind, then what would two do? She took a sip of sherry to calm her nerves.

She had decided that she'd been sleepwalking earlier, kind of in a waking dream state, even if she'd been sitting down. She'd always had a full fantasy life, had she not? Playing fairies in the woods around Broughton Park with little Cee, sure every dragonfly was a sign. Believing in Father Christmas long past his prime. Thinking her pony could talk if she listened hard enough. Keeping Rupert faithful if she anticipated his every need. The latter had proved more difficult than communicating with bugs or horses. French silk knickers couldn't do it all.

Addie's inadvertent summoning of Rupert was an indication that she'd overdone in all her planning. Spent too much time in the hot sun chasing a tennis ball, too. Hot weather made people go crazy; everyone knew that. There were riots and uprisings and crimes of passion and murders. Addie didn't have any idea how a proper English person could survive in India or the Argentine; she had enough trouble right here at Compton-Under-Wood, where the weather was temperate, if a little rainy.

The French doors to the garden were open to let in a pleasant breeze. Now that the sun was setting over the Cotswold Hills, the air was cooler, and her guests looked comfortable, having moved from the impressive Great Hall to the more modest proportions of the drawing room for the second round of drinks. There were squashy sofas to sit on just in case one's liquor consumption had gone to one's head, and more substantial nibbles were being passed around while they waited for Forbes to announce dinner.

Rupert wasn't lurking in any corner of the freshly papered space. Wallpaper had gone out of fashion during the war because of the paper shortage, but the drawing room now had sedate cream and gold stripes on the walls, with a few modern paintings that were just avant-garde enough without being inscrutable.

Addie had convinced noted decorator Elsie de Wolfe to help her with the renovations, and was very pleased with the results.

She wondered what Rupert would have thought of the redecoration. More than half the rambling house was still shut up—Addie was not made of money, despite what everyone thought—but on the whole she was glad she was able to bring new life to the old place. It wasn't too modern; that would have been sacrilege. The house had been in Rupert's family for generations, hopscotching between uncles and cousins and grandmothers. Rupert's own granny had left it to him when she died right before the war, and Addie had been brought here as a youngish bride after.

Then it had been cold and cheerless, its furniture rotting, the carpets moth-eaten, the curtains shredding, a definite smell of rheumatism liniment and mouse everywhere. Addie had done what she could at the time, but Rupert was far more interested in collecting motor cars to put in the newly repurposed stables. If he'd purchased a decent period dining table instead of the Hispano-Suiza, he might be sitting at the head of it tonight, she thought somewhat unkindly.

Addie supposed at some point she should try to sell the house back to one of Rupert's relatives, but for now she was very much enjoying being the lady of the manor. Her spacious flat in London was gathering dust, and her friends there had wondered if she had died right along with Rupert. Thus the reason for the house party.

"Who are these people?" her mother asked myopically. She hadn't joined them at lunchtime, pleading her own headache.

There would be thirteen at dinner, unlucky, but it couldn't be helped. Edward Rivers, the young vicar from the village, had bowed out at the last minute, claiming he was sitting with an ailing parishioner. Addie had no reason to disbelieve him, but she remained annoyed at the unknown parishioner's thought-lessness in falling ill when she'd gone to all this trouble to get the numbers right.

"You know most of them. Lucas, of course. His cousin, Eloise. The Shipmans—he's a financial wizard in London and they live next door to me on Mount Street. The man by the fireplace talking to Pansy and George is Colonel Mellard, who was Rupert's commanding officer. You met him at the funeral. Barbara and her new fiancé."

Addie couldn't remember the name of this one. There had been four previous fellows. Two had died in the war and two had discovered their feet were very cold, and no amount of Barbara's money spent on socks would alleviate the problem. Barbara was not the easiest of fiancées or friends, but Addie was nothing if not loyal.

Her mother sighed. "I wish you hadn't invited David Grant."

Addie had deliberately not pointed him out. "Cee likes him."

"That is the problem, Adelaide. Surely you know my objections."

Yes, she did. Sir David Grant was divorced, with three young sons. His ex-wife Kathleen was so infamous he'd had no trouble about the custody of the children. And he was almost fifty, far more suited to Lady Broughton than her twenty-five-year-old daughter.

"You know as well as I do, if you forbid her, she'll think she loves him all the more. She hasn't met the children yet. That might put her off." Three boys! Addie shuddered. Not that girls were any better, or at least she and Cee hadn't been. Addie had done her best to lead her little sister astray from the time Cee could crawl.

Her mother launched into the speech Addie had heard several times already over the past few days. "This house party is all very ill-advised. In my day, one mourned one's deceased husband for two solid years before one allowed oneself any sort of amusement. I don't know what the world is coming to. You young people with your cacophonous music and barely-there skirts—smoking and lip rouge! It's a very good thing your father is dead."

No, it wasn't. Addie had a feeling her papa would get right into the swing of things. He'd always enjoyed a glimpse of a lady's ankle. And after the privations of the war and the misery of all those young men's deaths, followed by the fatal sweep of influenza, wasn't it past time for some fun? A whole generation lost. But she said nothing, just took another sip of sherry and watched as one of the maids passed around a silver tray of shrimp toasts and olives.

"Your sister will be the end of me yet. Do you know she's joined the Vegetarian Society? I ask you, lentil cutlet in tomato sauce! Plum pudding without the suet! She wants me to tear up my flowerbeds at the Dower House and expand the kitchen garden. I won't do it."

Addie had heard this story too. "Of course you won't. Flowers bring you so much pleasure," she murmured. Her own simple borders were at their peak, the scent of lavender wafting in through the open windows. Since the war, Compton Chase's gardens had been turned over to vegetables, first for the country, then for the household. Cee would approve. With just one elderly man and a handful of village boys to help, flowers were an indulgence. Addie had spent almost as much time on her knees this spring as her gardener Mr. McGrath.

Sometimes she'd been praying. For what, she wasn't sure.

"You need to talk to her. It will come better from you."

Addie raised a plucked eyebrow. "It?"

"You know. Sisterly advice. What she owes the family name. Her appropriate place in the world. She's going to waste away like those suffragettes who starved themselves in prison and had to be force-fed. People already think she's peculiar since she reads so much. What she needs is red meat and a good rogering. But not from David Grant."

Addie nearly spit out her sherry at her mother's bluntness. Prior to this evening, Lady Broughton had been a staunch proponent of virginity. Addie remembered the endless lectures from her pre-war debutante days, and had mostly heeded them until Rupert came along. "I'm hardly an expert in anything, Mama. How can I advise Cee, or anyone?" An hour ago, she was under the influence of a powerful mania that made her doubt her very sanity.

"You made what looked like an excellent marriage, on paper at any rate. Rupert was perfectly desirable. Charm personified. Eton. Cambridge. A decorated war hero. Related, distantly I admit, to the Duke of Sheringham. The Comptons are one of the oldest families in England. Why, the whole village is named for them. In another era, people wouldn't have blinked even once at Rupert's indiscretions."

"I did a lot of blinking, Mama." Glasses or not, the evidence of Rupert's perfidy was strewn across the county.

Her mother patted her bare arm. "A man was meant to have his way in the old days, although if your father had got up to a quarter of Rupert's hijinks, I would have resorted to a dull kitchen knife. You kept your head and composure and have nothing to be ashamed of."

And consequently hadn't been hanged for mariticide. "Well, we've moved on, haven't we? It's a new age. If you'll excuse me, I need to move on at the moment and circulate amongst my guests again."

"Of course, dear. You always do the right thing, except for this party. Now if only your sister could follow in your footsteps."

Little chance of that. Cee had a mind of her own now, erratic as it sometimes was. Addie wondered if Sir David and his sons would settle her down.

Did the man know he was in Cee's hunting grounds? He was speaking to Eloise Waring, and looked rather weary, circles under his dark eyes. His light brown hair was fading to white, giving him a bleached-out look, and beneath his summer tan, his skin had a gray cast.

Perhaps he'd been up all night with one of his children—did divorced fathers do that? He had to be both parents now, not that

Kathleen had ever been much of a mother. Addie didn't know her well—well enough to know they had little in common—but Rupert had known her *quite* well. If she could ask him, he'd probably be able to describe her every mole and freckle.

"A heart-shaped spot right next to her left nipple. It was very intriguing."

Addie dropped her glass. Rupert yanked her back so that her new frock wouldn't be splashed with Amontillado, and she nearly screamed.

"Sorry," he whispered in her ear. "I couldn't help myself. Aside from your blood-thirsty mama's hair-raising revelations—dull knife, indeed—this party is putting me to sleep, my dear. I'll leave you to it."

Addie looked behind her. There was nothing but a table and a lamp on it whose fringe wiggled very slightly.

Lucas rushed across the room and clasped her empty hands. "Are you all right? You look like you've seen a ghost."

"Ah…silly me. The glass slipped right out of my fingers. I must be getting arthritis at my advanced age." She waved to one of the maids and pointed to the stain on the new carpet. Fortunately, the heavy Waterford glass had not shattered.

"Nonsense. If you're ancient, what does that make me? I'm three months older. You're as fresh as springtime! That dress is awfully, um, becoming. I expect your mama doesn't like it much."

"She didn't say. You don't think it's too short, do you?" *Rupert* was not here. Rupert *was* not here. Rupert was *not* here. Rupert was not *here*. Rupert was nowhere, as it should be.

"I think you may wear anything you want," Lucas replied, ever the diplomat.

Lucas would always support her decisions. He had a history of it. Whether it was locking Cee up in the family chapel or climbing the tallest tree in Broughton Wood, Lucas was right by her side in her every youthful endeavor. Why hadn't she married him?

Well, the truth was, he'd never asked.

Chapter Three

Dinner lasted an agonizingly long time. Cook had outdone herself, but Cee's running description of all the vegetarian dishes and their health benefits rather put a pall on those chewing their creamed chicken. Barbara was obviously bored to death, even though Addie had placed her fiancé right next to her as she'd requested. She lit cigarettes between courses, earning glares from Addie's mother, especially when she stubbed one out into the pea-studded aspic, even after John the footman placed an ashtray at her elbow. The quivering mass of jelly was bad enough without a lipsticked Lucky Strike stuck into it.

Barbara seemed especially high-strung this evening. She'd changed the color of her hair again, and no subtle candlelight could douse the flaming red of her sleek bob. Addie suspected she was on something beyond the Sidecars she'd had at the cocktail hour, and almost regretted asking her down for the weekend.

Perhaps she could collar Whatshisname—ah, Gerald, that was it—and have a frank chat with him about the care and feeding of her oldest friend. Barbara, like everyone, deserved some happiness. Four fiancés and a huge fortune were a high hurdle for anyone to overcome.

Her other guests were also in sharp focus, thanks to Addie's tortoise shell cheaters. Pansy Halliday was flushed and a little loud, for her. Too much wine. She really should know better; she'd never had a head for spirits, even when she and Addie were sneaking in sloe gin at Cheltenham Ladies College as teens. Across the table, Pansy's husband, George, was pretending not to notice his quiet wife's sudden exuberance, giving Angela Shipman his undivided attention. Angela's husband was a financier—maybe George was trying to winkle out the Next Big Thing on the Exchange. Pansy hadn't said, but Addie suspected the Hallidays had hit a rough patch. Pansy was in a dress from two years ago, and had cut her dark hair herself, possibly wearing a blindfold. Perhaps there was something to Rupert's dismissive attitude toward the latest hairstyles.

Good grief. What was she thinking? Rupert had said nothing about hair because he was *dead*.

At the end of the table, Colonel Mellard was relating a rose-grafting mishap to Addie's mother, who appeared fascinated. Good. Things were going just as Addie had hoped. Her mother had been widowed now for four years and it was time to get her out of black—she was outdoing Queen Victoria in her devotion to her late husband. Herbert Merrill, Marquess of Broughton, had been a capital fellow—Addie ached with missing him—but life was short and her mother was still young enough to enjoy herself with a kind, intelligent man. The colonel had been a godsend to Addie when Rupert died, making most of the arrangements and fluffing over the exact nature of the accident. He'd moved to Compton-Under-Wood on the strength of his friendship with Rupert, once he'd left the army three years ago, and had been a wonderful source of strength these past six months.

Cee and Sir David were talking so quietly—hopefully, not about vegetables—that Addie couldn't catch a thing. Dessert had been served—orange soufflés—and judging from the scraped plates it looked like it was time to leave the gentlemen to their port and walnuts.

Addie opened her mouth, but felt a cold breath on the back of her neck. "I wouldn't break this up just yet. You'll miss the fireworks."

"Wh-what?" Addie stuttered. This was too much. She would have to make an appointment with a psychiatrist in London first thing on Monday. Dr. Bergman might refer her. Even though he was technically retired, he still read medical journals, and he'd said once that he'd met Freud himself in their native Vienna. Addie could take the train up, do some shopping. Beckett could go to a matinee *and* a double feature.

"I didn't say anything, Addie," Lucas said. "Sorry, lost in thought. I'm not a very good dinner partner tonight."

"Neither am I. Perhaps this weekend was ill-considered. It's— it's too soon to have a party."

Lucas laid a hand over hers. "You've been a brick, Addie. No one could fault you for wanting your family and oldest friends close. I know I shouldn't speak ill of the dead, but after all that Rupert did to hurt and humiliate you, you are entitled to our support."

"Suck up. Lord, how can you stand his bloody Boy Scout earnestness? He reminds me of a blocky yellow Labrador. Too stupid to know he's in the way, looking vacuous, tongue out, tail wagging."

"Be quiet!" Addie said. Not to Lucas.

Lucas removed his hand instantly. "I've overstepped. Of course you don't want to talk about…it."

"No, I don't. Sorry for snapping." This was becoming intolerable. Should she find an exorcist as well as a psychiatrist? Addie was desperate enough to hold an impromptu séance right here at the table to get rid of the annoying voice in her head, but she didn't believe in such fol-de-rol.

Her butler, Forbes, was gliding toward her with more dignity and deliberation than usual, probably wondering why she hadn't risen. He was the best of butlers—she'd pinched him from Broughton Park when her cousin Ian had inherited, much to Ian's dismay. Served him right for the iniquities of primogeniture.

"Lady Adelaide," Forbes said, bending over, "might I have a word?"

"Of course."

"Out in the hallway, if it's not too much trouble."

Addie's heart jumped. Heavens. Had Cook gone after someone with a cleaver? Was Rupert haunting one of the pretty young housemaids? He'd not soiled his nest before, but apparently anything could happen today.

Rupert snorted behind her chair. "Give me some credit, love. I've learned my lesson. I'm on an Improvement Plan, remember?"

Addie squelched the impulse to stick her fingers in her ears, excused herself and followed Forbes outside the room.

"What is it?"

"Perhaps you should sit down, my lady."

Addie recalled the icy February night the last time he'd said those words to her. Well, Rupert was already dead, and the only people she loved or really liked were in her dining room.

Except for Fitz and Beckett! She sank into the chair he'd pushed toward her, his face all solicitation.

"Tell me. It can't be worse than what I'm thinking." She'd grown very fond of the little scamp, and furry Fitz was dear to her as well.

"I'm afraid a body has been found in the tithe barn. A, ahem, a naked body." His cheeks colored. "Two of the estate employees were, uh, out, uh, walking when they discovered it. They had the evening off, Lady Adelaide. No one was shirking their duties and taking advantage, you can be sure."

"A body! Who is it? Have you called Constable Yardley?"

"Not as yet. Mrs. Drum and I thought—well, it's a delicate matter. I have not seen it for myself, as I was serving in the dining room, as you know, but Mrs. Drum took the liberty to walk back across the south lawn with some torches, and two of the grooms for protection. They were accompanied by Fred Johnson from the Home Farm—I'm afraid his female friend, Josie Allen, was unable to bear the sight again and is gulping Cook's tea as though India was shutting down all exports, and blubbering more than she should. Center of attention, she wants to be."

Forbes' disapproval was evident. He might stumble upon a hundred naked bodies but never let his emotions get the better of him. "She works in the dairy and Fred is a cowman. Things have reached their inevitable conclusion, I'm afraid."

"Never mind about the course of true love, Forbes! Who is the dead person? Not one of our servants or neighbors, I hope?"

Forbes cleared his throat. "Mrs. Drum thinks not. In fact, she is fairly certain that the woman is, or rather was, Lady Grant, that is, the former wife of Sir David Grant. She has been a guest in this house before."

Addie felt cold all over, and it had nothing to do with any ghostly presence. "Kathleen Grant? Here? But I didn't invite her!"

"Of course not," Forbes said soothingly. "May I get you a brandy? You're very pale."

"No. I've got to keep my wits about me. Do you think—was it natural causes?" And where exactly were her clothes?

"Mrs. Drum is an excellent housekeeper, but no doctor, my lady. However, she thinks not, from the position of the body. I shall be happy to ring the proper authorities, if Frank Yardley can be called such. Dr. Bergman, as well, though he's too late to do any good. One of the grooms is with Lady Grant now. I did think Sir David ought to be informed first, however."

"Y-yes, you're right." How would Sir David take it? She knew what it was like to have lived with an unfaithful spouse. Divorce was still frowned upon by everyone who mattered, especially the Anglican Church. Now Cee might marry Sir David at Compton St. Cuthbert's with a lesser breath of scandal. He no longer had a living wife.

What was she thinking? The scandal would be worse! His ex-wife, dead—and nude—in Addie's barn during a dinner party! While they were munching on canapes, the poor woman might have been gasping her last breath and no one knew a thing.

Suddenly she felt every hairpin poking into her scalp. "How did she get here, I wonder? There's no extra car on the drive."

"She may have walked from the train station, Lady Adelaide. Or taken a taxi. She lived in London after the divorce, didn't she?"

"I believe so. Maybe she tried to visit the boys and found out Sir David was here for the weekend." His manor house, Holly Hill, was at the edge of the next village, less than two miles away. Addie couldn't see Kathleen walking on the dusty lanes in her usual high-heeled shoes, however. Pretty, vivacious Kathleen had been a fashion plate come to life.

And now she was dead.

Chapter Four

"Please ask Sir David to join me out here, and then make all the calls you need to," Addie said, removing her glasses and rubbing the bridge of her aristocratic-if-freckled nose. She'd not been lying earlier about headaches. Since Rupert's death, she'd been prone to more of them than she'd ever suffered in her thirty-plus years. She had attributed the twinges as a sensitive response to the smell of new paint or the stain on the sanded floors or the wallpaper paste. The lack of sleep, the loss of appetite, the paperwork dealing with an estate as complicated as Compton Chase. Whatever Rupert's faults, he'd managed to bring it back from the brink, and Addie felt a responsibility to be at least as good a steward as he'd been.

"Why, thank you. Faint praise, but praise."

She put her glasses back on, and there he was, lounging against the wall. "I don't understand, Rupert. Do you know everything I'm thinking?"

"Not everything, thank God—the female mind remains a mystery, despite all the time I've spent trying to get to the bottom of it. To get to someone's bottom, at any rate. I'm not a bit clairvoyant. Sometimes I pick up the odd phrase here and there. It's rather like static on a radio most of the time. But with you, I've become sensitive to changes in the astral atmosphere and can read you loud and clear. This murder—"

"Murder!" Addie gasped. "No one's said anything about murder!"

"Well, they wouldn't yet. But trust me on this; I feel it in my bones. Perhaps this is why I've been sent back here, to become a spooky sort of Sherlock Holmes and solve the case. But I refuse to don the deerstalker hat—it would muss my hair, and hair tonic is in short supply where I've been. It's apt to get very awkward, Addie. Be careful." With that, he faded into the wood paneling, his hair brushed back just as the undertaker had pomaded it.

Ah, well, she'd had a good life. A family that had loved her and provided every material advantage. Loyal friends. An attractive husband who'd pursued her with a flattering single-mindedness until he didn't. If she was going mad or had some sort of brain disease, the good still outweighed the bad. She was ready to meet her Maker if she had to. That would stop Rupert in his tracks, wouldn't it? She doubted they'd wind up in the same place.

"Lady Adelaide, you wanted to see me?" Sir David loomed over her, looking a tad anxious. Despite the length of their acquaintance and mixed history, they were still somewhat formal with one another.

"Yes, I did. Why don't you pull up that chair?"

"This sounds serious. Wait, it's not my boys, is it? Has something happened to them?" He was poised to run out the front door.

"No, no. I'm sure your children are all right." Goodness. Were they? They might be lying in their beds, throats cut. Smothered with goosedown pillows, their faces blue. Addie pushed the gruesome image out of her mind. She was indeed going quite barmy. "Please sit down." It gave her neck a crick to look up at him.

"But I'm afraid I do have some bad news," she began, once he was seated. She reached a hand out to him. "Your wife's body—Kathleen's body—was discovered this evening on my property."

"Body? Do you mean she'd dead?"

Addie nodded. "I'm so very sorry."

Sir David stood up, his dark eyes sparking. "Are you? I'm not! I won't lie, even if I should. Where is she? How did she die?"

"I don't know the details. She was found in the tithe barn by two young lovers tonight. Hardly the outcome they were expecting. Forbes is calling the constable and Dr. Bergman."

"Bergman? He doesn't practice anymore, does he?"

"No, but I'm sure his observations will be useful until someone else is sent." Addie realized her house was about to be descended on by suspicious official strangers, and shivered. Her mother was right—she never should have hosted this house party. Now her guests would be trapped here for who knew how long while clumsy policemen interviewed anyone they could get their hands on, from the few maids she had left to the Dowager Marchioness. If her mother had been displeased before, she was about to go off like one of the Kaiser's incendiary bombs.

Murder. Could Rupert be right? Or had she just read three new Agatha Christie books too fast and her temporary derangement had let loose all of her scattered and bloodthirsty thoughts? If she got through the next few days, Addie vowed to go to the south of France, sit on a beach, and pretend she'd never heard of Rupert Compton or Kathleen Grant, dead or alive. She'd go to Paris, have tea at Ladurée, and order too many Worth gowns in person.

And maybe even find a French lover.

"I should go to her," Sir David said, not sounding especially keen.

"That's probably not a good idea. A groom is guarding her, and the fewer disturbances to the scene, the better."

He gave her a sharp look. "You appear to be well-versed in this kind of business, Lady Adelaide."

"I read a great deal of crime fiction for amusement. Not that I'm saying a crime has been committed," she said hurriedly. "It's just best to be cautious."

"You're probably right. Good God, my boys. They'll be devastated. They loved her despite everything." He sat back down in the chair and ran a hand through his hair. His earlier bravado was inching away, and he looked more exhausted than ever.

"It's much too late to tell them tonight. And you'll want to know more, I'm sure."

"Will I?" he asked, bitter. "Sometimes it's best to be ignorant when it comes to Kathleen."

Addie knew the feeling. Heart-shaped moles! "Was she in good health, Sir David?"

"I presume so. The last few times I saw her she looked like the cat who'd gotten a monopoly on all the cream in the kingdom. She was a beautiful woman. Too beautiful for her own good. And mine. I really don't know what I was thinking when I asked her to marry me. Or what she was thinking when she said yes. It was a disaster from the outset." He covered his face with his hands.

Were they the hands of a murderer? Addie shivered. "I expect you'd like to go up to your room. I'll explain things to the other guests and let you know when the constable arrives."

He glanced up at the elaborate plasterwork on the ceiling. "I don't know anything—why she was here. I never told her *I* would be. I hadn't really made my mind up until the last minute, as you know. It seemed silly sleeping here when my own bed is just over the hill. And I hate to leave the boys. They've had enough disruption."

From what Addie understood, they were the disruptors. What one didn't think of, the next one did. "You have an excellent governess in Miss Patterson. If you need anything—aspirin, a cup of tea, or something stronger, please don't hesitate to ring."

She watched as Sir David mounted the broad staircase, his shoulders stooped. Even if he hadn't loved his wife anymore—hadn't even *liked* her—it was still a great shock.

She knew this from experience.

Smoothing her gown down, she opened the door to the dining room. Her company was still *in situ*, waiting for their hostess' directions. Addie was a little surprised her mother hadn't taken charge.

She cleared her throat. "Something awful has happened. Sir David's ex-wife was found dead this evening."

There were cries of surprise and confusion around the table. Barbara knocked her wineglass over. Cee leaped up but thought the better of it, falling back into her seat. Lucas looked—Addie hated to think it, blast Rupert—vacuous, as if he didn't understand the meaning of her words. Eloise turned paper-white.

Addie felt it was important to note these reactions, and made an effort to sweep her gaze from one end of the dining room to the other. Neither of the Shipmans registered anything but mild concern; Addie didn't think either of them had known Kathleen. An odd look passed between Pansy and George. The colonel showed no emotion—he'd probably seen enough death in his career to be entirely immune. Gerald Dumont studied the ruby pinkie ring on his left hand and frowned. Her mother's entire focus was on Cee, as if willing her to complete silence. Stoic, the servants waited for someone to tell them what to do.

Lady Broughton stepped into the breach. "I think under the circumstances we should not leave the gentlemen to their cigars," she said. "Let's all go into the drawing room for coffee. I assume the appropriate authorities have been called?"

"Yes, Mama. Forbes is taking care of it."

"Then we'll wait. What a bother, to be sure. That woman is as much trouble in death as she was alive."

"Mama!" Addie's mother could be blunt, but this was beyond her usual.

"H-how is Sir David?" Cee asked in a small voice.

"Upset, as you can imagine. Worried for his children. He'll probably drive home tonight and tell them in the morning." Addie leaned against the door, waiting for Rupert to pop out of the sideboard.

The room was unnaturally quiet, no Rupert, no one making an attempt to leave the table, until Barbara broke the spell. "What a lousy way to end the evening," she said after lighting up another cigarette. "Do you think the rustics will call in Scotland Yard?"

"Why should they? We have no reason to think anything untoward happened." *Yet.*

"Just out of curiosity, where was this woman found?" Ernest Shipman asked.

"In the tithe barn."

"Just a few meters away. I wonder how long she'd been there," George said, causing everyone to unwillingly contemplate rotting flesh.

They might all turn vegetarian by morning.

"Garden tools are stored there. I can't see Mr. McGrath missing a dead body. Come, my mother is right. Let's have coffee in the drawing room where it's more comfortable. Brandy, too." Addie nodded to a footman, who nodded back.

The group shuffled out like sheep in need of a sheepdog. Addie held back, waiting for something—someone—who didn't appear.

Chapter Five

Sunday

The phone rang at seven o'clock Sunday morning, never a good sign. Inspector Devenand Hunter picked it up on the second ring and listened. It was Deputy Commissioner Olive himself, which made Dev sit up straighter and be grateful the old man could not see through the wires that he'd slept naked. It was hot already, and the day had barely begun.

Important People had evidently called Commissioner Horwood all night, and Horwood had called Deputy Commissioner Olive. Dev scribbled the particulars of the incident in question in the notebook he kept at his bedside, his heart dropping with each detail.

This assignment had his father's fingerprints all over it. He might be retired from the force, but the force had not retired in him. As an old army man, he'd always had Horwood's ear. Had they cooked this up between them in the middle of the night?

All Dev needed to do was go to the flat next door and ask. His mother, Chandani, would feed him a full English breakfast *and* Methi Ka Thepla, and his father, Harry, would pretend to be deaf and read his paper. Since his retirement, Harry Hunter bought every reputable newspaper—and some disreputable— from the newsagent's shop on the ground floor of the building and spent hours pouring over them to keep himself abreast of news from around the world.

Thirty-five years ago, he had rejoiced in first-hand knowledge of Indian affairs, serving in the military police force in Her Majesty's army. It was in Jhansi Province where he met and married his wife, returning to London for a job in the Metropolitan Police Force. A year later, Devenand ("Joy of God") Hunter was born.

Dev might have been born on British soil, but most days he didn't think God was feeling the joy. He would always feel like an outsider. He didn't really mind it; it only sharpened his instincts. And right now his instincts told him that his father's ambitions for him were going to give him a pain in his bollocky-bare brown arse.

He was perfectly happy solving urban crimes. Jaunting to the Cotswolds to interview guests at a fancy house party had no appeal whatsoever. From what Olive said, the local constable had kicked up a hornet's nest. Formal complaints had been filed already by influential banker Ernest Shipman and the deceased's husband, a baronet, to the Commissioner himself, waking him up several times during the night. It was a proper cock-up, and the authorities had been involved for less than ten hours. The Cirencester constabulary wanted nothing more to do with the mess and had passed it up as high as it could go. A car had been requisitioned for Dev and his sergeant, and arrangements had been made at the Compton Arms.

Dev would have to remember to address the hostess as Lady Adelaide, not Mrs. Compton. She was a marquess' daughter, and bound to be a snob and a stickler. Dev paid no attention to the gossip columns—if he'd been feeling more in charity with his father, he might have asked him what he knew about the cast of characters at Compton Chase.

He did seem to remember hearing about Rupert Compton's death a few months ago, though. The man had made his name in the British Royal Flying Corps, surviving the odds over the Somme battlefields. Dev had been below on the ground before he was wounded and spirited to a field hospital, where he'd almost lost his foot. He'd been lucky to live; over a million in the Somme campaign alone had not been so fortunate. All he needed was his specially fitted boot and he could fox-trot with the best of them, not that he had time or interest in going dancing.

Dev called Bob Wells, his sergeant, then washed up, dressed, and over-packed. He hoped they wouldn't have to stay more than a few days at the village pub, but he liked to be prepared.

His first order of business would usually be to interview the local constable, but Yardley had raised so many hackles in such a short time that Dev decided to postpone that and meet the group with fresh eyes. Unruffle some feathers, if possible. The medical team was already in place, and a local doctor had also examined the body. With any luck, the dead woman had just tripped on a rake, hit her head, and expired amidst the hay.

In less than an hour, Dev heard the horn of the police-issue vehicle outside in the street. He was sure his mother was peering through the lace curtains as he reached the pavement, so he waved in that general direction and climbed into the car, tossing his bag in the backseat.

His sergeant was wearing a painfully new navy blue suit, probably purchased for his soon-to-be-born baby's christening. "Morning, Bob. Good day for a Sunday drive."

"It might be cooler out of the city," Bob Wells said.

"We can hope. How's the missus?"

"Hot, sir. And cranky."

"How much longer?"

"The midwife says two weeks or so left. I hope we get this business settled well before then, or Francie will have my bal—head."

Bob had a certain delicacy of speech that always amused Dev. They had been working together now for two years, and there was none of the undercurrent of resentment that had been present with Dev's other sergeants. Bob might not be brilliant, but he paid attention to detail and had a way with folks who were too startled by the color of Dev's skin to be comfortable confessing to him.

"Her mother's there, so she's not alone," Bob said, more to reassure himself than to inform Dev. "It's probably best I'm out of the way."

Dev understood many women were inclined to contemplate murdering their husbands during childbirth. He had no experience of that himself, having assiduously avoided his mother's matchmaking within London's Anglo-Indian community. He was only thirty-four—his father hadn't married until he was forty, which he reminded his mother of regularly. It was her opinion Harry had been too old to change, and she wouldn't wish such Hunter stubbornness on any future daughter-in-law.

Dev was not stubborn. Dogged, perhaps. Thorough. Traits that served him well in his profession. He pulled out his notebook and read out the information he'd received so far, knowing that Bob would remember every detail.

They passed the rest of the hundred-mile drive in companionable silence, stopping when necessary to refuel and stretch, arriving in Compton-Under-Wood just before the pub stopped serving, according to the sandwich board outside, "the best roast lunch in the Cotswolds."

The gentle roar of the dining room ceased as the two men took their table. Strangers in a strange land. Dev decided not to take it personally, and tucked in to what was a surprisingly delicious meal. He'd long abandoned any adherence to the vegetarianism of his mother's Hindu religion; for that matter, so had she. She now sat in a rear pew in Chelsea Old Church every Sunday, dressed like any other respectable English matron. She saved her saris for home and her elderly husband's nostalgia.

Their lunch was interrupted by a packet sent from the cottage hospital in Painswick, along with Yardley's garbled notes. Dev was used to such things, and it didn't interfere with his appetite. He apprised Bob of the current findings and ate his pudding—a somewhat tart blackberry crumble—and drank two cups of coffee to counteract the heavy meal. It wouldn't do to fall asleep mid-interrogation.

Once they had finished and checked into two plain but scrupulously clean rooms, Dev asked the landlord if he could use the telephone to call ahead to Compton Chase and alert Lady Adelaide of their imminent arrival. After speaking to a butler who sounded more like King George V did than King George V, they traveled the half-mile from the village to the Compton estate. A serpentine brick wall led to a gatehouse, which was unmanned. Bob rolled the Crossley onto the crushed stone drive.

"Blimey."

"Is that your professional opinion?" Dev asked with a smile.

"Wouldn't Francie be impressed at how I've come up in the world? Glad I wore my new duds. How many rooms do you think this place has?"

Too many. There really was no justification for anything this size, as far as Dev could see, unless it was housing orphans. He was perfectly satisfied with his three-room Chelsea flat, even if his parents were down the hall. "I wouldn't want to pay to heat it."

"Not on our salaries, even after we went on strike. Look at the undertaker."

"I believe that's the butler, Bob. Let's get the lay of the land." Dev swung out of the passenger side before the butler could open the door.

"Mr. Forbes? We spoke on the phone." Dev knew better than to offer a hand.

"Inspector Hunter, welcome to Compton Chase. A sad business."

"Indeed. This is Robert Wells, my sergeant. Is Sir David here?"

"He left last night to tell his children once Constable Yardley was done with him, but we expect him back any moment. I took the liberty of phoning Holly Hill after I spoke with you. Lady Adelaide and her family are waiting for you in the Great Hall. Please follow me."

If the Great Hall was meant to intimidate, it was doing a pretty fair job. A floor-to-ceiling window wall with hundreds of panes of glass gleamed in the bright August sunlight, briefly blinding Dev as he entered the cavernous space. Three fair-haired women were seated around a games table, no sign of any amusement on the marquetry surface or their faces.

Before Forbes could introduce them, the one wearing spectacles rose. She extended a slim white hand. To Bob. "Inspector Hunter? How kind of you to come."

Bob's face turned the color of a very ripe tomato. "Not me. This is my guv, Inspector Devenand Hunter. My, um, lady."

"Easiest promotion you'll ever get, my lad. How do you do, Lady Adelaide? We're so sorry to intrude on your time of mourning." Dev gave her what he knew to be a devastating smile, no pun intended. Just enough of his white teeth. Dark eyes radiating warmth and sympathy. He clasped her hand and gave it the gentlest of squeezes. She wouldn't mistake his authority again.

Her hand was cold and trembled in his. His thumb alighted on a massive diamond and sapphire ring on her right hand, the sale of which could have fed quite a few orphans for quite a few years. He reminded himself he was every bit as equal as this fluffy society beauty, who probably didn't have a thought in her head beyond buying her next new hat.

Ah. Who was judging who? One didn't get anywhere with a closed mind. He recited the Nyaya verses to himself.

Perception, Inference, Comparison and Word—these are the means of right knowledge.
Perception is that knowledge which arises from the contact of a sense with its object and which is determinate, unnameable and non-erratic.
Inference is knowledge which is preceded by perception,

and is of three kinds: a priori, a posteriori, and commonly seen.

Comparison is the knowledge of a thing through its similarity to another thing previously well known.

Word is the instructive assertion of a reliable person.

It is of two kinds: that which is seen, and that which is not seen.

Soul, body, senses, objects of senses, intellect, mind, activity, fault, transmigration, fruit, suffering and release—are the objects of right knowledge.

"My husband has been dead six months. Some intrusions are welcome. Oh! You mean Kathleen. I didn't know her well at all, so I wouldn't say we were in mourning for her. Please sit down. Have you had lunch? Shall I ring for coffee or tea? Beer or ale? The others are in the drawing room. I thought you'd want to meet me first, since Kathleen was found on my property. No one knows how she got here. She wasn't invited."

Lady Adelaide was flustered. Talkative. And remarkably pretty. Not too tall, not too slender, with none of the boyishness of figure that was so in vogue at the moment. Her black crepe tea gown probably cost more than Dev had earned so far this year, but he wouldn't let himself hold that against her.

"Addie. Darling." Those two words were enough of a warning for Lady Adelaide to remove her hand and sit back down in the crewel-work chair.

"I'm sorry—excuse the chattering. It's my nerves. Bodies don't usually turn up here. Dead ones, anyway. Until recently. May I present my mother, the Dowager Marchioness of Broughton? And my sister, Lady Cecilia Merrill."

Dev and Bob nodded to the women. Lady Broughton inclined her chin a fraction. She was small and blond, growing older beautifully, but Dev was not fooled—there was a martial glint in her hazel eyes. The sister was pretty as well, with her riot of short golden curls and pink cheeks which owed nothing to cosmetics.

He and Bob took the available chairs. "I understand my colleague in the village was somewhat ham-handed last evening. On behalf of the Commissioner and Metropolitan Police Force, I apologize and want to assure you we will discover precisely what happened with as little discommoding your family and friends as possible. I know your guests are anxious to leave. Will you be able to put them up one more day?"

"Of course. Only Mr. Shipman has made a fuss about staying—he's very anxious to get back to his bank. His wife told me when she accepted the Saturday-to-Monday that they couldn't stay past Sunday afternoon."

"I'll speak to him." He turned to Lady Broughton and Lady Cecilia. "Would you mind very much if I talked to Lady Adelaide alone for a few minutes?"

"If we did, I don't suppose it would matter. You're not going to bully her like that idiot Frank Yardley, are you? The family employs an excellent firm of solicitors. I could get one of the Mr. Pullings down here on the next train, even if it is Sunday."

Dev smiled again. "Pulling, Pulling, Stockwell and Pulling. Very impressive gentlemen. I don't think that will be necessary, Lady Broughton. I've never had any complaints filed against me in all my years on the force."

"And how many has that been? You seem awfully young."

"Clean living, my lady. It's been over a dozen, but with my army service tucked in the middle, so not consecutive." He left out the lost year of slow, painful recovery.

"You are English then?"

"Half. I was born at St. Anne's Hospital, Chelsea." He refrained from asking her where *she* was born.

She stood. "Very well. Come along, Cee. If you need us, Addie, we'll just be down the hall."

Like his family, Dev realized, hers was only too ready to "help"…and interfere.

Chapter Six

"You are sure I cannot get you gentlemen anything?" Addie said, wondering how long "a few minutes" was. She really had nothing to add to any investigation, and Rupert had not chosen to reveal all and come forth with the murderer's name, motive, and method. Addie took this as a very good sign that her insanity was lapsing, and soon she would be restored to robust mental health. It couldn't come soon enough.

It might not even *be* murder. After being roused from his brandy and a good book, Dr. Bergman had been unable to identify the cause of death. It was late and very dark; he was tired and rusty, and perfectly honest about his shortcomings. Addie should have invited *him* to dinner instead of Reverend Rivers so he would have been handy. He was only able to give an approximate time of death, which, she supposed, was a start.

The police had taken the body away to the little hospital in Painswick around midnight to do whatever it was they did, thank God. Going to church this morning had been out of the question. She'd actually managed to rest some with the draught Beckett had dug out of Addie's lingerie drawer.

After Rupert's death, she'd found it almost impossible to sleep and had needed something nearly every night—she'd been too angry. At Rupert. At herself. The waste. Though Reverend Rivers had held her hand and talked about God's will at the time, she had wanted to club him over the head with his Bible.

"Tell me about your house party, Lady Adelaide," Inspector Hunter said, drawing a small notebook out of his pocket. His sergeant followed suit.

"There's really not much to tell. I decided about a month ago to have a few people come for a Saturday-to-Monday. As I said, my husband died in February, and I'd lost touch with friends. I did some redecoration while I was getting myself and the estate's affairs sorted. The house needed it—ask anyone—and it kept me busy and my mind off...things. This was to be a grand unveiling." She spun her platinum and diamond wedding band around. She had been unable to bring herself to take it off, although she'd lost count at the number of times she'd thrown it at her husband in the heat of battle.

"I gave the guest list to Frank Yardley, seating and room arrangements etcetera. The local vicar backed out at the last minute, da—uh, drat him. I should have known thirteen would be a disaster."

"What's the vicar's name?"

"Edward Rivers. But he can't help you; he wasn't here. Frank Yardley has questioned everyone save him, I think. Have you met with Mr. Yardley yet?"

"I've not had the pleasure," Inspector Hunter said, his voice dry.

Addie rolled her eyes. "I'm afraid it will be a challenge for you—he's put everyone's back up, accusing just about everybody of killing Kathleen. We don't even know she was killed, do we?" If she'd been naked and having sex in Addie's barn, maybe she simply died of a delicious orgasm, that "little death" business writers went banging on about.

Addie wouldn't know about such things anymore.

"Not as yet. There was information left for me when I stopped at the Compton Arms, but it was inconclusive. You say you were not well-acquainted with the dead woman."

"No. I mean, I knew her. She'd been here occasionally with

her husband before they divorced last year—she lived in the next village. It's a very small world here, Inspector. Our social set is somewhat limited. I wouldn't have called her a friend." Addie was going to say absolutely nothing about that heart-shaped birthmark.

What if this Hunter fellow and his sergeant found out that Kathleen and Rupert had had an affair? Addie would cross that bridge when she came to it. Goodness! She'd be a suspect—the betrayed wife, out for vengeance.

"When did your guests arrive yesterday?"

"By eleven-thirty or so. And they all arrived within minutes of each other, except for the Hallidays—my driver picked them up a little earlier at the train station. It was a veritable parade of cars, and Forbes had his hands full. My mother and sister have been here since Thursday helping me get organized, doing the flowers and such. They live at the Dower House at Broughton Park, about fifteen miles away. We got everyone settled quickly and had lunch at noon on the terrace."

"How long were you seated outside?"

"No more than forty-five minutes. It was a very light repast, salads and cold meats. Even with the shaded umbrellas, it was a bit uncomfortable. It was so hot."

"After lunch, what did everyone get up to?"

"Well, we shouldn't have, because the sun was almost unbearable, but some of us changed and played tennis. Mixed doubles. You know we English bask in any scrap of good weather we can." Addie could have bitten her tongue. Would he be offended by the "we English" remark? He was as English as she was, she supposed, even with his foreign good looks.

"Cee partnered with Sir David, and Lucas, that is Lord Waring, was mine. Eloise, Pansy and George—the Hallidays—watched, then the Hallidays played the winners. Eloise complained of the heat and went back to the house quite early on. The Shipmans took a short drive around the countryside. Barbara Pryce and her fiancé walked around the grounds, then—I should let her tell you herself, but everyone knows because she bragged about it—they spent the rest of the afternoon in her room." She felt her own face growing warm. Barbara's mother's lectures on virginity before marriage must have fallen on deaf ears. But after five fiancés, it would be too much to expect a thirty-year-old woman to be completely chaste.

"Colonel Mellard walked back to his house in the village to get his afternoon post after lunch—he was expecting a letter from his brother in South Africa but he said it didn't come. My mother skipped lunch altogether—she had a headache—and read and rested under a cucumber mask as she always does every afternoon. I took a nap myself. I had an awful headache—too much sun. Mrs. Drum, my housekeeper, sent tea trays to everyone's rooms so they could relax instead of trying to bear up through the heat in yet another change of clothes. At seven-thirty we all convened in the Great Hall—here—for drinks."

She took a breath. "I only know all this because we talked about where we were when Kathleen may have died. Dr. Bergman came in for a cup of tea after he examined the body and told us his opinion of the time." Everyone had seemed more than anxious to present their alibis. Was that a sign of innocence or guilt?

"Did any of them seem different at drinks and dinner? Nervous, for example?"

"Not at all. If anyone was nervous, it was I. I dropped a glass of sherry. It's been quite a long time since I entertained, and I wanted everything to be right. Go smoothly." Be ghost-and-dead-body-free.

"When was the last time you saw the deceased?"

"Gosh. I'm not sure. Sometime in the spring or early summer? My sister and I were out walking my dog. We stopped in the village and she—Kathleen—was having lunch outside in the pub's beer garden." The less said about that encounter, the better.

"Alone?"

Addie nodded.

"Do you know of anyone who might have wished her harm?"

"No," Addie said too quickly.

"What kind of relationship did she have with her ex-husband?"

"Sir David wouldn't have killed her! If you could have seen how upset he was when I told him she was dead, so worried for his children. I believe he and Kathleen tried to be civil because of the boys. I know she came to visit the boys when she..." Addie trailed off.

"When she?"

"Had time in her social schedule. She was not, if I might say so, the most devoted of mothers."

Both men were busy scribbling. Addie wished she could read upside-down.

"I see. Is there anything else you'd like to add?"

"I don't think so. If I think of anything, I will of course let you know."

There. They were done, and it hadn't been too painful. Why should it be? Addie really didn't know anything. If she'd wanted to murder Kathleen Grant, she certainly would not have done it in her own tithe barn, and Addie would have made sure the woman was still dressed up to her chin like a nun when her body was found.

The inspector looked up from his notes. His eyes were nearly black, and Addie had the sensation of being spelled by a cobra. "You didn't like her."

"I—I wouldn't say that," she stuttered. "There are just some people you know who aren't meant to be bosom-bows. She was one of them."

"I see."

Ugh. It sounded like he really did. She would have to be careful showing her antipathy to Kathleen, and Rupert's responsibility for it.

He turned to his sergeant. "Bob, I'll leave the servants to you.

Thank you for your time, Lady Adelaide. If you'll conduct me to the drawing room, I'll see how swiftly I can leave your guests in peace for today. You don't mind if I use this room to question them one by one, do you?"

"Not at all. Come this way."

Her drawing room was large enough so that a dozen people in its confines did not make it feel crowded, but she noted the couples had chosen to sit as far away from each other as possible. Wariness had set in. Sir David Grant had returned, and Addie gave him a quick hug.

"This is Inspector Hunter, Sir David. I imagine you'd like to go first. Oh, am I overstepping? Perhaps the police have their own routine. Alphabetical order or something."

"No, you're right, Lady Adelaide. Your intuition serves you. There might be a spot on the force for you yet. Good afternoon, everyone. I'm Devenand Hunter of New Scotland Yard, and this is my sergeant, Robert Wells. I am truly sorry to disturb your Sunday afternoon, and even sorrier you had the unpleasantness of last night. I will be speaking to Constable Yardley at my earliest opportunity. If you can be patient and bear with me, I'd like to begin the interviews now. We'll stop at dinnertime, and finish up tomorrow morning if necessary. Lady Adelaide has graciously offered to extend her hospitality to you another day."

There was a quiet ripple of response, and just one outburst.

"Outrageous! I am Ernest Shipman of the Shipman Bank. I'm needed in the city tomorrow. Angela and I didn't even know the dead person. She has nothing to do with us and we had nothing to do with her…unfortunate circumstances."

Shipman was almost portly, his cheeks ruddy from too much good living, but Addie considered him to be relatively attractive for his type: a middle-aged man of considerable importance, who knew it. His temples were silver, and he looked every inch the successful banker—bespoke suit, heavy gold watch chain and fobs, handmade shoes. He was dressed for the boardroom, no touch of relaxing country tweeds.

He wasn't apt to relax *now*.

"I appreciate your irritation, sir. I shall see you directly after Sir David. But if there are any further developments after I've spoken to everyone, I shall need your presence on Monday to clarify matters."

"There are such things as telephones, Inspector," Shipman blustered. He'd wanted to leave last night, but Yardley had forbidden it and had practically arrested him on the spot for perverting the course of justice, which, Yardley sneered, carried a life sentence. Addie liked Angela, but her husband thought altogether too much of himself sometimes. But rumor was he had the King's ear and some of his children's loans.

The inspector had better watch his step.

Hunter shook his head. "Until they invent a talking device where one may see the communicator's face, I'd just as soon ask questions in person and gauge a subject's reactions."

Gosh, that would be interesting. Addie wondered if she'd live to see such a thing. One might never answer one's phone again.

"I'm almost certain they can manage a day without you, Ernest," Angela said, trying to soothe her husband. "We can go on another lovely long drive after. The countryside is so chocolate-box, don't you agree, Inspector?"

"Indeed." From his tone, Addie thought he'd probably appreciate it more if there were dead bodies sticking out of the hedgerows.

Chapter Seven

Sir David Grant looked wrecked, but Dev had seen plenty of guilty husbands put on a good show. Of course, he was an *ex*-husband. But a judge's decree absolute didn't necessarily mitigate years of misery. One could still harbor violence and reprisal years after the dissolution of a marriage.

"When was the last time you saw your wife alive, Sir David?"

"Three, no, almost four weeks ago. She came down to see the boys in the middle of the week for two nights. I stayed at my club in London, but was there when she arrived. I could look up the exact dates."

"Did you know she was coming to the area this weekend?"

"No. We usually communicate by letter, so I can make arrangements to leave. She would have written, unless the letter went astray. We put up a good front for the boys, but try to avoid spending time under the same roof."

"Why was that?"

Sir David gave him a sour smile. "Why do you think? We don't—didn't get along. Kathleen could be cruel. She had a great many admirers, before and after the divorce, and often compared me most unfavorably. I suppose I'd be as good a candidate as any to want her dead."

Well. "Was your wife—ex-wife—a drug user?"

Sir David looked at him blankly. "What? Why would you ask that?"

"The test results are preliminary, but we have reason to believe she died of a drug overdose. There are indications on the body." Dev watched closely to see Grant's reaction.

Shock. The man was a good actor, or truly surprised. "No! Her physical beauty was everything to her. Her currency, I suppose you could say. And Dr. Bergman would have said something."

"He might not have noticed. There were fresh needle marks between the victim's toes. No obvious places to attract attention."

"She never would have—my wife was squeamish, Inspector Hunter. She could barely insert a brooch on a collar without being afraid to prick herself. Fainted when the boys brought her a cigar box filled with pinned butterflies. I can't imagine her injecting herself with such poison. I never saw her take anything stronger than two aspirin for a hangover!"

"Did she drink?"

"No more than any of us. She liked a gay life, and found things here in the country boring. Found me boring. It won't take much digging to discover she was unfaithful. Repeatedly." The man met his eyes, daring Dev to say something. He felt an unwelcome sympathy for Grant, and that wouldn't do.

"Did you notice any change in her behavior once your marriage ended?"

Grant expelled a breath. "She was much happier. More…"

"More what?"

"Just more. Alive. Free. Excitable."

All of which could be attributed to cocaine.

"Where were you yesterday between four and seven?"

"Here. In my room. I played tennis for a couple of hours, then came up to take a long bath. It was so blo—blasted hot. Around seven I called home to say good-night to the children from the telephone in the upstairs hall. Then I dressed and came down for cocktails."

"Did anyone see you?"

"I don't know. A tea tray was delivered while I was in my

bath, but I never spoke to anyone. Maybe the maid heard me splashing." He gave an approximation of a laugh. "I have no alibi, and all the motive in the world. Kathleen was a nuisance, blowing in and out of our boys' lives at her whim. Always wanting more money too. I won't lie, Inspector. I'm...I'm almost glad she's dead. I hope she didn't suffer, but I understand she was not wearing any clothing when she was found. I imagine she met a lover here. An odd place for an assignation, but then she always did like to take risks. If you can find the man—or woman—you might have your answer."

Dev stopped writing. "Woman?"

Grant shrugged. "Kathleen considered herself to be beyond rules. She had, in my opinion, an over-developed libido."

The psychological jargon was unexpected. "So, you are saying she took female lovers too?"

"I don't know it for a fact, never saw it with my own eyes, but I wouldn't be at all surprised from the way she spoke when she was taunting me."

Spreading the blame around, then. "Thank you for your help, Sir David. We'll be in touch."

"I can go home, can't I? I'm quite nearby and will come back if I have to."

"Yes, of course. How are your children taking the loss of their mother?"

"Well, they've lost her before. I'm not sure they understand this time she's never coming back. When do you think we can hold the funeral?"

"I'll let you know when the body can be released. Does Lady Grant have other family?"

"Just her grandfather. Her parents were on the *Lusitania*, and her brother was killed in the Second Boer War when she was just a very little girl. I'm glad they won't know how Kathleen's life ended. Her grandfather's in a retirement home in Yorkshire, quite dotty, as I understand it. I'll let him know, but I don't expect him to attend the funeral. There's a cousin somewhere, but the family was estranged and Kathleen didn't know them."

It did seem especially sordid to be found naked in a barn and pumped full of cocaine. Dev was glad he wouldn't have to explain it to a confused elderly gentleman.

Grant stood. "So, are you saying it could have been an accident? An…an overdose?"

"Could have been." Unlikely. There was no drug paraphernalia found near the body or in Kathleen Grant's purse. Her clothes had been neatly folded, her silk stockings rolled into expensive shoes. The body had been laid out on a faded hand-pieced quilt, a bundle of straw between her folded hands.

Someone had an odd sense of humor.

"Shall I send Shipman in?"

"Give me five minutes, please. And I'd appreciate it if you said nothing about the circumstances of her death to anyone else."

"Of course not. I can hardly believe it myself."

Dev checked what he'd written and added a few details. Grant seemed legitimately upset. Honest to a fault. He tried to appear that way, at any rate—he must know he was the prime suspect. He might have lived the most blameless of lives, but being known as a cuckold was apt to bring out the worst in anyone.

The extraordinary window next to the card table where Dev sat overlooked the drive, a well-manicured lawn, and an ornamental lake. A family of ducks was paddling aimlessly. The property was beautiful, and must be a burden to keep up. If they had been lucky enough not to be blown to bits in the war, most young people today had no interest in going into service. Dev wondered how Lady Adelaide was managing.

Shipman entered without knocking. His color was high with temper and the heat. A break in the weather would be a relief, or Dev would consider stripping down and joining those ducks himself.

"Mr. Shipman, please make yourself comfortable."

"I'll be comfortable when I'm back on Mount Street! As I've told you, I never met Katherine Grant, or if I did, I don't remember—we go to so many functions. Wouldn't recognize her if I saw her on the street. Didn't meet her husband until yesterday. I'm sorry I let my wife talk me into this weekend. Lady Adelaide is a neighbor in Town, so she felt we had to accept. The poor thing's been shut up here since her husband killed himself. No good deed goes unpunished, and here I am, talking to a *policeman*." Shipman made the word sound equivalent to *cockroach*.

Dev ignored the insult. "Killed himself? You mean he committed suicide?"

"No, no. Nothing like that. Car crash. Died instantly and his mis—um, his passenger with him. Shocking business. Fellow was a flyer in the war and loved his speed, I guess. Angela and Lady Adelaide have grown close over the years when Lady Adelaide was in Town. It was our duty to come and cheer her up."

Not if he was hollering to go home. "As best as you can recollect, tell me about what you did yesterday."

"We arrived before noon. Made a very early start. I drove myself, and the trip west was uneventful. We had lunch outdoors with the other guests, although in my opinion it was much too warm for the lobster mayonnaise. It didn't sit right with my digestion, but my wife insisted on tootling around the area for an hour or two to see the sights. Sheep and more sheep, I ask you. A total waste of time. I cut the drive short as I wasn't feeling up to par. When we got back, I locked myself in and had a lie-down and so forth. Took a bath and dressed for dinner. Knocked on Angela's door at about quarter past seven and helped her with her zipper. Made myself useful."

"Did you have tea sent to your room?"

"No. As I said, I hung that 'Do Not Disturb' sign on my door handle. Didn't want to be bothered when I had a gyppy tummy. Caught at a disadvantage, you know."

Dev blocked the thought of a naked Ernest Shipman on the toilet. "I trust you're feeling more the thing today, Mr. Shipman."

"I'm all right. Look, I have half a dozen appointments tomorrow I really can't miss, and then a business trip scheduled." He put his hand inside his jacket pocket, drew out a thin diary and a thick billfold, and laid them on the table between them. His plump fingers tapped them lightly. "Don't you think you can see yourself clear to letting us go back to London? I can make myself available for anything else you need to ask at the drop of a hat."

Dev stiffened. "I'm sorry. No."

"I can make it worth your while." He said it as if Dev were too stupid to understand the significance of the wallet.

"Again, I apologize for the inconvenience. Would you ask your wife to step in?"

"Goddammit! Do I need to make another call to my friend Sir William Horwood?" The police commissioner was a Brigadier-General, recipient of a GBE, KCB, and DSO. He would be most unimpressed with Dev if he'd agreed to a bribe, although there already were plenty of newspaper stories about corruption and misconduct within the ranks that Horwood was accused of ignoring.

"You may call whomever you please. I suggest phoning your secretary to cancel tomorrow's appointments," Dev said evenly.

"Your superiors will hear about this!"

"My report will be thorough as well. Thank you for your time, Mr. Shipman."

The banker stormed off, and Dev sighed. It never did one any good to poke the society bear in the eye, but it couldn't be helped. For a man like Shipman, everything was solved with money and connections, with little work involved. For a man like Dev, it was usually just the opposite.

Chapter Eight

A substantial tea had been laid in the drawing room, but no one had much appetite, waiting to be grilled like the tiny cheese puff sandwiches that were Cook's specialty. As people cycled in and out of the Great Hall, Addie found herself alone in a corner with Barbara, who lit Lucky Strike after Lucky Strike, making Addie somewhat nauseous. She opened another window, but the air was as dead outside as in.

Barbara leaned forward. "So, tell me, were you handled with kid gloves by the glorious inspector? Gloves or not, *I'm* looking forward to being handled by the man. So attractive, don't you think? In a sub-continental way."

"Barbara!" Really, at this point nothing Barbara said should surprise her. There seemed to be no filter between what she thought and what she said. Addie had known her all her life—her mother and Barbara's had been childhood friends—and she'd only gotten worse with age.

"Admit it. He's almost as divine as Rupert. One can picture him in a turban with a ruby. And only that."

"One *cannot*. Honestly, Babs, get your mind out of the gutter. The man is a policeman."

"But a pretty policeman. I wouldn't mind being arrested by him. Handcuffed to his bed."

Addie set her teacup down. "Speaking of bed. I'm such a

rotten hostess, but I must go upstairs for a little while. One of my headaches is coming on again." It would if she had to listen to Barbara's nonsense any longer. "You can manage on your own, can't you?"

"Certainly. Gerald is about somewhere. If I must, I'll talk to Pansy or your mother or Cee. But not Eloise. She's such a bore. Why do you always invite her?"

"She's Lucas' cousin. They live in the same house. It would be very odd if I didn't."

"There's something odd there, all right. I don't see how he can bear breakfasting with her day after day. If anyone needs murdering, it's Eloise."

"Barbara! How can you say such a thing? Look what she did during the war. She was at a field hospital in France for three whole years. While you and I were rolling clean bandages in London gossiping, she was up to her eyelashes in blood and amputated limbs." Addie grimaced at the image. Her mind had taken a gruesome turn lately; dead husbands were surely responsible.

"Poor little orphan. Such a goody-goody. We did our bit, and more." Barbara never talked about the men she'd lost, but she must still be suffering.

Addie tried to win her over. "Plus, since Rupert died, she and Lucas have visited or called to check up on me several times a week. I don't know what I would have done without them."

"You know I was traveling, or I would have been checking up on you, too!" Barbara said with asperity.

And would not have been as calming a presence as Eloise, for sure. Being a good dozen years older than Addie and Lucas, Eloise had been more like a kindly big sister than a playmate. She had come to live with the Warings after her mother passed; her father died out in Africa trying to make his fortune.

"I admit, she's not the most scintillating conversationalist, but what has she ever done to you?"

"That's a story for another day. Go on upstairs and get your nap in. I shall make your excuses if anyone asks."

Addie sped up the stairs, hoping to avoid everyone. A nap, a cool bath, clean clothes from the skin out—she'd feel right as rain in a few hours. Tomorrow all this troublesome activity would be over, her guests gone. She'd encourage her mother and Cee to leave too. It had been lovely having them about, but it was somewhat exhausting living up to her mother's exacting standards. The woman had apparently forgotten how naughty Addie had been as a girl and had placed her on a pedestal that Cee was anxious to knock down.

She closed and locked her bedroom door behind her.

And yelped.

"Is Babs right? Is that Indian fellow as good-looking as I am?"

"He's half-Indian," Addie said, feeling obliged to respond to phantom Rupert's phantom provocation.

"Which half? Top or bottom, or split down the middle? Ouch, the thought of that isn't very amusing. She's never had good taste in men. Do you know, she turned me down once? September of '21. The Lancasters' shoot, do you remember? I wasn't really serious in my pursuit—I might even have been a trifle squiffy, which may have clouded my judgment. But never doubt her, Addie. She's a true friend."

"And you were an awful husband! Why are you telling me this? Am I going to find out you made advances to Cook and Mrs. Drum next?"

"You know I never once interfered with the help. That sort of thing is beneath me. Or was. In this state of limbo, I'm not sure what the protocol is. But Cook has a whisker or two on her chin and a good three stone on me. I think she's safe from my predations for the time being."

Addie burst into tears. "Go away, go away, go away! I can't bear it any longer. I'll have to throw myself in front of a bus or something, and then what will become of Fitz?" Speaking of which, she hadn't seen her dog since yesterday afternoon. He'd been at the tennis court until he'd stolen too many balls and she'd asked one of the maids to take him away. She'd been too upset last night to wonder where he was. Being a fairly bright dog, he often spent the night in the kitchen, hanging around for midnight snacks.

"Not a bus, please. You'd scar the poor driver for life. You know, old girl, I was wandering about the estate this afternoon for old time's sake. Considering everything, you're doing a nice job keeping up appearances. And your doggie's tied out at the gardener's cottage, happy as a clam, big bone between his paws and a bowl of water he hasn't managed to tip over yet. He did growl at me, but that's to be expected. We wraiths have that effect on animals. The little brutes have extra-sensory-something." Rupert adjusted his tie pin, the gold nugget that Addie had given him for their first anniversary when she'd thought nothing but golden days were ahead.

He seemed so very *real*.

She collapsed onto a chair. "Mr. McGrath has him? I don't understand."

"I didn't say Mr. M. has him. The man was nowhere in sight. I did peek in the downstairs window. Everything was ship-shape, but no gardener puffing on his pipe by the fireplace. When did you last see him?"

"Friday. We talked about mowing the tennis court as close as possible, and he did it. Or one of the village boys he employs did."

"Hmm. I don't like it. You never saw him yesterday at all?"

"No. He doesn't work Saturday or Sunday. Or Wednesday afternoons. I'm not a slave driver." Addie made numerous concessions to the staff to keep them sweet and on the payroll.

Rupert opened up her armoire and tsked. "All black. The color really doesn't suit you, and you know better than anyone that I'm not worth it." He fingered a pleated chiffon dress she hadn't worn yet. "Poor Kathleen is found in his barn. It makes one wonder what he was up to."

Addie had never heard anything so absurd, and she'd listened closely to Rupert for five long years. "It does not! Mr. McGrath wouldn't kill Kathleen! How would he even know her?"

"The mists are as foggy as ever. But I'd mention Mr. M.'s disappearance to that inspector chappie."

Addie jumped off her bed. "I'm going to get Fitz. I can't imagine why someone would tie him up there."

"At least that someone thought to feed the little fellow. What, you mean you're leaving right now in the middle of our chat?" he asked plaintively as she slammed her door in his face.

She took the servants' staircase, slipped out a side door, and followed the grass path between unkempt hawthorn hedges to a small cluster of very modest estate cottages. Only one was being lived in at the moment; the others needed work done that Addie hadn't gotten around to yet. Since she employed far fewer people at Compton Chase than used to work there in the last century, the question of housing was easily solved by the ample servants' quarters on the top floor of the house, a wing below stairs, and rooms over the stables.

Mr. McGrath had been in his little cottage for decades, and raised a family there. He was a nice old man whose wife had died long before Addie married Rupert. One of his daughters was in Scotland with a grown family of her own, the other was a teacher in Bristol. Addie knew how proud he was of both of them—their photographs, well-dusted, were on every flat surface of his home.

She went around back, and there was Fitz, sleeping under the shade of a lilac bush. He had dug himself a little hole, which Mr. McGrath would not be happy about. A long rope ran from the handle of the back door to the jaunty red leather collar Addie had bought in London on her last trip.

"Some watchdog you are."

The dog gave a happy bark and made a beeline for her. She brushed the dirty pawprints off her skirts and struggled with the knot around his neck as well as the one around the doorknob, resorting finally to cutting the rope with a pair of hedge clippers she found in the shed.

Addie knocked on the back door. "Mr. McGrath! Are you home?" She tried the handle, and the door swung open. Everything in the kitchen was as neat as a pin. She called once more to no answer. She didn't want to trespass, so shut the door and left, Fitz just behind her watering every bush he encountered on the way back to the house.

It was a puzzle. Addie would have to find Jane, the maid she'd asked to mind Fitz while they played tennis. Maybe she'd fobbed him off on the gardener; Mr. McGrath was fond of dogs, even though Fitz could be very naughty, rolling in freshly turned earth and digging up prized plants.

The huge whitewashed kitchen was empty, signs of tonight's dinner preparation neatly organized along the table. Addie could hear conversation in the servants' hall, where most of the indoor staff must be having their own tea.

Sergeant Wells was in their midst. They all stood up in a rush, and Addie waved them down.

"What's amiss, your ladyship?" Beckett asked. "Do you need me?"

"Not for a couple of hours. We're not dressing for dinner tonight, though—it just seemed too insensitive. Where's Jane?"

"It's her afternoon off, Lady Adelaide," Mrs. Drum said. "Why? What's she done?"

The housekeeper could be a regular Tartar, but between her and Forbes, the house ran like clockwork. "I don't want to get her in trouble, Mrs. Drum. I only wanted to ask her a question about this little ruffian here," she said, stroking Fitz's wiry coat. "She took him away for me yesterday at the tennis court, but I found him tied up at Mr. McGrath's cottage this afternoon. It seemed a bit of a mystery."

"Maybe the dog is a *witness*," Beckett said, her eyes widening.

"A witness to what?"

"To the murder! Everyone knows Lady Grant was found laid out like some effigy. She didn't die of no natural causes." When Beckett got excited, her command of the King's English was on shaky ground. Under ordinary pre-war circumstances, a girl like Beckett would be no one's lady's maid, but one had fewer choices nowadays. Addie liked her for her cheek and sense of humor. She had a cunning way with hair, too—she'd made Cee look nearly normal last night.

"That's enough, Beckett," Mrs. Drum said sternly. "Sergeant Wells has warned us not to discuss the manner in which Lady Grant was found."

An effigy? Addie hadn't heard anything like that. Why didn't Rupert tell her?

Oh, Lord. Her mind was definitely lost.

"The news will get around sooner than later, I expect, after all those people seeing the body last night. It's hard to keep quiet about such a thing." Sergeant Wells pushed himself up from the table. "This was a very nice tea, Mrs. Drum, Mrs. Oxley. Thank you. Who is this Mr. McGrath?"

"My gardener. He's been here donkey's years. My husband's grandmother hired him when he was just a boy. He came with his own grandfather from Scotland as a kind of package deal."

"Well, I might as well go talk to him too. Thank you all for your information. You've been very helpful." He picked up his notebook. "If you'd tell me the way to his cottage, Lady Adelaide?"

"He's not there. At least I don't think he is. I knocked and called, but I suppose he might be taking a nap. I think he does most afternoons. He's getting on in years. Here, I'll show you the way. Beckett, please see that Fitz is fed and walked again, then shut him up in my room before he gets into any more trouble."

Addie had no idea what to say to a police sergeant—that had never been covered in any courses at Cheltenham Ladies College, and it certainly had never been part of Lady Broughton's agenda—so they walked in awkward silence down the path.

"Here it is!" Addie said brightly. "The back door's unlocked. I know that because Fitz's rope was tied to the doorknob and I tried to get it loose. In the end I had to resort to some hedge trimmers."

Sergeant Wells gave her a very direct look. "You seem nervous, Lady Adelaide, if you don't mind me saying so."

"Of course I'm nervous! Someone died here yesterday, and you and Inspector Hunter think that one of us is responsible, don't you? It's enough to make anyone nervous. All I wanted was a party, and I got…this." Her vision blurred, even though she had her glasses on.

She took the proffered handkerchief, which seemed clean enough. "I'm sorry." She sopped up the tears from her cheeks, but refrained from blowing her nose in a stranger's handkerchief. "I'm not usually so emotional."

"Murder can do that to a person."

Addie swallowed hard. That word again. "Murder? Are you sure? It wasn't suicide or something?"

"There's usually a note when someone tops themselves." Sergeant Wells banged on the kitchen door, causing it to swing open. "Mr. McGrath? Police. I need to ask you a few questions."

He turned to Addie. "Stay here. I'll just nip in and take a quick look around."

Addie sat down on a willow-work bench in the yard and waited. Within a few minutes, Sergeant Wells emerged, looking grim.

"Would you be so kind to alert my guv'nor that there's another dead body?"

This time, Addie truly did faint, with none of the grace her mother had instilled in her.

Chapter Nine

"Someone who could kill a man in his bed, but not a dog." Dev sat back in the rickety chair and rubbed his eyes. The medical team had finished at Mr. McGrath's cottage, and he was sitting in an empty one next door with Bob. There was a small hole in the roof, a lot of dust and a paucity of furniture; poor Bob was relegated to squatting on a lower stair tread.

"Sounds like a woman to me," Bob said.

"Maybe the murderer didn't know the dog was tied out back. The front door was unlocked too." He sighed. "Two murders in roughly the same time frame. We'll have to start all over again." The police surgeon estimated the gardener had died an hour or two after Kathleen Grant. A syringe of cocaine was again the weapon of choice, this time left behind in the bedclothes. There were, of course, no fingerprints.

A mistake, that. A man of Mr. McGrath's age might be expected to expire in his sleep, arousing no suspicion, even if a murder had been committed elsewhere on the estate. He might have heard about it somehow, and it disturbed him and taxed his heart.

But leaving the syringe behind meant it wouldn't be discovered in an incriminating location if the police searched the guests' rooms, which he and Bob should do at the earliest opportunity.

"The killer creeps in, injects the napping old fellow with the drug, leaves quick as you please to sit down to dinner at the big house. We're dealing with one cold character," Bob said, shaking his head, "except for the bit about letting the terrier live another day. Who do you make for it?"

"I haven't even finished interviewing everyone. Mr. Shipman is not going to be happy." It would serve Dev's father right if he got demoted for this case—that might teach him to keep his nose out of Dev's career.

Bob bounced up. "The maid Jane must be back by now. I'll see what I can find out about the dog."

"You do that." Dev looked at his watch. "And see if any of the servants noticed anything near the estate cottages. The toffs will be having dinner soon. You grab something in the kitchen for yourself, won't you? I won't be too long upstairs after they finish eating." If he could get them to agree to talk to him tonight. It had been a very long day for everyone.

"What about you?"

"I'm not hungry." Two murders to deal with tended to depress his appetite, and the Sunday roast lunch had been substantial.

Bob left, and Dev went next door and took one more turn in Mr. McGrath's cottage. It was twilight now, golden light limning the gray-green hills. Not a thing seemed out of place. If anyone had heard the dog bark or seen the murderer enter this grassy little lane, it would have been Mr. McGrath, and he was dead.

It was obvious the old gardener had been somewhere and seen something he shouldn't have yesterday. He hadn't thought to write it down in a journal, which would have been a great help. No message was fingered in the dust, because there wasn't any dust in this pristine little cottage. Dev hoped the man had been dreaming and never woke to the terror of his end. Perhaps, as the Hindus believed, his soul was now passing into a new body, the karma of a good, hard-working man elevating his stature in his next life. Dev felt the man's daughters' eyes follow him about the house from their picture frames, and vowed he'd bring the murderer to justice.

He took his time walking back to the house. There had been something ritualistic about the way Kathleen Grant's body had been displayed. Mr. McGrath's was much more a murder of expedience. Dev was mostly sure the same person committed both crimes, but who?

The Shipmans claimed to be unacquainted with Kathleen Grant, although Mrs. Shipman admitted the name was vaguely familiar. Ernest Shipman had even made a point of calling her the *wrong* name, Katherine, which had raised Dev's antenna. London was a big place, but Mayfair was smaller. Lady Adelaide, the Shipmans, and Lady Grant lived quite near each other in very fashionable digs. It would not be out of the question for them to frequent some of the same establishments. The same gatherings. Pass each other on the street on the way to the chemist or dry cleaner. Dev needed more information there.

He was relatively certain he could rule out Lady Broughton. He doubted the woman would lower herself to actual murder—the cut direct would do it. She'd made no secret of her dislike of Kathleen Grant. In her day, a woman kept her marriage vows and that was that, but Dev didn't sense her personal animus had real heat to it. One simply couldn't be bothered by a woman like Lady Grant if one was a dowager marchioness.

Her daughter, Lady Cecilia, however…

Earlier, she claimed to know a lot about legal procedures and said she was within her rights not to speak to him at all, then blurted she was in love with Sir David, and oh, yes, she was glad his ex-wife was dead because she was an evil bitch and was driving poor Sir David mad. Always calling to complain about money, or the lack thereof. Telling him how he should raise his sons. If she hadn't cared enough to stay and raise them herself, how dare she interfere? The interview made Dev feel like he was watching a ferociously fast tennis volley; Lady Cecilia's back-and-forth gave him whiplash.

Did she know what she told him could be damaging to her

would-be lover? And she, like everyone else he'd spoken to, had no alibi to speak of. This uncorroborated resting in their room business would be the death of *him*.

Lord Lucas Waring had been next up, an amiable viscount who'd motored over from Waring Hall, his estate next door to Broughton Park, and seemed entirely at ease with Dev's questions. He'd been Lady Adelaide's partner at tennis. They'd lost badly— not his fault, but he didn't want to speak ill of his childhood friend, he said with a broad smile—and then he'd fallen asleep for his sins. He barely knew Kathleen Grant and was sorry she was dead for her boys' sake. All very proper.

His cousin Eloise Waring had nothing much to offer, either. It had been too hot for her; she suffered from heat rash at the slightest provocation. It was so embarrassing—she looked like she had the measles! She'd spent the afternoon with a cold cloth on her cheeks, reading, crocheting, and listening to the gramophone player in her room.

One interesting wrinkle. Yes, she'd known Kathleen Grant slightly through her late brother—twenty-five years ago. Peter Shaw and Miss Waring had had "more or less an understanding," but he was killed in the Second Boer War. When she'd known her, if that was the correct verb, Kathleen was just a tiny child, still in nappies. She'd lost touch with her until she'd met her a few times at Compton Chase after Addie had married Rupert, but they were not at all close.

With her conservative clothes, braided bun, and sensible shoes, Eloise Waring's photograph could have illustrated the dictionary entry under "old maid," if there was such a thing. There were a lot of old maids in Britain now, the consequence of a generation of men slaughtered across Europe. A woman in her forties like Miss Waring had little hope of making a decent marriage now.

Dev had gotten about halfway through with Pandora Halliday—watched tennis, played tennis, napped and bathed, and of course was alone—when all hell broke loose. Poor Bob had carried Lady Adelaide home, with her yelling at him at regular intervals to put her down at once. It had taken some time to unravel what had happened, and by that time Mrs. Halliday was in charge and put Lady Adelaide to bed upstairs. Dev had excused himself to the waiting interviewees and gone to the gardener's cottage, leaving Bob to call for reinforcements.

Four—and a half, counting Pandora Halliday—people to go. His original plan had been to get back to the Compton Arms at a reasonable hour, compare notes with Bob, scrounge up some dinner and a pint, go to bed. Now he'd be lucky to sleep at all.

One thing was clear: Kathleen Grant was not very popular with this particular crowd, and would not be missed. Dev wondered if it was worthwhile to gather a list of her *amours*, although his instincts told him no strange man had come to Compton Chase at her invitation. He'd send Yardley to make inquiries at the train station and taxi line, but his hunch told him the murderer was right here, pretending to "rest" while he really gave Kathleen the kiss of death.

Or murderers? He supposed it was possible two of them could have collaborated. Someone with access to cocaine, which was unfortunately readily accessible in all its forms nowadays, even in the country. General knowledge of the estate. Someone damn lucky not to be seen by a houseful of servants and guests. All the doors had been left open for the easy access of the guests and to help with air circulation, so people had moved about the estate during the day at will without Mr. Forbes' or a footman's assistance.

Bob had been meticulous in taking statements from all the servants present, and no one had noticed anyone tiptoeing toward the tithe barn yesterday. Of course, they'd been run off their feet with tea trays, drinks, hors d'oeuvres, and dinners to prepare and present. Mrs. Drum ran a tight ship with a limited number of staff. And if Dev was sure of anything, the butler did not do it. Forbes, like Lady Broughton, wouldn't lower himself.

He let himself in, then went to the Great Hall, where his notes were as he left them on the games table. That was careless, but he'd devised a code that would prevent an ordinary person from reading what he'd written. Dev doubted anyone here knew the Hindi alphabet. He pulled a drawer open, and found a muslin bag of chess and checkers pieces. The board was wood inlay on the tabletop, squares of walnut and maple.

Ruthless strategy. Who possessed it?

By reputation, certainly Colonel Mellard, who'd campaigned successfully across the Empire all his adult life. The banker Shipman, who'd single-handedly created a financial empire. Probably Lady Broughton, whom any sensible person would be reluctant to cross. Wasps were small, but had a devastating sting.

Lord Waring possessed above-average intelligence, but didn't strike Dev as a man with a murderous passion. Sir David Grant appeared too worn down to feel anything. Dev had yet to speak to Gerald Dumont, George Halliday, Barbara Pryce, or the colonel. He'd like to remedy that tonight.

He looked up to see Lady Adelaide in the doorway. She'd changed her dress into something nun-like, black with a tight white collar and cuffs. Besides her wedding and engagement rings, a long strand of pearls was her only adornment. She'd made an effort with the paint pots, but he could see how pale she still was.

He stood up. "How are you feeling, Lady Adelaide?"

"Like a fool. I don't know what's happening to me. Where is your sergeant? I wanted to apologize for screaming in his ear like a banshee."

"No need. He's seen and heard everything in our line of work, believe me. Won't you sit down?" Dev pulled a chair out for her.

"Just for a moment. My guests are at dinner without me. I should see how they're doing."

"But you don't want to."

"No, I don't! I think one of them must have killed poor Mr. McGrath, who saw something he shouldn't have, don't you? I don't care about Kathleen—isn't that awful of me to say?—but he was a lovely man. He deserved much better. I don't know what I'm going to tell his daughters."

"You don't think a stranger might have committed the crime?"

"What is it you say at an inquest—'murder by person or persons unknown'? How would a stranger—a tramp or a vagrant—know where the gardener's cottage is?"

"How would your guests?"

"They've all been here before. Well, except for Barbara's latest fiancé. Rupert used to do a guided tour and march all over the place, introducing our company to the biggest pig on the home farm and so forth. He was proud of everything, and very funny."

"And a war hero, too."

"Yes. I sometimes think he would have been better off if he was still fighting somewhere. Peacetime bored him. I bored him."

Dev was reminded of Sir David's words, and something clicked. "Was your husband friendly with Lady Grant?"

The spots of rouge stood out on her white cheeks. "What do you mean by that?"

"Nothing. I'm trying to understand the relationships here. One thinks of the country as quiet, but it can be a hotbed of vice, don't you agree?"

"You're making me sorry I stopped in to see you, Inspector."

He heard a marquess' daughter, and was reminded of her mother too. Dev smiled. "Now I'm the sorry one. I don't mean to offend."

She wrapped the pearls around a finger. "Oh, you'll find out sooner or later if you're as clever as I think you are. Kathleen and Rupert had a fling. It didn't last long, and it didn't mean anything. Both of them were not meant for marriage."

"Now I really *am* sorry."

Lady Adelaide shrugged. "So now you can move me up the suspect list. Wronged wife and all that. Concerned sister, too, if you want more ammunition. I know what Cee's told you, the little idiot. If she ever wins Sir David over—and my mother, who is opposed to the match with every fiber of her being—having Kathleen dead is a great convenience. She would have made any second wife's life a misery."

Dev raised an eyebrow. "Do you want to confess?"

"Not especially. I've never been a good liar."

"That's a relief." He sat back in his chair. "I don't have you on my list at all."

"Really? Why am I innocent?"

"It's just a feeling I have. It rarely lets me down. You can tell your mother she's safe at the moment, too."

Her face fell. "Not Cee?"

"Not quite yet. I haven't had a chance to complete the preliminary interviews. If the colonel, the Hallidays, Miss Pryce, and Mr. Dumont could make themselves available for a few minutes tonight, I would be most grateful. I'll have to speak to everyone else again tomorrow morning."

If he could somehow stay awake.

Chapter Ten

"You *are* a widgeon. It wasn't necessary to share my petty prurient peccadilloes with the Maharaja. Why did you tell him about me snizzling Kathleen?"

Addie hardly jumped. Thank goodness she'd dismissed Beckett for the night and was behind her dressing screen. "Don't be vulgar! And prejudiced! You never used to be such a snob." Or so alliterative.

"No, I was a modern man, wasn't I? Friend to the downtrodden. Beloved by all." Rupert plunked down on her bed and gave Fitz's ear a scratch. The dog didn't wake up. So much for extra-sensory-something.

"I wouldn't go that far, Rupert," Addie said. "You yourself mocked all those glowing newspaper articles about your wartime exploits. You said if you were that perfect, you would have been so insufferable that you would have had to kill yourself."

Oops. He more or less had.

Rupert didn't get the inference. "I was right to mock. All those medals and accolades—they've got me nowhere! Stuck here like a poor relation, a maiden aunt or some such, invisible and without any influence at all. It's…depressing. I might as well take up knitting. Eloise and I can share patterns. Knit one, purl two, right?"

"Eloise doesn't knit. She crochets. I can't believe you're complaining. You led a charmed life when you were really here.

Women dropped their drawers and dropped at your feet left and right—even men fell in love with you."

He waved his hands in protest. "Don't bring up boarding school, I beg you. We all experimented out of sheer boredom. Anyway, that was a long time ago. Didn't you and Pansy ever—?"

"No, we did not!" Addie stepped out from behind the chintz panels, a thick woolen robe over her tissue-thin nightgown. She might die of heat prostration, but Rupert was not going to get an undeserved eyeful before he left her alone.

She *could* make him go away, couldn't she? Chant some curse or something? Circle counter-clockwise on one foot? She'd have to go to the lending library at the post office and see if there were any books on witchcraft.

"There must be some way to get you out of my head," she muttered.

"I'm not in your head, Addie. I'm on your bed."

"La la la. I can't hear you." Addie went to the wall of open windows overlooking the garden. The air was still, the sky blanketed with clouds that covered the stars. Perhaps it would rain tomorrow and wash away the heat and all her troubles. However, if witches floated in water, what about ghosts? They were likely impervious to everything. Monsoons. Cyclones. Hurricanes.

She really did need to consult with an expert without letting on that she was crazy. What had Edward Rivers learned about the afterlife in divinity school? She'd have to find out. Addie was surprised actually that he hadn't turned up today, what with all the dead bodies in need of blessing and several of his parishioners in need of reassurance. He used the slightest excuse to drop in, usually around teatime. Addie suspected his housekeeper at the vicarage was nowhere near as good a cook as Cook.

"You've got to come to accept my presence at some point."

She turned to Rupert, who looked very comfortable, all her pillows tucked under his dark head. "I do not. I'm going to see a doctor as soon as I can. Maybe I need electroshock therapy. A lobotomy. You are a figment of my overtaxed psyche."

"Psyche *schmyche*. Don't tell me you've fallen for that psycho-analytical claptrap."

"Why not? It makes as much sense as having a dead husband turn up after six months and dogging my every step." Addie sat down, took the pins out of her hair, and began to brush.

"As we're talking about dogs, don't I get a thank you for rescuing yours? How did he come to be there anyway?"

"Jane bumped into Mr. McGrath, and he volunteered to take Fitz for the afternoon. He had a soft spot for him, even if Fitz dug up his dahlias. He told Jane the dog cheered him up and gave him hope for this wicked world. Or at least that's how she remembers it. He was supposed to bring him back by suppertime. The poor dog must have been tied up outside all night."

"I can't ask him, even if *I* bump into him in this limbo state. Not allowed. There's a no fraternization policy whose rules elude me. What I need is a Debrett's for the afterlife," he said, appearing thoughtful, a most unusual expression for him. Rupert had always been a man of action, leaping before he looked.

"Oh, Rupert! I can't believe he's dead! If you do happen to see Mr. McGrath, and you can, will you tell him how sorry I am? What the hell am I saying?" She threw her hairbrush across the room, her aim off, as she had removed her spectacles. It slapped against a wall and tumbled to the rug. Fitz slept on. He was an utter failure as her defender or retriever. Why hadn't he barked when poor Mr. McGrath was getting murdered in his bed?

Would her dog recognize the killer? Maybe Beckett was right. She'd have to watch to see if Fitz's hackles were raised by any of her company.

Rupert sat up on the bed. "Now, now. No tears. You know I can't bear them."

"I don't care what you can bear." Addie wiped her nose on the sleeve of her robe. "I've had quite enough of you and everyone. I want to be left in peace so I can enjoy my Last Days."

"*You* aren't dying, and won't for ages. Trust me."

"How can I trust you after everything you've done?" Addie cried. She wouldn't lower herself to ask him the specifics about how long she'd live—it wouldn't be cricket, although it was tempting.

And, really, it was like asking herself, because *Rupert wasn't here*.

"I never meant to hurt you, Addie. I was…oh, I suppose you'd say let-down after the war. All the excitement was over. I was at loose ends, and one thing led to another."

"You should have taken up a bloody hobby. Golf. Fishing."

"Sinking a little white ball into a hole with a stick when I could be in a lady's boudoir sinking into something entirely more satisfactory? Come now, Addie. Even you must see the absurdity of that. I acknowledge I was weak. A sinner. Perhaps my nanny mistreated me once too often. Withheld my puddings and paddled my bottom with too much zeal. And now I'm paying for it. I wonder what it is I'm supposed to be doing here to help you out."

"I don't want your help! I want you gone! Right this bloody minute!" She covered her mouth with a hand, almost expecting her mother or Rupert's maligned nanny to swoop in with a bar of soap and wash out the naughty word.

"You'll have to take it up with the Fellow Upstairs. I really have no control."

Addie wanted to scream, but the police were still downstairs finishing up. The last thing she needed was to be carted off to a padded cell.

"Look, I'm exhausted. Can't you go wherever it is you go when you're not aggravating me? A cloud or a closet or a crypt? I want to go to sleep, damn you!"

He patted the bed. "Curl right up. I'll watch over you."

"No thank you," Addie said tartly. "I hardly think you're my guardian angel."

Rupert brushed some invisible lint off his cuff. "You have no faith in me."

Addie was pretty sure she'd lost what little faith she had some time ago. She knew she should be grateful for her circumstances in life, and she was. It was far better to be Lady Adelaide Compton than anyone else she knew, including her mother. It was a gift she should be using wisely, but she seemed to be tripping over her own expensively shod feet lately.

"*Now*, Rupert. I feel as dead as you are."

"All right, all right. I'm leaving. I heard the coppers say they're going to search everyone's rooms tomorrow. Do you have any contraband? Needles? Cocaine?"

There was a box of chocolates in a night table drawer. The packets of sleeping powder. A nearly empty bottle of French brandy in one of her Wellington boots. All unexceptional.

Oh! The dreadful life-like dildo Barbara had sent after the funeral was in the other boot! Addie blushed to the roots of her hair.

Rupert winked. Of course he would *know*. "Put it in a box and I'll take care of it."

"Throw it away!"

"You're not dead yet, my dear. It may come in handy on a long winter's night. A long summer's night, for that matter."

Addie rummaged in her armoire, searching for the buried boots, and pulled the incriminating evidence of her solitary state out of the left one. Not quite tall enough to get purchase on a shoe box, every single one of them fell from the top shelf in a rumble.

"Look what you've made me do!" She kicked a box across the floor and immediately regretted her throbbing toes. Addie dumped out a pair of velvet pumps and stuffed the pink marble thing in the box they came in. She tossed it in Rupert's direction and he made an easy catch. "Thank you. Now please, please go."

"Your wish is my command, my lady." He disappeared, shoe box included.

Addie collapsed on the bed next to Fitz, thought the better of it, sat up and untied the bathrobe. She felt immediate relief. The bedroom was still sweltering. She wished she'd bought electric fans, but she'd been a little afraid of blowing up the new wiring and burning down the house just when it was to her liking. She pulled open the bedside table drawer, found her little red leather notebook and a silver mechanical pencil, and wrote:

Call Harrods re fans. Ask maids in attic if they are surviving. Several for them. 1 for me, 6 spares for guests if I ever entertain again? (unlikely)

Letters to Mr. McGrath's daughters. DO NOT PUT OFF!!!

Invite Edward R. for tea to pick brain re heaven/hell. Reading list? Call Hatchards

Inquire discreetly about psychoanalysis (Dr. Bergman)

She flipped back a few pages. There was her guest list for the Saturday-to-Monday. One of those people…

She set the notebook down. Why was Kathleen Grant killed? Besides the fact, as Cee said, that she was an "evil bitch."

And that wasn't really true. Kathleen had been beautiful, lively, and selfish. It would never have occurred to *her* to supply fans to her servants, Addie thought with a touch of smugness. But Kathleen had never been deliberately unkind, except when it came to Sir David. Easily bored. Up for anything.

And a drug addict? That was the rumor. Addie had difficulty believing such a thing.

She remembered the time Kathleen jumped into the lake in her vest and knickers, her taffeta dress tossed on the lawn, a casualty of one too many gin fizzes. David had been mortified, but Rupert laughed and joined her. It was the last time they had socialized as couples before David sued her for divorce.

Addie picked up the notebook and made notes.

The most logical explanations for her death:

Because she did something

Because she didn't do something

Because she knew something

Like poor Mr. McGrath, someone might have wanted her to be quiet. Permanently.

Chapter Eleven

Dev allowed himself one gasper a day, and, both God and Vishnu knew, he had earned it tonight. He'd been puffing away at the back of the house when he heard the most extraordinary conversation from the bank of open windows above.

No. It wasn't a conversation—it was completely one-sided. Lady Adelaide was talking to herself. Crying a little too. There had been the sound of flying and falling objects, a few unladylike curses, some talk of golf, of all things. Dev was as fond of puzzles as the next person, otherwise he'd never be a detective. But what she'd been saying—what he could hear clearly—made no sense at all.

At first he thought someone was in the room with her, but unless he'd gone deaf or the person was using sign language, there were long silent pauses between her utterances. The woman was, sadly, somewhat unhinged. A pity, as she was so attractive. But the upper classes were known for their idiosyncrasies, which people like Dev could not afford.

He hadn't meant to eavesdrop. Oh, who was he kidding? The more he knew about the people at Compton Chase, the sooner he could leave it. He'd eliminated Lady Adelaide as a likely murderess, based on his gut instinct. He hoped it wasn't because he found her so physically appealing, which any red-blooded man would do. Even Bob was a bit bowled over. She reminded Dev of a schoolmistress with those specs sliding down her nose, her enormous hazel eyes wide, her lips a perfect cupid's bow.

But perhaps he'd been too hasty. If she was deranged or drugged-up in some way, why couldn't she have walked across her lawn and killed Kathleen Grant, then gone after her gardener?

Dev felt a tap on his shoulder. Where were his instincts now? He could have been knifed where he stood.

"Guv, here's the last of them. The colonel's waiting for you, and then he wants to go back to his own place in the village. He'll come back early tomorrow, if that's all right."

"I suppose. Ready for bed yourself?"

"Close. I'll just go and have a last word with Mr. Forbes while you finish up."

Dev had thought it odd that several of the guests stayed overnight to begin with, when they lived such a short distance away. There was Grant, Colonel Mellard, the Waring cousins, even Lady Broughton and her younger daughter. But if everyone drove home, no doubt a little tipsy, a house party wouldn't be a house party then, would it? He wondered what entertainment Lady Adelaide had planned for Sunday before everything was spoiled by death.

Dev ground out his cigarette beneath his boot, then picked it up and put it in his pocket. He didn't want complaints that the boorish half-caste police inspector defiled the pristine grounds. It would be bad enough tomorrow when a squad from Cirencester came to sweep through the house. He'd have to give them strict instructions.

Constable Yardley had been told to stay away.

The house was still lit up like Christmas, though everybody had drifted upstairs to bed some time ago. Dev had spoken with Barbara Pryce of "Lowest prices at Pryce's" fame before he cadged his cigarette. Her father's business might be based on odd job lots and damaged goods, but his daughter was one elegant and exalted customer.

It appeared no one had told her the guests were not dressing for dinner tonight. Her teal beaded evening gown must have come straight from Paris, not some burnt warehouse, and she'd made a point of telling him her mother was a baron's daughter who'd given her the emeralds she was wearing as she lit American cigarette after American cigarette. She'd flirted outrageously during the interview—she must have forgotten she was engaged to Gerald Dumont.

To be fair, Dev had found Dumont to be forgettable—he was handsome enough, but a cipher. A few years younger than Miss Pryce, he was "between jobs," and had known no one at Compton Chase before he arrived yesterday in Barbara's new cherry-red Lancia Lambda. He swore he and Miss Pryce had lounged about in her room until the dinner gong, turning cherry-red himself at the admission.

The Hallidays had provided no pertinent information, either, although they admitted to socializing with Kathleen Grant on numerous occasions in Town but were "only casual acquaintances." Dev had a list now from them of people to contact when he returned to London, but he hoped the case would be cleared up before then. All he needed was someone to confess!

The colonel was pacing in front of the Great Hall's massive fireplace, and looked pointedly at his watch when Dev entered. His military bearing evident, he looked as fit as he must have been as a younger man. He'd volunteered to go last, but probably had not expected the late hour.

"Sorry to keep you waiting, sir. Won't you sit down?"

They moved to a pair of chairs, and the colonel took a cigar out of his pocket, rolling it between his palms. "I spoke with your sergeant. You have no objection to me sleeping in my own bed tonight?"

"No, Colonel. As long as you don't do a bunk."

"No chance of that. Terrible business. I knew Kathleen well. Too well, I'm afraid." He reached into his jacket and held another cigar out. "Want one?"

"No, thank you. Can you tell me what you mean by that?"

Mellard took his time clipping the cigar and lighting it up. Dev waited, patience fraying. He looked down at his own watch. Midnight had come and gone.

Blowing a smoke ring, the colonel sat back in his chair. "No one knows. I'm not sure I should even tell you. It will look bad. That's why I waited to go last. Indecisive. But the truth is the right thing to tell."

"Tell me what?"

"I had asked Kathleen to marry me. You'll think there's no fool like an old fool, but it wasn't a love match on either side. I knew about her affairs—it would have been hard not to know—but I believe we could have muddled along together. She would have been closer to her boys for part of the year, too."

This was rather a bombshell. No wonder the colonel had been indecisive. "I was under the impression she didn't like country living," Dev said carefully. Or fidelity.

"She didn't. We would have traveled some, and she would have been a wonderful companion. She is…was…so energetic. Curious. I miss it, you know. New sights, new sounds, new smells, some not always entirely pleasant, of course. I'm still not used to waking up in the same place every morning. Odd, when one is posted abroad, all one wants is home, and now—" He shrugged.

"Anyway, I keep a bolt-hole in London that would have suited as a base as well. My income is sufficient to have kept her in every comfort. Grant kept her on a tight leash, saddling her with three children one after the other. He's a dull, judgmental sort of fellow. Mean, too—perhaps not in temperament, but when it came to money, he could barely part with a penny. Kathleen was wasted on him. She was much too full of life to be buried down here."

And now she was full of death, to be buried here forever.

"I must ask you, Colonel, was she here to see you?"

Dev was surprised to see the old soldier blush. "Yes. We had an assignation of sorts. Entirely innocent. She came down on the train, and took a taxi up to the turn-off. She thought it great fun to hide in plain sight as it were, slipping through the woods to the tithe barn. But I swear to you, when I left her, she was very much alive. And dressed," he emphasized. "I would never be so ungentlemanly as to take advantage of a lady in a barn. My housekeeper is away for a few weeks, and Kathleen planned on spending the night at my house. Said she was going to measure the windows for new drapes." His voice thickened. "She didn't like my curtains, you see. Said my place needed a feminine touch."

"Did you plan to see her again last night?"

Mellard nodded. "Once the party had broken up, I would have gone for a midnight walk. I do that sometimes—everyone in the village knows it. I like the stars. The quiet. One can think."

Maybe Dev should make it a point to do the same. It might help this investigation that was going nowhere.

"Would you know anything about her possible drug use?"

The colonel winced. "I wouldn't say drug use, per se. Not that she hadn't experimented—so many of these Bright Young People do nowadays. And when she was finally free of Grant, she may have overindulged in any number of activities to make up for lost time, I'll admit. One must make allowances for youthful high spirits, eh? But I doubt she was addicted. One can tell. Take Miss Pryce, for example—there's something wrong *there*."

Of course. Dev had been too stupid and flattered to see it. Barbara Pryce had been high as a kite when he interviewed her.

"You're a man of the world, Colonel Mellard. What do you think about these crimes? Who would want Lady Grant dead?"

"I can't imagine. Grant, perhaps. He didn't want her, but he might have got wind that I did. Kath was not always as discreet as she should have been. It was part of her charm."

Rubbing her ex-husband's nose in her newfound love was not especially charming, but Dev refrained from saying so. "How was she fixed for money? Did she have outstanding debts that might have led to retribution?" Drug dealers were not known for the milk of human kindness when they were owed money.

"Grant had given her an allowance. I've been supplementing it for a few months. One couldn't expect her to live on what he gave her. As I said, he was a Scrooge. Eventually, she would have come into a bit of money. There's a grandfather up north. She'll share with a cousin when he passes." He realized what he'd said. "She *would have* shared. I'm sorry. I can't believe she's really gone."

"Do you know who this cousin is?"

"Haven't the faintest. Kath had never met her. Or him. I don't know which. I can find out the name of her solicitor. He might have that information."

"I'd appreciate that." Dev had to tread lightly now. "I'm going to ask you an uncomfortable question for both of us. Is it possible she was seeing someone else, romantically speaking?"

Mellard looked him directly in the eye. "Absolutely not. She was done with all that. It was part of our arrangement."

"Did you see anyone about when you left her? The gardener, for instance?"

"I can't recall. I wasn't really looking, you see. I did have to run back to my house to unlock it for her and check my mail. I wasn't paying much attention. When I got back here, the house was wide open and all the young people were otherwise occupied. I read in my room and took a cold bath. Devilish hot it's been this past week. Reminds me of India."

"My father served in Jhansi Province. Bedfordshire Regiment."

"Hunter. Was your father Harry Hunter? Military Mounted Police?"

"Yes, sir. Do you know him?" Dev really would have to talk to his father now.

"By reputation. He was a tough old nut."

"Still is. He retired from the Metropolitan Police Force a few years ago as a Detective Chief Inspector."

"Like father, like son, eh? Still, you probably haven't had an easy time of it, no matter who your pa was."

Dev let that go, and rose. "Thank you for your time, Colonel. And I am sorry for your loss. Have you packed up yet?"

The colonel tossed his cigar butt in the empty fireplace. "No. I expect you'd like to rootle around in my room. Do you want to pat me down before I leave?"

Good grief. "No, sir."

"I'll come back for my kit tomorrow. I have plenty of extra tooth powder and mustache wax."

"Do you want Sergeant Wells to run you home?"

"No. I'll walk, as is my custom. Count the stars and think. Keeps one young. I'll just borrow a torch. Lady Adelaide has some in the front hall. Good night, Inspector. And good luck."

Dev sat back down to think. Exactly what he should be thinking *of* was elusive. Feeling light-headed, he was beginning to regret skipping supper.

Kathleen Grant, laid out like a virgin bride, a crumpled bouquet of hay in her hands. Someone knew about her impending marriage. But who?

Chapter Twelve

Monday

"Pills. Several kinds. No sign of anything injectable."

"Thank God. Are they going to arrest her?"

Rupert shook his head. "All legal, if ill-advised. Barbara says she has a prescription for both the barbiturates and the amphetamines. Not with her, of course. They were phoning her doctors in London last I looked." He loosened his necktie. "Damn, it's hotter than hell, not that I'd know. Yet. What kind of quacks does she go to? The men should lose their licenses not to recognize Barbara was fooling both of them."

Addie agreed. She knew Barbara had been restless and unhappy. Or *too* happy. Money didn't buy everything, but it did buy drugs, unfortunately. "So, they found nothing incriminating. I must say, the police were very respectful. One could never tell they'd been in my drawers."

"Nobody's been in your drawers for yonks, my dear. And I'm sorry about that, believe it or not."

Addie lobbed a pillow at him and missed. "So that's it? They're just leaving?"

"The Cirencester bunch is. Your friends and family are free to leave as well. I understand Hunter and his henchman are staying another night in the village. He wants to talk to you, by the way."

"I should ask them to supper. Something informal. On the terrace. It will only be Pansy and George, I think."

"Why aren't they going home?"

"I thought you knew all." Addie stuck her tongue out. She was getting used to these odd encounters with her dead husband. Obviously, she must have overheard everyone's plans herself; she just couldn't remember the details because she was hot and tired.

And going mad.

"There must be a short-circuit somewhere. How many more days are they sponging here?"

"Not sponging. They can stay as long as they like. Their flat is being painted."

Rupert curled a lip. "You believe that? I think they've been thrown out. They haven't paid the rent for almost a year."

"What? How can that be?"

"If Germany can default, why not George? His downfall? Speculation in Canadian wheat, of all things. If only the world ate more cereal, the Hallidays would be hunky-dory."

"Pansy never said a word."

"Well, she wouldn't, would she? She's always been jealous of you, and doesn't want to appear vulnerable."

Addie gaped at Rupert. "Jealous! Don't be ridiculous. We've been the best of friends since school."

"That's what you think."

Oh, no. No no no. "Don't tell me that you—and she—"

"All right, I won't tell you." He did have the sense to look shame-faced.

"Oh, Rupert! How could you?" It wouldn't help to scream or throw more pillows, but she wanted to. Very much.

"You needn't blame me! If you must know, it was her idea. You think she's a shy, quiet little thing, but you would be wrong. She's always wanted what you have, and what you had was me. I succumbed. I'm not proud of myself. But if it makes any difference, it happened before we were married."

It didn't. "I want you out of this house this instant!"

Rupert gave her a sad smile. "Oh, we've had that fight before. Several times. This time, I really can't leave. Sorry."

"At least get out of my bedroom!"

"All right. That sounds reasonable."

She blinked, and he was gone.

Such betrayal. Addie should be used to it by now, but she wasn't. How could she look Pansy in the face? Worse, how could Pansy look at hers? Why, she'd put Addie to bed yesterday afternoon after she'd been carted home like a sack of potatoes by Sergeant Wells, rubbed a cool cloth on her forehead, and said comforting things like a true friend would. All the while she was probably snickering up her sleeve.

To think Addie had thought of loaning—no, gifting—the Hallidays some money to tide them over if they truly were in trouble financially. They could starve, for all she cared.

But if they needed school fees for their son away at prep school—

Really, there must be a sign around her neck that said "FOOL." She expected people to behave better, but they never did. She'd been hopelessly naïve, and it was time to smarten up.

Beckett rapped once and poked her head in. "People are scrambling to leave, Lady A. And that personable inspector wants a word. He looks a little like Charles Farrell, don't you think? He's just a bit player, but he's going places."

Addie wouldn't know Charles Farrell if she tripped over him. She'd have to look him up in Beckett's magazines. "I'll be down in a few minutes. Do me a favor. Get one of the housemaids to help you pack up the Hallidays. I've changed my mind about them staying."

Sir David and the colonel had already vacated their rooms, but had come back after breakfast for a final interview, then left again before lunch. While the house was being searched attic to cellar by the police, Inspector Hunter had gathered up her guests and gone over everyone's time lines, i.e., their alibis, for both murders. They sat in a circle like a group of fidgety Sunday School children. Addie had paid close attention, but not as close as the inspector.

He must be enormously frustrated—no one had seen or done anything unusual Saturday afternoon and they sounded so… honest, at least to Addie's ears. But someone was lying, weren't they?

Addie patted her hair, dusted her face with a bit of powder, and went downstairs. The ancient studded front door stood open, the cars had been brought around, and luggage was scattered on the black-and-white-tiled floor. She stopped herself from rubbing her hands in glee.

But there was a fly in the ointment. Two, if one counted correctly.

"Forbes, have you seen either Mr. or Mrs. Halliday?

"I believe they are in the gold drawing room, Lady Adelaide."

"Thank you. Could you get someone to take them to the station as soon as possible? Plans have changed. I'll be right back to bid farewell to my guests. They'll probably never come back again."

Which was almost all right with her.

Addie could see George smoking on the terrace through the open French door. Pansy glanced up from one of Beckett's cinema magazines and smiled.

"You look *much* better than you did yesterday."

"Do I? Looks can be deceiving. I'm frightfully sorry, but I'm going to have to renege on my offer to let you both stay on for a few days. I feel wretched—this has all been too much for me. I want to be left alone." She placed a hand across her brow for emphasis.

Pansy shut the magazine. "Is that wise? We could help you get through this difficult time."

"How?"

Pansy opened her mouth, but had no prepared remarks. "Um, uh, we could go walking. Get some fresh air."

"And die of heatstroke. No, I want to lock myself in my room and sleep for days. Naked. I know you understand. I've taken the liberty of having your things packed, and Forbes will see to it that you're on the next train. I'm sure you miss London."

"But the flat—I told you it's being painted."

"You'll get used to the fumes. I know I did during our renovations. Or go to a hotel. Forbes can call the Savoy for you. Or the Ritz." Goodness. Addie didn't know how bitchy she could be. If they were broke, she was offering the impossible.

Pansy shook her head. "That won't be necessary. We'll work something out."

"Excellent. Well, toodle-oo. Thank you so much for coming." Addie left before she had to receive a good-bye kiss.

She did give Angela a peck, though, as Ernest practically knocked her over running to his car. Assuring her mother and sister that she was quite looking forward to some peace and quiet, Addie waved them on their way too, then hugged Eloise and shook Lucas' hand as they followed soon after.

Barbara and Gerald were last to leave. Her friend was wearing large sunglasses and a guilty expression. Addie chose not to mention the drug business; there would be time when Barbara was more clear-headed.

"There! All gone. Forbes, I cannot tell you how happy I am to have the house back to myself."

"About that. Inspector Hunter is waiting for you in the Great Hall."

How could she have forgotten?

Chapter Thirteen

"These are your family and friends, Lady Adelaide. I know it's unorthodox, but I'd like your opinion."

Her mouth formed a little O of surprise. There were faint smudges under her gold-green eyes, a sign that she hadn't slept well.

Dev hadn't slept at all.

"You know them well; I do not," he continued. "And I couldn't hold them here any longer without the wrath of my superiors raining down upon me—or perhaps Mrs. Oxley's. I've warned them all to let me know where to reach them, not leave town, etcetera. I'll be damned if this is a case of 'murder by person or persons unknown.' I'm missing something that's right in front of me."

"You still believe I didn't kill Kathleen?"

"You never would have killed your gardener too." Bob had sworn she'd been genuinely upset, so upset he'd put his back out carrying her back to the house as she squirmed and raved.

"I wrote to his daughters before sunrise. I still feel responsible. If I hadn't planned this stupid party…"

Dev lifted a hand. "If not here, then elsewhere. In my experience, another opportunity would have come along if the murderer was truly determined to kill Lady Grant. They would have made sure of it."

"But not Mr. McGrath, too! I still don't understand why she was here when I didn't invite her. What on earth was she doing hiding in the barn?"

"Ah. You haven't heard. You're not a gossip, are you?"

"Well, sometimes," Lady Adelaide admitted. "I listen more than I repeat, though. I don't know if that makes me any less guilty."

Dev found her honesty appealing. "Since I'm confiding in you—let's say temporarily deputizing you—I'd appreciate it if you said nothing to anyone else. Not even when you're talking to yourself."

Her fair eyebrows knit. "Talking to myself?"

"I, uh, overheard you last evening when you were upstairs. The windows were wide open—I assure you I wasn't spying. And I really couldn't understand everything you were saying anyhow. Maybe I've made a mistake. Were you talking to your maid?"

"What? Oh. Oh! No. Not to Beckett. And, yes, sometimes I do talk to myself. Even fight with myself. It clears my brain and gets the cobwebs out." She turned that massive engagement ring until only the band showed.

"You'll always win the argument, won't you? Anyway, Colonel Mellard and Lady Grant had an understanding. They were making plans to be married."

"You can't be serious!" Laughing, she quickly covered her mouth. "Oh, you are serious. Who told you such a thing?"

"The colonel himself. Do you think he was lying?"

"Goodness! How did Kathleen get her hooks into him, too? He must be beside himself. I never would have suspected a thing—he's so dreadfully dignified, isn't he? Stoic. He didn't bat an eye when I announced her death after dinner Saturday night. I checked everyone's reactions especially."

"I believe their relationship was more about companionship than great love. He was well aware of her faults."

"And he's old enough to be her father. Grandfather, if he started early enough."

"But not too old to want a pretty face across the breakfast table." Or in bed.

"Did Sir David know?"

"I'm not sure. For obvious reasons, Colonel Mellard doesn't want the news to get around to the general public. I'm going to stop at Holly Hill on the way back to London tomorrow and see what Sir David has to say. I'm seeing your vicar this afternoon."

"He's not *my* vicar. I find him a little annoying, to be frank. I know I shouldn't say anything like that—it's very un-Christian, but when you talk to him, you'll understand. He's such a Mr. Collins. Why do you need to talk to him? He wasn't even here."

"Exactly." Dev had no idea who this Collins bloke was, but would find out.

"Oh! I can't see Edward Rivers creeping about and plunging a needle into Kathleen. I don't think they were even acquainted. He's only been in the parish since December. Kathleen moved to London over a year ago, although she was back and forth to see the children."

"I like to tie up loose ends."

"Don't we all?" She turned the ring again, and the sapphires and diamonds sparkled. "Nothing will happen to Barbara Pryce, will it?"

Two women in charming Compton-Under-Wood, both with nasty drug habits. Was there a connection? "If she doesn't stop taking those pills, then yes. Something very unpleasant will happen. I'm not sure that fiancé of hers has the will to stand up to her. Do you know him well?"

"I don't know him at all. I doubt Barbara does. They met on the Riviera a few months ago. Maybe *he* did it. Killed Kathleen, I mean."

Dev bit back a smile. "Why do you say that?"

"He's not a friend or a member of my family, so that would be the perfect solution. It would make me feel like a much better judge of character than I've been for thirty-one years."

"You sound, if I may say so, a little bitter."

"Well, I am! My late husband was a cad of the first order, and my friends are not who I thought them to be. Whom? I can't even think properly in English." She pushed her spectacles, which had begun to drift, back up her nose. "Oh! I don't know what's come over me. I usually try not to let my feelings get the better of me."

"You're only human. Sometimes we can't see things because we're too close. That's kind of how I feel about this case. On the surface, there are few reasons for anyone here this weekend to want Lady Grant out of the way. They say they either didn't know her at all, or knew her only slightly. Her husband had already divorced her. Even if she made the occasional demand over seeing their children or wanting more money, Sir David doesn't strike me as the type to resort to murder. He's a steady sort of fellow, isn't he? Conservative."

Lady Adelaide nodded. "I've always thought so. Even when Kathleen was making a fool of him, he kept his dignity. I suppose he could have snapped, though. We all have our breaking point."

"What did he do in the war?"

"Something at the War Office. Very hush-hush. He met Kathleen in London and married her in 1917 after her parents died. Her much older brother was lost in the Battle of Ladysmith years ago. I only know that because she made a joke of it—she was so young she thought there was a fight over Lady Smith. Her parents were on the *Lusitania* when it was torpedoed. Sir David must have been her port in the storm at first. But then..." She shrugged. "Kathleen was easily bored. He was over twenty years older than she, and they had different interests. They moved down to his country house once the war was over. It didn't suit."

"Did you know her before you became neighbors?"

"Not really. We might have attended some of the same parties in Town. She was a few years younger than I was."

Really? At this point, Dev had seen the body and not much

of his bed at the Compton Arms. Lady Adelaide appeared much fresher and more youthful, not only because Lady Grant had been dead for forty-eight hours. Drug use tended to have adverse effects on the human body. No matter what the colonel believed in his semi-bridegroom state, Dev thought Lady Grant had done more than "experiment."

"Was she especially friendly with Colonel Mellard during her marriage?"

"I never would have said so before, but now that I know they were engaged—" Lady Adelaide paused. "The thing is, Kathleen flirted with everyone. Even my butler, poor man. That rattled him terribly, and Forbes is not one to rattle. I don't think she could help herself. If one wore trousers, one was a target. She hadn't many close women friends, I don't think."

If Kathleen Grant had female lovers, she'd been discreet, which was somewhat out of character. But perhaps she drew the line somewhere. Dev didn't bring up the subject, not wanting to shock Lady Adelaide unnecessarily. "I spoke to some of her acquaintances in London by phone. They all found her to be rather a force of nature."

Lady Adelaide nodded. "She was hard to ignore. Mercurial. I told you, my sister and I met her a few months ago in the village. It was a lovely, warm day, and she was sitting outside having a drink alone. But maybe she was waiting for Colonel Mellard. She was awfully snippy with us, and practically ordered us to go away, which we did with the greatest of pleasure."

"You never heard any gossip about them?"

"No. It wouldn't be unusual for her to come to Compton-Under-Wood both during her marriage and after—there's no public house the next village over—church, either—and the Compton Arms is famous for its food. Plus, we have some excellent shops. If she met the colonel "by accident" in the beer garden, no one would think anything of it. He dines there regularly, even if his housekeeper is at home."

Dev tapped his notebook. "Next on my list. What about your sister?"

"What about her?" There was a touch of frost in her tone.

"Did she hate Lady Grant?"

"Hate is far too strong a word. I think she was frustrated for Sir David. She likes him very much, as I know she told you."

"Is the feeling returned?"

Lady Adelaide stared out the window, then gasped. Dev turned, but saw nothing that might cause any strong reaction. Lots of drooping greenery, wilting plants in pots. Someone should water, but it wasn't an emergency yet. Poor McGrath wasn't going to be doing it, though.

"Lady Adelaide?"

"What? Oh, your question. I'm sure I couldn't say. They're friends, considering the age difference. I think Sir David is wary of another entanglement. He has his little boys to think of. I think in the end, Cee's going to be…disappointed."

"The Hallidays?"

"They're having money issues, but I can't see how Kathleen's death benefits them. They barely knew her."

Dev jotted down this new information.

"Lord Waring?"

This time Lady Adelaide laughed openly. "He's much too *nice* to commit murder. I'd stake my very existence on it."

"Could he have had a relationship with the deceased that no one knew about?"

She frowned. "I just can't see it. She isn't—wasn't—his type. But I've been wrong about so many things before."

"Do his interests lie elsewhere?"

Her face became quite rosy. "I don't know."

Her first fib, Dev thought. She had been truthful about being a poor liar. "And his cousin?"

"The only needles Eloise has with her are in her crochet bag. Oh!"

Dev raised a brow. "Oh?"

"She worked as a nurse during the war. I expect she administered a few shots. But it would be absolutely ridiculous to suspect her."

Ridiculous or not, Dev added this to his notes.

"And, finally, the Shipmans."

"Again, they barely knew her. I like Angela a great deal. She's sweet. I'm not so crazy about her husband, so if you can pin it on him, I wouldn't object too strenuously."

He let himself chuckle. "That's not quite how police procedure works, Lady Adelaide. Thank you for your time. I'll be in touch if there's any break in the case." He closed his notebook and rose.

She sat, staring out of the window again. "I think I'll go up to London tomorrow for a few days. Get away from…everyone."

As half her guest list had returned there, she didn't make total sense, but then, Dev would be the first person to admit he didn't understand women. Especially a society beauty like Lady Adelaide Compton. His previous cases had never involved someone from so rarefied an environment.

He hoped he wasn't being too dazzled. Just because one talked to oneself, it didn't make one unbalanced enough to commit two murders, did it?

Chapter Fourteen

"What are you doing lurking about?" Addie whispered into the bushes.

"Not lurking. Until fairly recently, I was the lord of this manor. Let's just say I was surveying the property. And checking up on your welfare, too. You were unchaperoned. I don't trust that foreign fellow." Rupert stepped out from behind the hedge and brushed off his suit. For something that he'd worn now for six straight months under unusual conditions, it was holding up well.

"For heaven's sake—not that you'd know anything about that—Mr. Hunter is not foreign! He was born in Chelsea."

"Details. Nevertheless, that Bob Whosis should have been there looking like an earnest bulldog in his new suit, scribbling away. Or Beckett, if you could convince her to get her nose out of *Movie Weekly* long enough."

"You pressed *your* nose against the glass, crossed your eyes, and waggled your tongue at me while I was talking to him!"

"See? I don't understand how you could call that lurking. Lurking requires stealth. Tiptoeing. Near invisibility. There I was, plain as day."

Rupert always had an answer to everything. Addie wanted to slap him, but reminded herself he wasn't really there.

Or was he? Could it be possible that she was really, truly being haunted by the ghost of her husband?

Why was she being punished so? Just because she found Mr. Rivers' sermons dull as ditchwater? Even if she avoided church with the slimmest excuse—a slight cough, a bee-sting, a bunion—she'd tried to lead a virtuous life. Share her wealth with others. Be kind. In fact, she was as dull as ditchwater herself now, all her naughty childish exploits history. No wonder Rupert—

He pushed a branch away. "This isn't about you, my peach, and please don't think along those lines. I was never good enough for you. You just happen to be collateral damage at the moment. It's I that's being tested, sent here to perform some service that is as yet hazy. But I'll bet my life—ha, much too late—that my being here has something to do with those murders. I've been looking for clues."

"In the boxwood? Through the window?" Addie asked, sarcastic.

Rupert looked down at his feet. He'd been buried in brand-new shoes from John Lobb, and Addie wondered if they were comfortable. Did ghosts feel discomfort? It seemed unlikely.

"All right, I was jealous."

"Pardon?"

"You and that Hunter person. You looked very congenial when I peeked in."

"We were not congenial! And if we were, I was only helping him with his investigation. He asked me for my opinion, something *you* never did."

"That can't be true."

"I'm not going to argue with you. I don't even know why I'm out here. They're going to lock me away if they see me talking to the shrubbery."

"I won't let that happen, Addie, I promise." Rupert reached out to touch her, but she stumbled backward.

"Your promises are worth nothing."

"I admit my wedding vows were fudged a little, but as for the rest—I tried to be an honorable man. Didn't kick any dogs or someone when they were down and out. I wasn't a *total* cad. Why, your mother liked me despite everything! Still does. I can tell."

"You can believe whatever makes you feel better about yourself. I don't care anymore." Even as she said it, Addie knew that wasn't true. She'd been so deeply hurt by Rupert—*lessened*—she wondered if she'd ever recover.

Yes, what she needed was a stay in Town. A change of scenery. Addie had given a fashionable decorator *carte blanche* over Mount Street earlier this summer, and she'd barely had a chance to check out the changes. She'd send Beckett ahead to open up the flat and get in some groceries. Between the two of them, they could cobble together something edible for themselves. Order from the Connaught down the street, if they had to. Addie would go shopping, buy a new hat, something not black that she could look forward to wearing.

No, damn it. She'd buy it and wear it *now*. Life was meant for living. As Rupert said, he wasn't worth wearing black for. Besides the hat, she'd order a raft of new clothes in every color of the rainbow.

"It won't work, you know," Rupert said. "I can't be got rid of—I'll have to come along. Can we take the Daimler? The train can be so crowded, even in First Class. I think I'm meant to be near you to protect you."

"Protect me! Are you kidding? I'm not in any danger, except from you. And why can't you just fly to London? Flap your wings or something."

There was a wistful look on his face. "Would that I could. The happiest days of my life were spent in the air in my Avro. You've never seen blue until you've been in the middle of it." He plucked a few tiny leaves from the boxwood and let them fall. "There is a murderer on the loose, you know. It behooves us both to be vigilant."

"You mean I really can't get away from you?" Of course she could. This was England, land of opportunity. Green and pleasant. She simply needed to think positively. Think of any-thing—anyone—but Rupert.

"Sorry. No matter how hard you think to wish me away, that won't work either. You must come to terms that I am here, whether you like it or not. You aren't going mad. I'm not a figment of your imagination. Or a dream, which I'm sure you consider to be a nightmare. I have a job to do, maybe several, before I can leave this plane and ascend."

"Or descend."

"Please. As you said, we must think positively."

"I didn't say anything. You're inside my head, and I don't like it!"

"Uh, Lady Adelaide?"

Addie spun around to find Inspector Hunter and Sergeant Wells on the grass. Oh, God. How much had they heard?

Hunter looked at her with sympathetic brown eyes, as if he knew she was falling apart piece by piece, like the boxwood. "We're leaving now. I wanted to reassure you we've interviewed the last of your servants and have no reason to suspect any of them in the crimes. Mr. Forbes has given me your direction in London if I need to touch base with you. I hope you have a quiet, restful time. This, uh, event has been an ordeal for you, I know."

"Th-thank you. I...I was just fighting with myself. Again." Addie felt the need to explain, but could see the men were wary. "Good luck."

"We'll need it." He reached into his jacket for his card case. "In the event you think of anything—anything at all—that might be useful, please don't hesitate to contact me either at the Yard or...my home." He took out a pencil stub and wrote on the back of the card. "My hours are irregular, so it's best you try my office first. They'll know where to find me."

Addie took the card and slipped it into her skirt pocket.

"You're not going to call him at home, are you? That isn't done, my girl. A lady never calls a gentleman, even if the gentleman isn't quite top-drawer."

"Shut—should I recall anything, I certainly will." She turned and glared at Rupert.

Hunter tipped his hat, and his sergeant did the same. "Good day, then."

"Good-bye."

They walked around to the stable block, and she breathed a sigh of relief as their motor car started up without incident and moved down the avenue at a sedate rate.

"Good riddance."

"You were the one talking about a killer on the loose! Why don't you want them around?" A perfectly horrible thought occurred to her. "You didn't kill Kathleen, did you, with some sort of heebie-jeebie ghostly curse or something?"

"You *are* having a breakdown. Of course not. Heretofore, I've only killed Jerrys. As many as I could shoot down in the air and bomb on the ground. War really is hell, as that American General Sherman—the one with the funny middle name—said in the last century." He smoothed his silly little mustache down. "And I suppose, if one wants to be technical, I killed Claudette, I'm sorry to say."

"Do you see much of her?" Addie asked, imagining them cavorting in the afterlife, the wretches.

"No. In fact, I'm fairly sure she went directly to—ow! What was that for?"

Addie's fist was ice-cold, but it felt good on a hot day such as this.

Chapter Fifteen

Thursday

It was even hotter in London than in Compton-Under-Wood. When she wasn't shopping, Addie had spent the past two days in her slip in front of a bowl of ice and an electric fan. All thoughts of brassieres or therapy were temporarily postponed. It was too hot to think or care about anything. How did one ever get work done in the tropics? She could barely lift a finger to put a spoonful of sugar into her teacup. Even Beckett had given up her movie theaters and was lying in her room with an icepack on her forehead most of the day.

The one bright spot so far—Rupert had not materialized in their stark white London flat. Addie had come up by train, and he hadn't slithered into her First-Class compartment at the last minute. She'd been braced for it, prepared to ignore him, since it would be odd indeed for her to talk to herself in front of strangers. As it happened, she'd had the compartment to herself and was able to read a few chapters of Mrs. Christie's brand new thriller, *The Man in the Brown Suit*, with no interruption. The plot was a trifle complicated, involving death and diamonds and false identities. Addie was tempted to assume a false identity and travel to South Africa like the book's heroine for her own adventure.

Why not? It was a long way away, and if Rupert couldn't make it to London, surely South Africa would be safe.

Perhaps he was tethered in some way to the estate, and not assigned to be her personal guardian angel after all. Ha. As if he had any angelic qualities. Oh, why was she wasting time thinking about him when he was not around to provoke her?

If he proved to be a permanent fixture at Compton Chase—at least in her mind, what was left of it—she might have to abandon the house and live full-time in Town. That would be a pity—on the whole, she preferred the country. Her mother and Cee lived close by, and Lucas and Eloise had motored over regularly since Rupert's funeral.

Addie would miss her daily tramps about the gardens and fields with Fitz, the smell of honeysuckle and the hum of bees such a comfort. Now that the dwelling had been updated to her taste and at such expense, it would be most annoying not to reap the benefits of it, indoors and out.

The doorbell rang, then rang again. Fitz didn't bark, and Addie wondered if the dog might actually be deaf. Tongue lolling, he slept on the chaise in the corner, and hadn't moved at all except to go do his business in the little back garden when nature called. Addie's spacious flat was on the ground floor of a brick mansion house, and ran the length of it. She had exclusive use of a small but well-tended walled city plot, but even the chilliest champagne or ice lolly would not lure her out there today in the brutal sunshine.

Beckett knocked, and popped in without waiting for a response. "Are you receiving, Lady A.?" The maid had removed her black stockings, white cap, and ruffled apron in deference to the weather. Her dress crumpled, she really should have thought twice about answering the door. But Addie didn't mind. She was every bit as disheveled.

"That depends. Who is it?"

"Mrs. Shipman from next door."

"Angela? Damn it. I suppose I have to get dressed and see her."

"She does seem to be in a bit of a state, if you want my opinion."

Addie usually got Beckett's opinions without asking. "Why do you say that?"

"She's been crying. Her mascara is running down her cheeks. Looks a fright, she does."

Which was why Addie rarely bothered with mascara, even if her blond lashes were on the rabbity side.

"Oh, dear. Tell her I'll be with her as soon as I can pull myself together. I don't think she'll mind if I just throw on my wrapper—I cannot deal with layers of real clothing today. Can you put together a tray of something? Maybe a pitcher of martinis instead of tea or lemonade."

"Olives or twists?"

"Both. Let's live dangerously. But not in the same glass, please." Beckett tended to take things literally.

Addie entered her white-tiled bathroom and splashed some cold water on her flushed face. Her long hair was already braided and in the tightest bun possible, no charming curls or wisps around her ears or forehead to soften the effect. It was very tempting to contemplate cutting it all off, but she wasn't ready to become a thoroughly modern flapper.

She belted the lightweight cerulean silk robe over her slip, stuck her feet in mules, then spent two minutes on her face. Powder, lip rouge, glasses. She was almost presentable.

Angela Shipman was standing by the windows facing the street, wearing a darling purple cloche and what Addie thought was almost certainly a heather tweed Chanel skirt suit. She turned as soon as she heard Addie's mules hit the marble hall floor. Her face was indeed tear-streaked, unless it was perspiration arising from wearing her fashionable but unseasonal outfit.

"Angela! What's happened?"

"Oh, Adelaide, I didn't know where to turn. But of all my friends, you would understand best, and I heard through the grapevine that you were in Town. It's—it's Ernest." She covered her face and began to sob, her blood-red nails a contrast to her pale skin.

Addie stepped forward and put a hand on Angela's shaking shoulder. "He's not…um, dead, is he?"

Her friend looked up, black rivulets rolling down her face. "I wish! No, he's in Zurich at some bankers' meeting, the beast! I hope his train crashes on the way home!"

"No you don't. Come, sit down. Beckett is mixing up some martinis for us. Why are you so angry with Ernest?"

"Kathleen Grant," Angela spat.

"You don't mean to say *he* killed her?"

"How would I know? But I wouldn't put it past him. He was having an affair with her! Right under my nose. Do you know she lived just around the corner, more or less? All these months when I thought he was working late or out of town, he was with her. He promised me banker's hours. Bollocks."

"Are you sure?" Addie didn't know Ernest as well as she did Angela—he'd never gone shopping for gloves or hosiery with her or giggled over tea at Fortnum and Mason or had his hair done at Harrods hairdressing court. But he'd never struck her as a man with a wandering eye, unless a pound note blew by. He'd been totally consumed with his bank and its clients, as far as Addie knew.

"I found his appointments diary in a suit pocket when I went to take it to the cleaners. He must have forgotten to pack it in his rush, and I was going to send it on, but then I looked—oh, I can't believe how stupid I've been! " Angela collapsed on the white sofa—a foolish choice by the decorator, considering Fitz's frequently muddy paws—and opened up her handbag, tossing out lavender gloves, a handkerchief, a tin of mints, a tube of lipstick, and a twenty-four-karat gold pen. "Here. Read this. Proof." She shoved the slim brown leather diary into Addie's hands.

Addie sat down on the sofa, pushed a smoky-grey velvet pillow away, and opened it.

"Start in February."

When Rupert had died. Could Kathleen have been so upset

she sought comfort in another man's arms? Well, several other men—she must have connected with the colonel at about that time too. Addie scanned the pages. Most of the notations were indecipherable, business meetings during the day with one set of initials or another. But "K." kept turning up late afternoons. Evenings. Weekends. Addie flipped through to the date of her house party.

Saturday:

"K. 3:00-ish"

She sat back and exhaled. It all seemed so unlikely. "K. could be someone else—or stand for something else entirely. We don't know what this really means." It could be kitten. Kumquat. Kleptomaniac. Killjoy. Addie kept these suggestions to herself, however.

"Oh, don't we? Ernest might be the last person to ever see her alive! Either that, or he did kill her. How could I have been so blind?"

"Wait! Doesn't the letter k stand for a thousand? Maybe it's banker's shorthand for a monetary transfer."

"That would be a great deal of money over the months, Adelaide. We'd be broke, and we're not. How do you like my new suit? It arrived from Paris this morning."

That explained one thing. "Maybe Ernest was *receiving* the thousands. I don't know, Angela—why do you assume it has anything to do with Kathleen Grant?"

"Ha! Because I found a telephone exchange number next to the K in the back of the diary, and I called it! Guess who answered?"

"It couldn't have been Kathleen," Addie said dryly. Although if Rupert was on the loose, who knew?

"No, it was her maid, who very politely informed me she was closing up the flat because her mistress had passed away. So what do you make of that?"

"You don't know that they were having an affair. He could have been advising her about investments or something." At three o'clock in the tithe barn.

One of those naked investment consultations.

Angela gave her a disgusted look she deserved. Addie reached over the handbag and passed Angela her own handkerchief. "What are you going to do?"

"Call that police inspector, the Indian one."

Half. "And what will you say?"

"That I have Ernest's appointments book, and that he's been lying, and that he should be extradited from Switzerland for further questioning."

"That seems unnecessary, and internationally time-consuming. By the time the legalities are finalized, he'll probably be somewhere else. When is Ernest due back?"

"Not until the end of next week. He was going on to Bonn and Berlin and Vienna after the symposium." Angela blew her nose into the fine embroidered Irish linen. "I should have known something was fishy at your house. I've never seen him so anxious to get back to work in my life."

Addie made up her mind. "I'll call him."

"Who?"

"Inspector Hunter. You don't mind if I keep the diary to show him? And if the police are interested in it, I expect they'll want to hold onto it, and talk to you, too."

"I really don't know anything. I *thought* I knew Ernest," Angela said, blinking back more tears. "We've been married eighteen years. I was practically a child when we married"—Addie knew Angela was several years over forty, but didn't interrupt—"and was so flattered that such an important man found me interesting. It hasn't been all roses and rainbows, but, by God, I thought he'd been faithful! You know just how I feel, don't you? A fellow betrayed wife, abandoned and unloved."

Addie forbid herself any response. In all her years of marriage to Rupert, she'd never complained about his behavior to anyone save her family, never publicly acknowledged that the roses were dead and there was an eternal torrential downpour with no chance of sunshine. She wasn't going to say a word against him now; she still had her pride.

Beckett chose this moment—Addie expected she'd been eavesdropping shamelessly—to bring in the tray with three kinds of nuts in crystal bowls and a most-welcome pitcher of martinis. As tempted as she was to down every drop, Addie poured the clear liquid into one glass with olives (hers) and one with a lemon twist (Angela's) and settled in to listen to Angela expound on Ernest's every fault. She gave Beckett the secret hand signal, guaranteeing that in twenty minutes, she would be reminded she had to dress for Lady Grimes' drinks party.

There was, of course, no Lady Grimes.

Chapter Sixteen

Friday

Dev had spent the past few days interviewing or re-interviewing in person, or by phone and/or telegram one virtuous vicar—this Collins fellow must be quite a bore—one ex-husband, one alleged fiancé, one tearful maid, three bank managers, two solicitors in both London and York, and the city friends that Kathleen Grant still possessed after apparently sleeping with everybody's husband/ brother/father. The woman's reputation was quite shocking, and he wondered how much of it was true.

That was the thing about reputations—once one lost it, one became fair game for the most salacious of tales. Now that she was dead—*murdered*—there was no reason to not let one's imagination run wild.

Dev was beginning to feel sorry for Kathleen Grant. It was almost as if she knew she had to sow those wild oats while she could before she was plowed under.

Surprisingly, she hadn't engendered hatred or strong negative feelings—almost everyone had grudgingly agreed that she was charming, impulsive, and great fun, even the wives whose husbands had strayed. She was considered almost too beautiful. The life of any party she attended, and she was invited everywhere, despite being a divorcee. The recent change in the divorce laws had alleviated some of the onus, and Kathleen took advantage and was the most social of butterflies.

The only person she'd deliberately hurt was Sir David Grant, and that was by his own admission.

Dev had also made a point to speak with Mr. McGrath's daughters by telephone, to assure them that while the focus was on Lady Grant's death, his would not be forgotten.

What had the old man seen?

The inquests were next week in the Assembly Room over the Compton Arms. Dev was finalizing his presentation to the coroner, but so far he had nothing conclusive. If anything, he had too many suspects with no credible alibis. But motive? So far, that was lacking across the board, with the exception of her ex-husband.

And George Halliday, who, it turned out, was Kathleen Grant's long-lost cousin.

It was suspicious that the Hallidays had not mentioned the connection, but perhaps they didn't even know. According to the solicitors he'd communicated with, the two daughters of the dotty old gentleman in Yorkshire had a serious falling out and hadn't spoken in decades. Both were dead now. Their children had never met each other and were only vaguely aware of the other's existence.

Contrary to his explicit instructions, Dev had been unable to locate the Hallidays for further questioning—their flat was empty of their personal belongings, and the landlady had no idea where they'd gone. And if, she'd said tartly, Dev was able to find them, he had to tell them they were about to be sued for breaking their lease and owing several months' back rent.

Coming into some money would be handy for them—even better, now they wouldn't have to share.

Dev supposed either Pandora or George Halliday could have committed the crimes, or they could have worked together. Money was always a motivating factor. They were each other's alibis, although they were alone in their respective connected rooms during the times in question. Compton Chase's ancient walls and doors were thick and soundproof, so it was perfectly possible to sneak out without being heard.

And now they'd flown the coop completely.

But—and here Dev had no good explanation—he didn't think either one of them was guilty. The way the body had been presented told a tale that had nothing to do with money or cousins. He would talk to Lady Adelaide about his hunch.

He'd been surprised to answer the phone last night and hear her somewhat breathless voice asking him to come to tea "to discuss a new development." He'd been in his shirtsleeves, and felt a little awkward speaking to her in such disarray, as if she could see him. He'd taken care with his clothing today, so much so that Bob had given him a wolf-whistle.

He was going to tea in Mayfair, wasn't he? Had to dress the part.

Dev signed out for the day. Her flat was only about a mile and a half away from the Yard, but he decided to take the Tube from the Embankment station. He'd arrive hot either way—the weather still had not broken.

Was Lady Adelaide enjoying her break in Town? Shopping, lunching, gossiping? Was she going to smoky jazz clubs and society parties?

Probably not. She was still in mourning, wasn't she? And she didn't strike him as any sort of rule-breaker. She was one of those women whose good breeding oozed from every tiny white pore. Dev would bet his paltry salary that she lived for good works and charitable endeavors. If she could have, she probably *would* turn her house over to orphans.

He'd asked around, even his father, who was up to his sandy eyelashes in the scandal sheets. No one had a bad word to say about Lady Adelaide Compton. Her name had never appeared in the newspapers, except for the occasion of her marriage and in her husband's obituary. Dev knew rather more about that man now than he had before, and Lady Adelaide had his sympathy.

Damn it. He was getting soft. It wouldn't do to fall victim to sparkling hazel eyes and golden hair. And, worst of all, a title. He'd be a laughingstock.

Determined to be as professional as possible, Dev arrived as the clock inside was striking four. The little maid Beckett opened the door and gave him a cheeky grin, as if she knew everything he'd been thinking on his way over here. She took his hat and guided him into a blindingly white drawing room, very sleek and modern, a contrast from the more traditional Compton Chase. The flooring beneath a fluffy white fur rug was gray-veined marble, and Dev caught his multiple reflections in the large silver-framed mirrors that lined the walls.

It was, to be frank, a little disorienting. Cold. His own flat was rather basic, his parents' much cozier with colorful Indian fabrics and sentimental objects to catch the eye. Dev actually paid attention to physical surroundings; they often told him a lot about the personality of the person he was interviewing. This apartment simply said "money" and very little else.

"Lady A. will be right with you. China or Indian?"

"Indian, please," Dev responded, hoping she was referring to tea.

He wasn't ready to sit on the tufted white sofa, so he went to the large bay window overlooking Mount Street. Pristine red and white brick buildings lined both sides of the street. The Connaught Hotel was just around the corner. Before the war, Dev had been inside once, to arrest an ambitious pickpocket. She'd been a well-dressed, voluptuous young woman who made a habit of accidentally tripping against elderly peers in the elevators. If only she'd played her cards right and not concentrated on being light-fingered, she might have been a duchess instead of going to Holloway. Where was she now?

Beckett rolled in the loaded tea cart. Dev was sorry he was

too nervous to be hungry, for there was enough food for half a dozen policemen.

"Still no Lady A.?" the maid asked. "I'll just go see what's keeping her."

"It's all right. I'm in no rush."

"Let me pour you a cuppa before I go see what's taking her so long."

"No, really I—"

"Wouldn't want it to get cold. Or maybe we would. Sure is hot out, ain't it?"

"It is the end of August." Gracious, Dev was having a conversation about the weather with a maid. It somehow made him feel exceptionally British.

"Bet it's hot in India." She poured a stream of tea into an almost transparent cup. "Sugar? Milk?"

"Black, please. I don't know how hot it is in India. I've never been."

"Fancy that. Do you ever want to go?"

"I haven't given it much thought." This decade. When Dev was a boy, his parents' stories had seemed straight out of Kipling. He'd been curious about the different culture. But his Indian grandparents were dead, and his English side had the upper hand now. Even his mother could out-queen Queen Mary when she wanted to, only with an Indian accent.

"Stay put, and help yourself."

Beckett marched off. Dev didn't want to touch the towers of tiny crustless sandwiches and cakes without Lady Adelaide, so he settled for sipping his tea.

A good ten minutes passed. Surely she could not be agonizing over her clothing as he had. He poured himself a second cup of tea, and put it down hastily as Lady Adelaide entered the room.

She was not wearing black.

Dev swallowed. Her frock was a shimmery, flowy, sheer-ish thing of spring leaf-green, making her eyes appear twice as wide as normal.

It suited her.

She extended a hand. "I'm so sorry to keep you waiting. Someone, I mean, something turned up that I couldn't get rid of. I should have known it was too good to be true."

"Of course," he said, not understanding a word.

"I have something for you. Evidence, perhaps." She opened the credenza drawer and handed him a thin brown leather notebook. Dev flipped it open and skimmed as she busied herself pouring her own tea and making them both plates. "Aren't you going to ask me what it is?"

"It appears to belong to Ernest Shipman."

She looked up, her eyes huge behind the spectacles. "How did you guess?"

"The gold initials on the front cover, for a start. I recognize some of the abbreviations and locations for business meetings. I am a detective, you know." Besides, he'd seen it when Shipman attempted to bribe him, which he thought best not to mention. "Where did you get it?"

"You know Ernest is on the Continent?"

He did. Shipman had reluctantly given Dev his schedule before he left. "Yes."

"His wife found it in a suit pocket and, um, couldn't help but look through it." Lady Adelaide blushed a little, but continued. "The letter K is all through it. Ernest was having an affair with Kathleen Grant!"

"How did you come to this conclusion?"

"Her telephone number is in the back. Angela called and spoke to Kathleen's maid."

"I hate to stifle your investigative skills, but he was one of her bankers, Lady Adelaide." This, he and Bob had discovered during their third interview with the man right before he left, who still claimed not to "really know" the murder victim. Did Dev have any idea how many portfolios Shipman managed? He couldn't possibly remember all his clients, and Lady Grant had invested a very insignificant amount with him, if he could recall even that much.

That had sounded reasonable until Dev counted up the "Ks" in the little brown book, and the odd times they had been entered. "K. 3:00-ish" last Saturday was extremely interesting.

"But he said he didn't know her!"

"And that might be true. Although I rather doubt it now." He looked at the beautifully arranged plate she'd placed before him and realized he'd better eat some of it or appear rude. The first bite was, of course, delicious, so he forged ahead.

"Will you want to speak to Angela? I can call her—she's just next door."

Dev would have to speak to her, but didn't want to spoil this moment.

Oh, whatever god one worshipped, he was in trouble.

Chapter Seventeen

The doorbell rang. Addie nearly jumped out of her seat. She was still agitated, although she hoped Inspector Hunter didn't suspect. Rupert had better be in her bedroom doing whatever ghosts did and not pranking at her front door. How and why he'd turned up at Mount Street was as yet unanswered, but she hadn't given him much of an opportunity to explain while she was whisper-shrieking at him.

Beckett was unusually prompt at answering, no doubt trying to give a good impression to the representative of Scotland Yard. Addie had to watch what she said in front of her, too, or Beckett would think she was working for a bedlamite and give notice. It had been a near thing as she'd been hissing like a demented reptile at Rupert while the maid knocked on the bedroom door as the detective waited.

"It's Lord Waring, Lady A. Shall I tell him to go away?"

"Certainly not! You don't mind if he joins us, do you, Inspector?"

Mr. Hunter shook his head, his mouth full of cress sandwich.

Lucas entered, his smile brilliant until he spotted the police inspector on her sofa. "I'm sorry. I didn't know you were engaged, Addie. Shall I leave you two alone?"

"Don't be silly, Lucas. Beckett, please bring another cup—you'll stay for tea, won't you? What are you doing in Town?"

"To tell you the truth, I came to see you and how you were getting on. Eloise is busy at the moment helping Sir David plan the funeral service and reception for Kathleen next week, and I was bored."

Addie puzzled over this news. "Eloise? I didn't realize they were so well-acquainted."

"Well, they aren't, really, I don't think. But she volunteered. You know how she likes to be useful. She did have an odd connection with Kathleen, you know. She and Kathleen's late brother were sweethearts twenty-odd years ago."

"I don't think I knew that. Did you, Mr. Hunter?"

"I did. Lady Grant was hardly more than a baby when her brother died, though."

"How dreadful. Is that why Eloise never married?" Addie asked.

Lucas shrugged. "She's never confided in me about her love life, I'm afraid. Or if she did, I never paid attention. I suppose I've taken poor old Ellie for granted all these years."

"He's such a shallow little shit, Addie. I don't see why you permit him to be at your beck and call all the time."

Addie dropped her plate, and a cascade of crumbs bounced into the white fur rug. Damn it, he'd promised—not that his promises had ever meant anything, as he himself admitted. She turned, and there was Rupert sitting in the white brocade window seat, evaluating the room and her company.

"I don't mind what you've done with the old country place, but this flat is much too white, my dear. It looks like some kind of clinic or laboratory. I dread to imagine the gruesome experiments you might attempt. Skewering me with a curtain rod, for example. Stabbing me with mirror shards. Whatever were you thinking?"

"The decorator—well, to change the subject completely, what do you gentlemen think of my flat? I gave the decorator leave to do as he wished, and I'm not sure of the final effect," Addie said, flustered. "And, uh, forgive my clumsiness. My nerves still haven't settled." And they never would, if Rupert kept jumping out like a smug jack-in-the-box.

"It's all the rage, this Art Deco, isn't it?" Lucas said, looking around. He, of course, did not notice as Rupert made a very rude gesture as his gaze swept over the windows. "I think it suits you—it's fresh and bright and clean. Like, um, that dress. Have you given up mourning wear?"

"Just for today. It's too hot to wear black." It was too hot to wear anything, but Addie wasn't going to admit *that* in mixed company.

"And, if I may be so bold, your decorator failed to capture your own warmth. The flat is a little impersonal. A touch chilly, Lady Adelaide. Though in such hot weather, that might be welcome," Inspector Hunter offered with a smile, as he bent to pick up the plate.

Chilly. Yes, that was exactly it. Tomorrow Addie would go to Harrods and buy some pillows and knickknacks to tart up the place.

If she wasn't in some mental ward.

She had three men in her sitting room—well, at least two—and didn't have the faintest idea what to do with them. A mental ward might actually bring her some relief. There would be a daily schedule. Shots of something calming several times a day. Plain nutritious food. No need to dress up. Yes, there were numerous benefits.

Mr. Hunter pulled out his little notebook and a pencil. "Lord Waring, this isn't a social call for me. Lady Adelaide and I were discussing the murder case. Perhaps you have something to contribute as well. How well do you know the Hallidays? They've gone missing, and left no forwarding address with their landlady."

Addie was about to speak until Rupert did first. "Paint fumes, ha! Just as I said, and you didn't believe me."

Lucas lifted a blond eyebrow. "Have they? I've known George

over half my life—we were at Eton together. He did say something about their flat being refreshed when we were at Addie's. Maybe they moved into a hotel for the duration."

"We've made inquiries and they aren't registered anywhere. And they were under an obligation to inform us of their whereabouts."

"Just as I did before I left Waring Hall this morning. I called your office *and* that idiot Yardley. You don't think they had anything to do with Lady Grant's death, do you?"

"Don't forget about poor Mr. McGrath!" Addie found it vexing that her gardener was always an afterthought.

"People like your precious Lucas don't count the help in the grand scheme of things," Rupert said with a sneer.

"He's not my pre—um, I still feel so responsible," Addie said. She really should take a vow of silence. Starting about three minutes ago.

"It's not your fault, Lady Adelaide. As I've explained, if the murderer was set on killing Lady Grant, he or she would have found a way and a location. But I too am sorry that Mr. McGrath got mixed up in it. I've spoken to both his daughters and assured them we are doing everything possible to find the killer."

"Thank you for that. He's going to be buried in Scotland on Saturday. I really should have made arrangements to go." Funerals were not her favorite event, especially after Rupert's, with so many of his paramours turning up crying more than she ever would.

"Not when you're still suffering, Addie. They wouldn't expect you to."

Addie frowned at Lucas. "Suffering? I'm still alive and fortunate beyond belief. If my nerves have gotten the better of me, it's nothing to brag about. I'm not *Camille*, wasting away from consumption." Beckett had dragged Addie to see the Alla Nazimova and Rudolph Valentino version of the film a few years ago and they both had wept buckets.

"Indeed, you are not!" Lucas responded, shocked. "You are a respectable woman!"

"He's right there. You are certainly not a courtesan signaling your sexual availability with flowers," Rupert said helpfully from his window seat.

"*Too* respectable," Addie grumbled. "If I wasn't—" *Vow of silence. Vow of silence.* She would not let Rupert goad her into any more unwise utterances.

Inspector Hunter cleared his throat. "Getting back to the Hallidays, if I may? Would either of you know where they might have gone? A cottage in the country? A relative?"

Lucas shook his head. "George's parents are dead. I don't think they own a country property. But you're closer to Pansy than I am to George, Addie. What are your thoughts?"

"Pansy slept with Rupert. I won't call us close any more."

Inspector Hunter dropped his pencil. Addie was happy to see that across the room, Rupert was covering his face with both hands. It was past time for him to feel some embarrassment.

Lucas reached across the table. "Addie, my dar—dear. You have suffered, no matter what you say. You are just too brave."

Rupert snorted. "Oh, put a sock in it. Always oozing concern. Why, I could tell you a few tales which would—"

"Enough!" Addie said irritably. She didn't care which one of them stopped talking. "Inspector, may I pour you another cup of tea?"

"I really shouldn't stay. You must have plans."

Would Lady Grimes be invoked later at some point? Addie wasn't particularly keen to be left alone with Rupert.

"They are unsettled as of yet."

"Perhaps I can take you out to dinner at the Ivy later, Addie." Lucas gave her a sunny smile, pointedly leaving out Mr. Hunter.

It was still considered somewhat daring for a lady of Addie's class to go to a restaurant like the Ivy, so Addie was surprised by the invitation. The Ivy attracted Bohemians and theater types, so Beckett would positively be green with envy if Addie went. She'd expect a full set of notes, not that Addie had been to a theater this year. She wouldn't recognize anyone important if she fell in their laps.

Lucas was generally all for the conventions, no matter what Rupert implied. What kind of tales? She'd have to grill him later.

"Don't go across the street with him, Addie. I don't trust him as far as I can throw him." Rupert scratched his chin, perplexed. "But then, I'm not sure if I *could* pick him up. The rules, you know, seem to vary with the circumstances. Something to do with physics and gravitational fields, and I now regret not paying attention in science class. If I couldn't understand science back then, that German bloke Einstein completely defeats me. Molecules and what-not."

"Excuse me for just a minute." Addie walked across the marble floor to the window and opened the sash another inch. "First you say he's a dull dog, and now he's just a dog. Which is it?" she murmured to Rupert, who scooched over on the cushion to give her room to adjust the window.

"Both. You can do better. Tell him to go home. Tell *them* to go home."

"I should like to say the same to you. But here you are."

"Home is where the heart is." His attempt to look winsome was futile as far as she was concerned.

"Oh, for God's sake. Give it a rest, Rupert."

"May I give you a hand with the windows, Lady Adelaide?"

She pivoted, and there was Mr. Hunter right behind her, who had most likely heard each of her mutterings.

"It is so hot, isn't it?" she said, looking up into his dark eyes.

"It is. The heat makes some people cross. Cross enough to argue with themselves."

"You've caught me again. I'm developing a very bad habit, aren't I?" Addie tried to smile but her lips were uncooperative.

"I'd never presume to criticize your behavior. I know my place." Mr. Hunter could and did smile, taking the barb out of his words.

Rupert rolled his eyes but looked extremely interested in the conversation, his arms folded over his immaculate suit.

"Don't be silly! There are no *places* here. It's 1924, for heaven's sake."

"You are a modern woman then." Mr. Hunter's voice dropped. "Would you allow *me* to take you out to dinner some night?"

"D-dinner?"

"You know, food. Knife and fork. Plate. You may say no. It's probably not a good idea. Unprofessional on my part. Not to mention, your mother would not approve. Nor would mine."

That did it. "I'd—I'd love to. Tomorrow."

"Oh, my giddy aunt. I didn't leave you a widow so you could find some exotic fellow to throw yourself away on."

Addie elbowed Rupert as she raised the next window, wishing she had the strength to toss him out of it.

"I say, how difficult are those windows? May I help?" Lucas sounded peevish.

Rupert sighed and merged into the drapes, just like that.

"Call me," Addie whispered, feeling very naughty indeed. "All done. They are a bit tricky. Painted shut in spots from the renovations. Thank you for your help, Inspector. And, Lucas—I've just remembered. I promised to visit Lady Grimes this evening. She hasn't been feeling all that well."

"Another night then. How about tomorrow?"

"I have a dinner engagement. And then, I think I'll go back to Compton Chase. I will see you at the inquest, won't I, Inspector?"

"And the funeral. In my experience, the murderer is often unable to stay away."

Addie shivered. "How grisly. I'll be so glad when this is all over." Surely that meant Rupert would move on…to wherever his ultimate destination lay.

Chapter Eighteen

Saturday

In this morning's telephone call, received even before Addie finished her first cup of tea, they had agreed that Mr. Hunter would have an early supper with her at her Mount Street flat. It would be easier, she claimed, and he didn't argue.

It wasn't that she'd be ashamed being seen with him; she just wasn't ready to be seen with anybody. Wasn't ready to face any sort of speculation. Be the center of inevitable attention. Some of the newspapers had got hold of Kathleen's death, and she could only imagine what they would make of her dining with the chief investigator. But even if the Prince of Wales himself was her escort, she simply couldn't manage it. She was safe there—he was meeting with Calvin Coolidge today after a cross-Atlantic trip on the *Berengaria,* according to the *Times.*

She'd have to wear black in public, too, and it was still so blasted hot. She'd bought a few frocks that were definitely not black this week, found a few more in the back of her closet, and had resolved to wear them when she could. Tonight, for example, she'd wear a pale pink one with embroidered yellow tulips on the hemline from Callot Soeurs, very fresh and light. Mr. Hunter could not accuse *her* of being chilly.

After her successful shopping trip for trinkets for the flat, she'd sat in a cold bath until her skin shriveled. She couldn't wait to get back to Gloucestershire and plunge into the lake, even if it was not especially deep. She'd shoo away the ducks and practice her backstroke.

It was nearly September, time to leave summer behind. Once Kathleen's funeral was over, Addie would see about making some fundamental changes to her own life. She'd already spoken to Edward Rivers and invited him for tea tomorrow afternoon, notifying Forbes of her plans and return on a late morning train. She and Beckett would be met with all efficiency and deference, and life could unravel as it would.

Hopefully Rupert would stay behind the white velvet curtains at Mount Street.

How did he get from one place to another? He'd been vague, claiming he wasn't sure himself. Poppycock. But he'd made himself scarce most of today as she plumped new scarlet, peach, and pink pillows about the furniture, and promised to be even scarcer later when Mr. Hunter arrived.

The new accessories popped against the white and gray that her decorator had been so enamored with. A painting of roses with lush greenery hung over the mantel, purchased straight from the window of gallery down the street. Real roses stood in crystal vases scenting the warm air, and Addie was mostly satisfied with the result. A few more cosmetic fixes, and the room would be perfect.

The doorbell buzzed at seven exactly; Mr. Hunter was very prompt. She'd given Beckett the night off to see a double feature, and was confident she could serve the cold collation ordered from the Connaught without mishap—vichyssoise, shrimp cocktail, stuffed quail eggs, green salad, slices of chicken, ham, and rare roast beef, gooseberry fool, and a cheese board. She could make the coffee herself, and two bottles of wine were breathing in ice-filled buckets in the kitchen.

She wasn't expecting Mr. Hunter to arrive in evening clothes, but the pinstripe charcoal gray suit he wore was very fine and suspiciously new.

How very handsome he was.

Don't think it, Addie reminded herself. Rupert would burrow into her brain and get wind of it, and somehow ruin the evening.

"You're on time!"

"Policeman's training. I hope you're ready. That is, you look ready. More than ready. Very nice. That dress suits you."

Addie detected a faint blush on the inspector's brown cheeks as he struggled with his compliments.

"I've been ready for ages. Beckett's gone out. To the pictures. She thinks you resemble the actor Charles Farrell, by the way. He's not very famous—you probably don't know him."

Mr. Hunter blinked. "What do you think?"

Addie had looked him up. "Maybe around the eyebrows. Your nose is all wrong. Not that it's not a lovely nose!" she said quickly.

"It works, which is all I care about. I've been told it's my grandfather's, but I never met him."

"Come into the dining room. I hope you don't mind—I've laid out everything on the sideboard and we'll help ourselves. Perhaps start with dessert, if we throw all caution to the winds!"

"I don't see you as a renegade, Lady Adelaide, even if you've invited a humble policeman to dinner."

"*You* asked *me*, remember. And you're right. I'm a dreadful stick-in-the-mud. I didn't used to be." While she'd never been as gay and daring as Kathleen Grant, once upon a time, she'd been fun. When had that stopped? Something else to lay at Rupert's feet, no doubt. The pile was getting dangerously high.

"This looks very elegant," Mr. Hunter said, appraising the food resting on beds of crushed ice on white and silver platters.

"I didn't cook any of it," Addie confessed. "I can cook a little, when Cook—Mrs. Oxley lets me into the kitchens, but that offends her sense of propriety. Everything tonight comes from the Connaught Hotel." A dreadful thought belatedly occurred to her. "Oh! I should have asked for your food preferences! Are you a vegetarian like my sister? I understand Hindus don't eat any meat."

"They don't. But I'm not a Hindu. I'm not really anything at the moment, although I've studied world religions and philosophy. But don't tell anyone, particularly my mother. She is a pillar of the Old Church in Chelsea."

"Really?"

"Don't be so surprised, Lady Adelaide. Things are not always as they seem." He filled a cup with the cold soup and sat down.

"I know that, even if I'm not a detective!" She spooned some soup into her own cup. "I talked to Angela. This is your second trip to Mount Street today. You've ordered that good-for-nothing husband of hers home. Bravo!"

"That's if he decides to obey my telegram. He can always say it didn't reach him."

"Not with Angela firing off her shots too. She spoke to him on the telephone—a rotten connection, but he knows you're onto him. Can't you go fetch him yourself?"

"I'm afraid the Yard frowns on that kind of expense, Lady Adelaide. If he were the confirmed killer, we might work with the Swiss authorities. But he's merely a person of interest at this point." He looked into his empty cup. "That was delicious. Refreshing."

"Any news of the Hallidays?"

Mr. Hunter shook his head. "I was hoping you might have heard something." He rose and returned with the two shrimp cocktails. It was rather nice to be served by someone other than Beckett, who tended to slap food down to get it over with.

"No, and I don't expect to." They polished off the shrimp, the inspector clearly waiting for further explanation.

When none was forthcoming, he rose again, filled a plate with an egg, salad, and meat, and gave it to her. There was just the right amount of everything.

"You had a falling out with Mrs. Halliday?"

"Thank you. She doesn't know it. But, yes. As I said, I recently discovered that my late husband and she engaged in an affair before he and I married."

"That's not very pleasant. But it could have been worse."

"Because we hadn't wed yet? *She* was married—a mother! And one of my oldest friends. We've known each other since we were fourteen. I trusted her. She made a fool of me behind my back." The food in front of her, pretty as it was, had lost all its appeal.

"Karma. A man is born to the world he has made. Your friend has made her bed in this lifetime. Now she must lie in it, and in her future life as well."

"Do you believe that? That we live again?" Could that explain Rupert?

"Finer minds than mine have debated. There are six schools of philosophy in Hinduism. None of them agree."

Addie sliced her tiny quail egg in half. "So, if I'm well-behaved in this incarnation, good things will happen to me in the next?" She was a shoo-in then for a totally boring existence.

Mr. Hunter smiled. "Some might say so. I do not presume."

"What about heaven and hell?"

"There you need to talk to your vicar—" he held up a hand—"who's not your vicar. I can see after fifteen minutes in his company why you don't want to claim him."

"Ugh. I'm having tea with him tomorrow." She had prepared a list of questions. Goodness, two nights of serious thorny issues she hadn't thought about since Sunday School, if then.

"Lucky fellow. And not on my list of suspects. He was indeed sitting with a parishioner all afternoon well into the night, and he has no motive for killing a woman he didn't know unless he's a complete maniac. I have met a few maniacs, and he doesn't fit the bill."

Addie reached for her glass, but realized the wine was still on the enamel kitchen table. "Oh! How stupid! I've forgotten the wine."

"None for me, thank you. And not on any religious grounds. The temperance movement is well-meaning but ultimately naïve. Men of all cultures have been drinking alcohol since standing upright, possibly even on all fours if they accidentally fermented something. But I never know when I'm going to be called out on a case, so it's easier to be on my guard. Don't let me stop you. I can get it."

Addie rose, folding her napkin next to the linen placemat. "No, no. I'll be right back. May I bring you some ice water?" She picked up the two empty wineglasses.

"Yes, please."

Addie swung the kitchen door open and stopped. There was Rupert, leaning against the kitchen sink, his jacket discarded and his sleeves rolled up. She bit back an oath, and made sure the door was fully shut before she uttered a word.

No, she wasn't going to say anything. Not a single solitary syllable. A few inches of wood would not prevent Mr. Hunter from hearing her—he was a very smart man with excellent senses.

"I thought you might need help cleaning up." Rupert pointed to the suds in the dishpan.

"Oh, you're nobody's sweetheart now," Addie began to sing, "'cause nobody wants you somehow." She shoved him away from the tap and filled a wineglass with water, then chucked in a few ice cubes from the tray in the icebox.

"That's not very kind. And I'm not wearing 'fancy hose and a silken gown.' That would be you. You look smashing, Addie, even with your specs on. I hope Hunter is suitably impressed."

"'You'll be out of place in your old hometown.' The kitchen too! 'As you walk down that avenue, all the people won't believe that's you.'"

"They won't see me, as you well know. I'm beginning to find it very annoying. One doesn't want to brag, but I was used to some admiration."

Too bad. "Paint your lips, paint your eyes," Addie extemporized, "wear a bird of paradise! 'It all seems wrong somehow, it seems so funny you're nobody's sweetheart now!'"

"You don't have to rub it in. This afterlife business is nothing like it's cracked up to be. And I wish you'd forget about Pansy. It meant nothing then. In fact, I can barely remember the event. It happened just the one time. Or perhaps twice. Three times, at the very most."

Addie set the water down and poured as much wine as could fit in the remaining glass and drank it down in one unwise gulp. Refilling it, she gave Rupert a bright smile. "Whatever did I do in a past life to deserve you? Now *that's* a mystery that needs solving."

Chapter Nineteen

Sunday

Addie had woken up dry-mouthed, her head pounding. Nevertheless, she and Beckett had caught their train with time to spare, thanks to the maid's never-fail hangover cures—raw egg with Worcestershire sauce and a cold shower.

Addie was mortified. The details of last night's dinner with Inspector Hunter were hazy in the extreme. Beckett believed she'd consumed two bottles of Alsatian wine on her own, but Addie suspected she'd had some help from Rupert, who had also washed the dishes and even put them away.

Unless Mr. Hunter had. All Addie knew is that he'd fixed her coffee—amazing that Rupert had not gotten in the way to sabotage that. When she'd spilt half of it on the new white sofa, he'd picked her up and carried her into her bedroom. Beckett had discovered her asleep on top of the covers, fully dressed, her glasses on the nightstand, and her shoes returned to their box in the closet.

The thought of Devenand Hunter fiddling with her stockinged feet made Addie feel squirmy inside. What must the man think? That she was clumsy, always spilling or dropping things. That she was barmy, arguing aloud with herself. That she was a drunk—she, who never over-imbibed. Addie would have to write him a thank-you note and try to explain.

She couldn't tell him what she was beginning to realize might be the truth—that she was haunted by her late and unlamented husband. Or not. Losing one's mind was a serious thing. One might make jokes, but she could very well wind up in Compton Chase's attics like Mrs. Rochester, only hopefully with less fire.

Back in a black dress, Addie had refused the sherry that Forbes had proffered and reviewed her discussion points. Mr. Rivers tended to drone on and on, so it would be up to her to keep him on task. The tea trolley was loaded with his favorites. If he could stop chewing long enough, she might get some answers to her questions.

"The Reverend Rivers, my lady."

Addie looked up from her notebook with a forced smile. "Good afternoon! How nice to see you. I'm so sorry I missed the church service today—I was on my way back from Town." She felt guilty fibbing already. Mr. Rivers tended to be condescending and superior, even when he was christening a baby, and was giving her That Look now.

"I paid you a visit earlier in the week to see how you were handling such a double tragedy, but they said you'd gone off to London." His tone implied that she'd been drinking champagne out of her slipper every night and generally raising hell in the wicked city.

"Yes. I had some electric fans sent for the servants' quarters and the kitchens. It's been devilishly hot, don't you agree?" Addie asked sweetly. "Shall I pour you tea, or would you like something stronger?"

That Look returned. "You should know by now I never indulge in alcohol. The Americans have the right idea of it."

"How silly of me. You are quite correct to abstain." Lord knows, she would do so for the foreseeable future to avoid a repeat of last night. She prepared the vicar's tea from memory—three sugars and milk, and encouraged him to take what he wished from the three-tiered cake stand.

After a few more comments over the weather, Addie got to the point. "I'm afraid I invited you today not just to be sociable."

Mr. Rivers stiffened. "Oh? *You're* not going to ask me where I was when that woman met her scandalous end, are you? I answered more than enough questions from that jumped-up policeman."

"I'm sure he was just doing his job," she said soothingly. "As you said, it's a double tragedy. No one ever talks about poor Mr. McGrath, though."

"I didn't know him either. I must say, church attendance from the residents of the Compton Chase estate has been disappointingly hit-or-miss since I arrived at Compton St. Cuthbert's. In my old parish, everyone from the big house would have attended, from the boot boy to the duke. Lady Ravenglass insisted upon it. A formidable woman is Lady Ravenglass."

"I think Mr. McGrath was Church of Scotland," Addie said, making no excuses for her own failings, and wishing the formidable Lady Ravenglass to the devil. In the olden days, Compton Chase's servants probably *would* have been ordered to attend church, but Addie considered it her Christian duty to allow them their own consciences. And, also, spare them Mr. Rivers' stultifying sermons. "But I would like to pick your brain a little. What is the church's position on ghosts?"

He set his half-eaten sandwich down. "Ghosts? Do you mean to say Compton Chase is haunted?"

Addie waited a beat, half-expecting Rupert to emerge from the Chinese urn like a demented genie. "Oh, no. I'm asking for a friend of mine. She lives in a very old property, much like this, and has experienced…some unusual activity."

Rivers leaned back, ready to expound. "According to Charles Wesley, one questions the truth of the Bible if one doesn't believe in ghosts. They are mentioned throughout. His brother John said they were proof of a spiritual realm. The rectory they grew up in was haunted for a time, you know."

Of course she didn't.

"There were nineteen children in that rectory. I suppose mischief may have counted for some of the odd activity, but the brothers were staunch believers in their poltergeist all their lives. Of course, they were Methodists," he said, dismissive.

"What do *you* think?"

"Perhaps we can survive the death of our bodies if we accept that our souls are immortal, as Christ taught us."

Hmm. Sounded a bit like reincarnation to Addie, but she said nothing.

Rivers ate the remains of his sandwich and reached for another. "Have you read Sir Oliver Lodge's *Raymond or Life After Death*?"

Addie scribbled the title in her book. "No. Who is he?"

"Quite a famous physicist and inventor. *And* a spiritualist. He lost his son in the war and believes he can communicate with him. Allegedly Raymond told him that people smoked cigars and drank whiskey on the other side! Just as heedless as here—for obvious reasons, I disapprove and doubt that's true. In my opinion, God would not be so frivolous. Does your friend want to communicate with her ghost?"

"No, she wants to get rid of him." She took a sip of her tea. "What do you think about séances?"

"My dear Lady Adelaide," Rivers said firmly, "don't get mixed up with mediums. They're most of them charlatans. I know spiritualism is all the rage—so many desperate people have lost loved ones in the last decade. But I cannot think God wants us banging on tables in the dark. Let us open our hearts to see what His plan is for us."

"Very sensible," Addie said, somewhat surprised at the vicar's gentle and nearly poetic words.

Mr. Rivers leaned forward. "You can tell me the truth. It's Major Compton who worries you, isn't it?"

"No! Not at all! I'm sure Rupert is fine, wherever he is." So far, she hadn't seen him today, which was perfectly all right with

her. Not on the train, not in her bedroom, not making a silly
face on the other side of the French doors right this minute.

"I know how lonely you must be. If you ever, um, need any
sort of private spiritual counseling at any time of the day or night,
any time, even the darkest hours before dawn, I would be more
than happy to provide it. And never breathe a word to a living
soul, of course. You can count on my discretion." Mr. Rivers'
normally pasty complexion was quite pink.

Was he *propositioning* her? That seemed absurd. To even think
such a thing must mean Addie was losing her marbles for sure.

She tugged down her skirt, just in case. "Thank you, I think.
But you mustn't worry about me. My family is nearby, and I
have plenty to occupy myself with on the estate. I have a dog,
too," she added, as if that would end the discussion.

"You may consider me too bold, but a beautiful woman
such as yourself cannot content herself with a dog. You need a
champion."

Mr. Rivers was not Addie's idea of a champion, or anyone's,
she suspected. She shut her eyes, clapped him in a suit of shining
armor, and gave him a worthy steed and a mighty sword.

Nope. Not even then. She could practically hear Rupert snickering. Thank goodness he wasn't here.

"Since coming to Compton St. Cuthbert's, I have tried to
fulfil my parishioners' needs, whatever they may be. Why, I even
minded the Post Office for a few minutes last Saturday. I was
sitting with Mrs. Franklin, you know. Or perhaps you don't.
That's why I couldn't come to your dinner party. She was having
one of her spells and asked me to pray with her. We were at it
on our knees until midnight." He seemed very pleased with his
diligence.

Mary Franklin was Compton-Under-Wood's postmistress
and news agent, and Addie could have told Mr. Rivers that her
spells were famous, and usually ignored by anyone with the sense
God gave them. The symptoms varied with her whims and the

weather, and caused great inconvenience when she decided she was too ill to open up her little shop for business.

Mrs. Franklin was more than likely lonely, too, Addie realized.

"How kind of you. Did you sell any stamps?"

"I did! To some disreputable old duffer who had a letter to Scotland. I made him tie up a wretched little terrier outside— Mrs. Franklin is allergic to dogs."

Addie's heart tripped. "What? Tell me again, please."

"Tell you what?"

"The man who came to the post office. Did you know him?"

"Never saw him before in my life. Scruffy old fellow—his fingernails were black with dirt. Must have been a day laborer."

Or a gardener.

"Did he speak with a Scottish accent?"

"I can't recall. We barely spoke, except for me to tell him to take the dog out of the store. Really, I know people are fond of their pets, but there's no place for them in a business. Fleas and worse! Mrs. Franklin's rooms are only through a flimsy curtain— she started sneezing like a fiend as soon as the animal came in."

"What time was this?"

"I don't know. The post office closes at four on Saturday, so it was before then. He was the last customer. Mrs. Franklin made me a lovely tea—not as nice as this," he said, gesturing at Addie's china and silver, "but more than adequate. Supper left a little something to be desired. Sardines are not my favorite, but one must take into consideration that she was not well."

"Can you remember the address?"

"The address?"

"Of the letter," Addie said, with as much patience as she could muster.

"Of course not. I barely looked at the envelope except to note the handwriting was atrocious. I'd be very surprised if the Royal Mail has even delivered the thing."

"Did you mention any of this to Inspector Hunter?"

Mr. Rivers raised his eyebrows to his receding hairline. "No. Why should I have?"

"Because," Addie said, "you are probably the last person, beside his murderer, to see Mr. McGrath alive!"

Chapter Twenty

The very last person Dev expected to hear from today was Lady Adelaide Compton—in fact, he would have wagered she was much too embarrassed to ever speak to him again unless she absolutely had to in the course of the investigation. He was amazed that she was not still lying prostrate upon a fainting couch nursing a bad head. Dev was not one to judge, but he'd watched her consume almost two entire bottles of white wine before he'd gently removed her glass from reach.

She hadn't struck him as a woman who drank to excess—her eyes and skin were too clear, and she was missing the telltale facial puffiness. But something had prompted her to swill—no, her wine was probably too expensive to use the verb *swill*—swallow many more ounces than she should have.

He'd made allowances. Lady Adelaide was not herself, what with her husband recently deceased, two additional dead bodies turning up on her property, and the hellacious weather—it was awfully hot still with no sign of relief. Chilled wine had seemed like a good idea at the time. Even he'd been tempted. Last night she kept going into the kitchen (singing, oddly enough—she had a nice alto voice) to refill her wineglass, until she'd finally emerged with a whole bottle.

Lady Adelaide had sounded tipsy on the telephone, too, although it wasn't past five o'clock on a Sunday afternoon. Hair of the dog? He'd had difficulty making out the garbled rush of words, but she wanted him to come to Compton-Under-Wood immediately. Something about Mr. McGrath walking her dog and mailing a letter to Scotland before he took the afternoon nap from which he never awoke. She was convinced the letter must hold clues, and was going to ring the gardener's daughters once she hung up with him. Unfortunately, she expected Dev to grill that annoying vicar again when he got there, too.

Dev rubbed his eyes. He was due there anyway. Lady Grant's funeral was Tuesday; the inquests were two days later. He'd leave poor Bob behind—Mrs. Wells was belligerently pregnant, and wanted Bob at hand so she could shout at him for putting her in this predicament. Dev could manage on his own, and with the invitation to stay at Compton Chase, there would be no added expense for the department.

It was highly irregular to stay with a suspect, but he could say with the utmost confidence that Lady Adelaide had murdered nothing more than two bottles of wine. A week ago Saturday, during the hours in question, she had been attended to and seen napping and bathing by Beckett, called down to the kitchens numerous times to make sure her guests were taken care of, and—well, there was no "and." He would stake his reputation on her innocence.

Ernest Shipman, on the other hand, needed to cut his Continental jaunt short. There had been no word from him, and Dev was anxious to confront him about his diary. Whether he was guilty of murder or not, Mrs. Shipman was ready for him to hang.

He would borrow his father's Morris to go to the country; it was just sitting in the garage gathering dust. But first, he'd have to ask, and no doubt answer too many questions. Dev buttoned up his shirt and slicked back his hair with cold water. Even though he was just going next door, his mother would expect standards to be maintained. Queen Mary or some other royal personage might be lurking in their hallway.

He knocked, and waited as he heard the bolts release. As a former policeman, Harry Hunter was taking no chances with his wife's safety or his own, despite the fact their neighborhood was safe as houses. With the church at one end of the road, a few convenient stores, green space, and newer, solidly built lower-middle-class housing, this corner of Chelsea was a prime location.

Dev's father opened the door. He was also in shirtsleeves, his wiry white hair tamed by oil, his mustache waxed to perfection. His bearing showed his military training, and Dev was reminded of Colonel Mellard. A retired soldier was never really at ease.

"Good evening, Father. I have a favor to ask."

"If it's supper you're wanting, you know your mother always makes too much." His father patted his slight paunch, a recent development since his retirement. "Come in, come in. Anything new on the Cotswold case?"

"Maybe. That's why I'm here. May I borrow your car for the week?"

His father raised a brow. "My car? Won't the Yard issue you one?"

"I'd like to avoid the red tape and head out first thing tomorrow morning, as early as possible. There's some new information."

"Says who? Not that blundering local constable?"

Dev's encounters with Yardley had not been fruitful. "No. I don't expect he'll have his job much longer. I had a phone call. There's a letter from one of the victims."

"What does it say?"

"That's just it. No one's received it. It was on its way to Scotland, but for all I know, it's sitting in a Dead Letter drawer between here and there."

"Devenand!" His mother emerged from the kitchen, a starched apron over a remarkably short navy blue dress. Her ankles were as trim as a woman decades younger.

"Ma, very stylish. You're turning into a flapper." He bent and gave her a kiss.

"I won't let her cut her hair," his father grumbled.

"If I wish to cut my hair, I shall," said Dev's mother. "No one can stop me."

No one had ever been able to stop Chandani Hunter, not even her strict parents when she told them she was marrying a British military policeman and moving halfway across the world. Dev's parents had conducted a stealth courtship that had taken everyone by surprise, especially Harry, who never stood a chance against Chandani's predations and had rather enjoyed that.

"You will stay to supper?"

"I can't. If I'm leaving at first light, I have to pack and go into the office tonight and grab my paperwork."

"Where are you going?"

"Back to Compton-Under-Wood. There may be a break in the case, which would be most welcome before the inquests." He didn't want to count on anything—the letter might be worthless in the end. Like Lady Adelaide, he would also call Mrs. Robertson, Mr. McGrath's older daughter, and tell her to be on the lookout.

Of course, if the missive had arrived this week, she would have already read it. That she hadn't contacted him meant there was nothing in it to help solve her father's murder. She, again like Lady Adelaide, had all his numbers.

"Will you be staying at the Compton Arms again if we need to reach you?"

"Um, no. Lady Adelaide Compton has very kindly invited me to stay at Compton Chase." Dev waited, but neither of his parents said anything, a most unusual occurrence.

The silence stretched, and Dev cleared his throat. "So, may I take your car, Father, or make other arrangements?"

"You won't drive it to Scotland?"

"No, I promise." Dev's father was very particular about the car, using it rarely. Dev couldn't remember the last time the Morris was out of the private garage his father rented at considerable expense on a side street. Every now and again he toyed with making his father an offer for the machine, but he had little use for it himself in the normal course of things. "If I need to travel much beyond Compton-Under-Wood for any reason, I'll take the train."

He might have to meet with Shipman in London, if he returned, unless he could persuade the man to return to Compton Chase again. But it would be handy to have a car for Kathleen Grant's funeral, as well as the official dealings with the coroner. Dev enjoyed driving, and rarely got the chance since Bob considered it to be part of his duties.

Dev's father opened a desk drawer and presented Dev with the packet pertinent to the Morris and its operation. "You know there is an electric starter. Don't let the car get stolen. It wouldn't do your reputation as a crack detective any good."

"I'll chain the car to a fencepost if I have to, Father. Thank you. I don't expect it will leave the stable yard very often."

"Does Lady Adelaide keep horses?" Dev's mother asked, clearly more interested in the woman than she wanted to let on.

"Only the motorized kind. Her late husband had the stables converted and was a bit of a collector. You'd be impressed, Father." Dev had at first been surprised by the lack of horses at Compton Chase—the Cotswolds were famous for their hunts. But Lady Adelaide was probably too soft-hearted to chase after a terrified fox, and horses were notoriously expensive.

Despite her apparent wealth, Dev didn't think she was profligate with her money, except for lavishing it on the staff—more than half the house was under Holland covers. Aside from a very young chauffeur who looked as if he needed to shave only every other week, she kept two elderly grooms on the payroll, who were now tasked with care of the motors and anything else Mr. Forbes could dream up. Dev had a feeling they played cribbage as often as they worked. Many of the senior staff were holdovers from Rupert Compton's grandmother's day and were close to, or past, the usual retirement age.

Good help was hard to find now. No doubt Lady Adelaide was grateful and paid accordingly for their loyalty. Dev and Bob had not heard one complaint about Compton Chase's mistress, and they had probed. It was a murder investigation, after all.

Dev kissed his mother goodbye, grateful to escape without a grilling. He knew he was being unwise, accepting Lady Adelaide's offer to stay. Frankly, he'd been so surprised by it—especially after last night—that he'd said yes before he thought it through.

He was a professional, wasn't he? Thirty-four years old, tested by war and villains and the vicissitudes of twentieth-century living. He knew his place, even if Lady Adelaide didn't.

Chapter Twenty-one

Monday

The invitation had just tumbled out last night. No, it was worse than that—Addie had practically ordered Mr. Hunter to come and stay for the week. She didn't know why, but she was convinced that Mr. McGrath had put something down in writing before he'd walked to the village with Fitz, and somehow Mr. Hunter would get to the bottom of it. Woman's intuition? She'd never believed in that before.

But then she hadn't believed in ghosts either.

"If only you could read. And talk," she said, scratching that special spot on the dog's flank that always made his rear hind leg flap back and forth. "You were there when he wrote it, weren't you? And good for you for making Mrs. Franklin sneeze. She's a hypochondriac. Like *The Imaginary Invalid*. Molière, you know. I read it at school. With pimply Pandora, though I never would have brought attention to all those pustules. *I* tried to be a good friend. I wonder how many of my beaux she slept with."

There really hadn't been that many. Despite being a marquess' daughter, or perhaps because of it, few young men had pursued her. When the war broke out ten years ago, those who had shown some interest were invariably killed in action, like two of Barbara's fiancés. Lady Broughton had been in despair, dreaming of orange blossoms and wedding breakfasts that were not to be. Like so many of her contemporaries, Addie had been on the shelf before Rupert flew in in his Avro and swept her away.

Barbara. She should call her. Offer support for her recovery. *She* hadn't slept with Rupert given the chance. Addie knew next to nothing about drugs and their negative effects—she'd been healthy all her life, but she could ask Dr. Bergman the best way for her to help. With the exception of the sleeping powders she used after Rupert's death, she'd never taken anything stronger than an aspirin for a headache or a spoonful of honey for a cough.

Yes, she should call Barbara. Invite her down too to be a demi-duenna, in case Addie decided to fall victim to Mr. Hunter's liquid brown eyes and disgrace herself further. Knowing Barbara, she'd probably try to push them together instead. Lock them in the conservatory or cellar or something and let them out at Christmas.

It had even occurred to Addie to invite the original attendees of her ill-fated house party to spend the night tomorrow after Kathleen's funeral. Somehow she felt their presence was required, although it was likely one of them was guilty of committing the murder. But with the Hallidays off to who-knows-where (suspicious, that), Ernest Shipman presumably still inspecting a Swiss bank vault, and Sir David comforting his children, she'd have to take a couple of leaves out of the table.

It would be enough to have Barbara, accompanied by Gerald Dumont, if Barbara couldn't do without him. He'd been nice enough—good-looking, attentive, well-spoken, and well-dressed. If Barbara really was going to marry him, it behooved Addie to get to know him better.

She placed the trunk call to London, spoke briefly to Barbara's maid, and then waited what seemed like eons. Addie had to remind herself that just because she'd been up at the first blush of dawn in nervous anticipation of Mr. Hunter's arrival, Barbara had no reason to follow suit.

"*Do* you know what time it is?" came the croak at the other end of the line.

"I do!" Addie said brightly. "How are you? I mean, really, how *are* you?"

"If you've called to lecture me, don't waste your breath. Mama and Papa have me on short rations, and I cannot turn around without the private nurse they hired reporting on it and spinning me in the opposite direction. I may as well be in jail."

"I'm sure they mean well," Addie said, feeling somewhat relieved that she was being looked after at home instead of being locked away in some grim sanitarium.

"They just don't want the scandal. It would be bad for the business. Even Gerald has given me hell."

Addie was surprised to hear it. "Has he? That's good! That means he must care for you a great deal." Or worry about his meal ticket. As far as Addie knew, he had no employment, but didn't strike her as the kind of man born with a silver spoon in his mouth.

Like Lucas. Well, she chewed on a spoon from the same set, and still tried to contribute to society in a positive way. They both did. Lucas was a renowned sportsman and supported local charities. He was *not* a "shallow little shit."

"Between the four of them, I'd like to run off to a desert island. Life is such a bore at the moment." Addie could hear her friend light up a cigarette and exhale.

Another bad habit to break.

"Listen, I'm calling to invite you to stay here for a few days. To make up for the house-party-from-hell. Kathleen's funeral is tomorrow. Were you planning on going?" As far as Addie knew, it would be a relatively small, private affair. She'd received a written invitation, but she didn't think Sir David would object if she brought Barbara. She and Kathleen had run in the same circles in London.

There was a lengthy silence. "I don't want to. But Eloise wrote. However did she get mixed up in planning Kath's funeral?"

"She was just being neighborly, I imagine. Poor Sir David has his hands full with the boys. You know how strongly Eloise feels about her Christian duty."

"If that's what you want to call it. She's an interfering old bitch."

"Babs!"

"Oh, don't sound so shocked. You know my penchant for telling the truth no one wants to hear. I love you, but you're a babe in the woods when it comes to people."

"You'll make me sorry I asked you to come down," Addie said, keeping her temper. Was she really so naïve?

Yes, she was.

"Oh, I promise to behave. I'll have no choice. Fraulein Schober will be attached to me like a limpet. Barnacle, more like. Or those things on trees that look like mushrooms but are not."

"Who?"

"My minder. Someone forgot to tell her the Germans lost the war. She's a brute and a bully."

"She sounds dreadful. *Must* she come?"

Barbara laughed mirthlessly. "They won't let me go to the loo without her. I might get up to my old tricks."

Addie paused. Maybe inviting her was a bad idea, more than she could handle as a friend. Even with Dr. Bergman handy, Addie might fail in her well-intentioned support. "You don't want to, do you?"

"I don't know what I want, Addie, and that's the truth. It's all impossible now anyway." Her world-weary sigh blew across the miles.

"Maybe not. It's always darkest before dawn, you know," she said, echoing Mr. Rivers and feeling silly for doing so. "When you get here, we'll have a nice long chat, just like old times."

"Whoopee."

"Don't be so enthusiastic. Do you want to bring Gerald?"

"If he'll come. He's around here somewhere, but we're on the outs." Barbara had a penthouse flat all to herself on Park Lane, courtesy of her father's generosity.

"I'm sorry to hear it. He's welcome if you want him. Do you think you can manage to get here on the two o'clock train? I'll have my driver meet it."

"That won't give me much time to pack. But we're about the same size—I'll raid your closet if I need anything. But no bloody black for me, thanks very much."

Addie's non-mourning wear was hanging neatly in her dressing room, awaiting the February day when she could put her blacks aside for good. It had felt wonderful wearing those colored frocks in London, even if she was sure she'd scandalized Lucas. But as a marquess' daughter—more to the point, Lady Broughton's daughter—she knew she had to abide by the conventions, no matter how dreary they made her feel.

Gosh, she was rivalling Eloise for who was the goodest of the goodies. If her current predicament ever ended, it was past time to kick up her highest heels.

Chapter Twenty-two

Addie had sent Mr. Hunter straight to the vicarage and Reverend Rivers, with a side stop at the post office to corroborate his story. She had apologized too—not for pushing him away before he had a chance to get settled in his room upstairs, but for practically passing out toward the end of their dinner Saturday night. He looked as embarrassed as she felt as she stumbled over her words, and assured her he hadn't given her erratic behavior a moment's consideration.

Which was a lie. He must be gathering up quite a list of her oddities; he had that little notebook, after all. If only they had met under less bizarre circumstances, Mr. Hunter might not think she was deranged. It was all Rupert's fault, of course, but Addie tried to block him from her head the second the first syllable of his name popped up.

She wasn't quite successful. If Ru**** was tasked to accomplish some kind of mission, perhaps he was far away in Egypt, investigating poor Lord Carnarvon's curse for disturbing King Tut's tomb last year. Several people associated with the dig had died. Even the earl's pet bird was eaten by a snake, and rumor had it his faithful dog dropped dead at Highclere Castle about the time Carnarvon did in Egypt. It was all very supernatural, not that Addie had reason to take such things seriously pre-Rupert.

Oops. There he was, both syllables, bouncing about in her

head again. As long as he wasn't bouncing around in her bedroom.

When she had spoken to Mr. McGrath's daughter last night—who had received no letter—she'd promised to go to the cottage and pack up his things. Addie could have sent a maid, but she felt she owed it to the family to do it herself. She had time to kill before Barbara arrived, told Forbes where she was heading, and set out.

Addie didn't have proper boxes or shipping materials, but at least she could make a preliminary sorting of the old man's belongings. Mrs. Robertson had laughed ruefully and said she didn't want her father's clothes. Mr. McGrath was not known for his fashion sense, and almost everything he'd owned had been hole-infested from his decades of laboring in the gardens.

Addie took Fitz with her, hoping the dog might dig up evidence somehow. But Fitz was no bloodhound. As soon as he got to the cottage, he returned to his cool burrow under the lilac bush and left Addie to go in the kitchen door and get started.

While Mr. McGrath's clothing might have been on the disreputable side, he'd kept his little cottage spotless. He wouldn't have liked the footprints and crooked pictures the Cirencester police had left behind. They had dusted for fingerprints, and Addie's first order of business was to wipe away the sticky powder from places like the sugar canister and a chipped commemorative teacup celebrating King Edward VII's coronation. Most of the kitchen equipment belonged to the cottage, and she didn't think Mr. McGrath's daughters would value a battered eggbeater.

She took the homely pictures off the walls of the little parlor, the Toby jug, the framed photographs, and transferware platter off the mantel. Mr. McGrath's pipe still rested on its ashtray, causing her a pang. Addie put everything together on a gateleg table. There were a few dusty books on a shelf, which disintegrated in her hands. Mr. McGrath was not illiterate, but had been orphaned and left school at a very early age to live (and work) with his only living grandparent, a Scottish gardener employed by Rupert's grandmother. Despite over six decades living in the Cotswolds, he'd never lost his Scottish burr. He'd been pleased as punch that his older daughter had married a Scotsman.

She looked around the tidy parlor. Where might he have written a letter? There was no desk or secretary. When she and Lucas had been children, they'd experimented with "secret" messages, revealed by lemon juice or pencil rubbings. There was no pad of paper with impressions, or blotter that could be read backwards in a mirror, unless the police had carried off such things.

Addie climbed the steep narrow stairs, wondering how Mr. McGrath had done the same several times a day at his age. He'd certainly slowed down over the past few years, but never complained. For the millionth time since he'd been killed, she wished he had retired to Scotland to be with his family.

One small bedroom was nearly empty, its bed stripped, its cupboard bare. This is where his daughters had grown up, but there was no trace of the girls they had been. Across the hall, the scent of cherry tobacco was strong.

Addie hesitated. Mr. McGrath had died here. A prickle of unease crept up her neck, but she took a few steps into the room. This bed was stripped too, the sheets gathered up for evidence. A Bible was on a bedside table, and she gathered it to her chest. There was a large, poorly executed watercolor of mountains and lakes that must have held some sentimental value. She'd have to get someone taller than she was to take it down.

The chest of drawers held very little of interest, except for a bundle of letters from his daughters and grandchildren, tied with a frayed green ribbon. Addie tucked those on top of the Bible and opened the closet under the eaves. Ancient muddy boots, the stitching coming undone, very worn tweeds. In their condition, they weren't really fit to even donate to the church.

It was odd what one left behind to be discovered after a sudden death. Addie was grateful Barbara's joke of a dildo would not be found if she fell down the stairs here. But it was clear to her after viewing Mr. McGrath's spartan cottage that she simply had *too much*.

Not that she wanted to join the Communist Party of Great Britain. If her mother objected to Cee's vegetarian interests, Addie could only imagine her mother's horror if she betrayed her class in such a fashion. But really, there had to be a happy medium somewhere.

She trod the stairs carefully, holding on to the rope railing and Bible with equal fervor. Returning to the parlor, she set everything down with the rest of the items. The table wasn't even half-covered.

Still, Mr. McGrath had seemed happy enough with what little he had. Addie envied him.

She flinched at the hand on her shoulder. "Don't cry, my dear. The old fellow wouldn't want you to. He was fond of you, you know."

Ugh. Rupert. "Where have you been?" She blew her nose on the monogrammed handkerchief the undertaker had tucked into his breast pocket.

"Here and there. I thought you didn't want me underfoot."

"I can't seem to keep you from turning up when it's most inconvenient."

"Ah, yes. You have company again. All the more reason for me to come and help if I can."

"Help! You've been nothing but a hindrance," Addie said.

"I did wash all those dishes. To be fair, Hunter cleared the table after he put you to bed. His stacking and rinsing methods leave something to be desired." He tucked the snotty handkerchief back in his pocket where it became miraculously pristine again. "You never could hold your liquor, my poor darling."

Addie stamped her foot, narrowly missing his. "I am not your poor darling!"

"No, nobody's darling, nobody's sweetheart. And that's a bit of a waste in my opinion. I've given it some thought, and I'm prepared to let you have your bit of fun."

"Let me! You have nothing to say in the matter! I'm a thirty-one-year-old widow. If I want to have my 'bit of fun,' as you put it, nothing could stop me!"

Rupert gave her a thoughtful look. "Except perhaps your mama. She has such high standards for you, and I know you don't wish to disappoint her."

What he said was the truth, so Addie couldn't argue. "I need to go home. Mr. Hunter should be back by now."

"Are you sure you don't want to take one more look around the cottage?" He examined his fingernails in a faux show of disinterest.

"Why? Do you know something I don't?"

"I might. Call it *man's* intuition."

"Rupert!"

"All right, all right. The police were a trifle careless, no doubt because Hunter wasn't supervising."

"Where am I supposed to be looking? And what am I looking for?"

"The Bible, my dear. Where else?"

Addie tripped over a rag rug and picked up the Bible. Bits of paper had been slipped between the pages, presumably marking favorite passages. Several of them had cramped, struck-out writing on it, and were virtually impossible to read.

"They're a whatchamacallit," Rupert said unhelpfully. "Like in the olden days, when they wrote over something that was already written upon to save paper or postage."

"Palimpsest," Addie replied. "Why do I know that? You went to university."

"Where I barely picked up a book, to my current regret. I have the strongest feeling Mr. M. marked a few passages the day he died."

Addie studied the strip of paper, flipping it around until

something came into focus. "I Corinthians 10:13." She found the verse and read it aloud. "'*There hath no temptation taken you but such is common to man. But God is faithful, and will not suffer you to be tempted above that ye are able; but will with the temptation also make a way to escape, that ye may be able to bear it.*' Goodness. What could have tempted him?"

"I think you need to check the sixth chapter of I Corinthians, verse eighteen. Just a hunch," he said with modesty.

"Actually, it's on the back side of the paper in my hand, if my glasses are on straight. '*Flee fornication!*' Rupert! He saw Kathleen and whoever she was with! Whomever? Whatever! It's a clue!"

"I believe you're right. But we knew this anyway, didn't we?"

Addie nodded. "It's even more important to find his letter now."

"I doubt he named names, even if he knew them. That would make all this much too easy. Somehow, I think there are a few more tests ahead."

Would they pass or fail them? For Rupert's sake, Addie hoped they'd get high marks.

Chapter Twenty-three

Despite the short notice, Barbara had packed enough to move in for the foreseeable future. The entryway was filled with trunks and suitcases, whose colorful stickers were a reminder of all the places she had visited since her debutante days. Of course, she was accompanied by two other people who might claim a bag or two.

Gerald appeared uncomfortable at his return, no doubt wishing to be far away from the scene of a crime, and possibly Barbara herself. And then there was Fraulein Schober, who was not at all what Addie expected: some Teutonic Valkyrie with a mustache and unplucked brows in a white uniform who would pummel poor Babs into submission if she stepped over the line.

Instead, Fraulein Schober was a petite blonde with sky-blue eyes who resembled a China doll in stature and delicacy. She was not dressed in nurse regalia, but a floral chiffon dress and a smart straw hat. Her command of English was near-perfect, her manners impeccable. She seemed unintimidated by the relative grandeur of Compton Chase, leading Addie to believe she'd had an upper-class upbringing in Germany, or had at least moved in good society. There was not a drop of perspiration on her porcelain complexion.

Barbara was pale and fidgety, but allowed herself to be hugged for an over-long time.

"It's only been a week," she laughed uncertainly, escaping from Addie's clutches.

"And what a busy week it's been! Forbes, would you please get our guests settled?"

"Very good, my lady. If you all will just follow me." He directed the footmen up the stairs, and even picked up a dressing case himself.

"Babs, come to my room after you powder your nose. We can catch up."

Inspector Hunter was out again, now armed with the knowledge of Mr. McGrath's Bible. After lunch, he'd decided to take a walk around the estate "to think," and go over the gardener's cottage once more. Addie had wished he'd asked her to accompany him, but she did have to meet her new guests.

Fraulein Schober cleared her throat in a discreet and musical way.

"Brigitta can come too, yes? She's my shadow." Barbara said, glum. She hadn't been kidding about the limpet part then.

"Of course. You might be bored, though, Fraulein Schober. We'll be talking about old acquaintances." One old dead acquaintance anyway.

"The more I can learn about Miss Pryce's life, the better I can help her. Don't you agree, Mr. Dumont? You have been a font of knowledge."

Which was odd, as Gerald had only known Barbara a few months. Not for the first time did Addie wonder why they had gotten engaged so suddenly. Barbara forgot he was there half the time. But that could have been a result of the pills.

"Um. Yes, I suppose." Color crept up from his collar.

Fraulein Schober smiled. "Mr. Dumont is, as you know, a medium. He has such fascinating insights, *ja?*"

"What?" Addie blurted. She sounded rude to her own ears.

"A medium. A facilitator from this world to the beyond. Even though I have had a scientific education in nursing, the metaphysical interests me." Fraulein Schober was full of surprises, as was quiet Gerald Dumont.

"That's how we met. He was presiding over a séance in Cannes. For a lark, I wondered what Billy and Paul were up to—you know, fiancés number one and number two," Barbara said, as if getting engaged to mediums was what one did after a séance.

Gerald examined his ruby ring. "I regret I was unable to open up the laws of attraction that evening. The electro-magnetic field was weak. But life is continuous even after we leave our physical bodies, and the language of the soul is strong. We all possess psychic energy and the ability to conduct its current, and we can try again to communicate with the other side in the future, if you wish it, my dear," He sounded extremely serious.

Well. Addie just stopped herself from giggling. It wasn't that she disbelieved him—he sounded like Reverend Rivers *and* Inspector Hunter—but her mental image of a medium did not resemble conventionally handsome, unobtrusive Gerald Dumont in the least. Somehow she expected a raddled female with gaudy clacking jewelry, shawls, and feathered headgear, a crystal ball at the ready.

"Uh, how long have you done this, Gerald?" she asked.

He shrugged. "All my life I've benefitted from flashes of intuition. I knew at once Barbara needed me."

"He's famous in France," Barbara interjected, lighting her cigarette before Gerald could get to it with his own gold lighter.

How was it Inspector Hunter missed this? It wasn't every day one bumped into a medium. Maybe Gerald could be persuaded to help with the investigation.

Maybe Gerald could get rid of Rupert!

"Can you see into the future?" Addie asked. Not that she really wanted to know what was in her future. That would take all the fun out of life, wouldn't it?

As long as it was Rupert-less.

"No, not usually. My job has more to do with the past. Unfinished business. So many of my clients have lost family and friends in the Great War, and even more died from the Spanish influenza epidemic. They have questions, and hope those who have passed on can provide answers. But one must be prepared to not always get the answer to the question one asks." Gerald was speaking with more force and confidence than he'd shown previously. Maybe he really knew what he was talking about.

Gosh. Ghosts and voices of the dead. If someone had told Addie seven months ago that she'd be having this conversation, she would have hooted with derision.

"Forbes, can you have a tea tray sent up to my room in half an hour? When Inspector Hunter gets back—"

"Hold on. You never said he was here!" Barbara gripped Addie's arm, hard enough to hurt. She sounded absolutely panicked.

Addie gave her a gentle squeeze to release her. "Didn't I? He had more interviews to do, and he's here for the funeral and inquests, too. I thought it would be easier if he stayed at the house rather than the Compton Arms. He got here this morning."

Barbara stumbled backward. "You most certainly did not! I don't want to see him!"

Fraulein Schober placed a gloved hand on Barbara's arm. "And you won't have to. Compton Chase is very large, *ja*? There is no reason for you to cross his path unless you want to."

This was all very odd. The last time she was here, Barbara practically salivated over the policeman, flirting as if her knickers were on fire. If anything, Addie thought she would be teased for harboring the man under her roof, no matter how innocent her intentions.

"He—he doesn't have to dine with us. I guess I can make up some excuse," Addie said with doubt. She didn't want to offend him, make him think he wasn't good enough to share the same table with her other guests just because his background was so different.

"Nonsense," Fraulein Schober said. "If Miss Pryce cannot face her fear at present, it is she who should be sequestered. We can have a simple supper sent to our room."

Our room? Addie had placed the nurse across the hall, with Gerald in the connecting room, just like last time. How awkward. Well, they were adults—they'd have to figure it out.

"I'll go inform Cook."

"No. Wait." Gerald gave Barbara a look. "It's time we told the truth, don't you think?"

Barbara took a long drag from her cigarette. "No, I don't think," she said, sullen.

"We'll talk about it upstairs."

"I knew you shouldn't have come. You'll ruin everything!" Barbara grumbled.

"This conversation requires privacy," Fraulein Schober said firmly. "Come, Miss Pryce, it's nearly time for your tonic. And we are keeping the poor butler waiting. One should never be disrespectful of the staff. Don't you agree, Lady Adelaide?"

"Absolutely," Addie said, wanting to flee. Tonic? Probably not quinine water. She hoped Barbara wasn't getting addicted to something else.

She remained alone in the hall while they went upstairs, wanting to smack herself for the spur-of-the-moment invitation. For Mr. Hunter or Barbara—it didn't matter which. Somehow she'd complicated things. Good intentions invariably led one straight to you-know-where.

"*That* was interesting." Rupert sat in the tall leather porter's chair by the front door, twirling his Lobb-shod foot.

"Here again?" She was getting less spooked at his imaginary manifestations, thank goodness. Her heart barely raced this time.

"I'm at loose ends. Believe me when I say I find these instant appearances beyond tedious. One can never get settled before one is whisked away to another responsibility."

"What's your responsibility now? You've done your Bible bit this morning. Mr. Hunter was very impressed with my—your—conclusions."

Rupert frowned. "I'm not sure what I'm here for. I never am. I do hope Dumont doesn't notice me."

"You mean he's on the up and up? An actual medium who receives and transmits information from the spirit world?"

"Oh, yes." Rupert adjusted his perfectly adjusted tie. "You'd never have guessed, would you? It's the quiet ones one has to watch out for."

"Why didn't you say something before?" She might have mentioned Gerald's "career" to Mr. Hunter, not that the inspector was apt to take a medium seriously.

"His abilities didn't seem pertinent at the time. And you never asked."

Frankly, she'd thought of Gerald Dumont as a plain old-fashioned gigolo. So much for *her* instincts. "Does he know who killed Kathleen?"

"No. But he knows something."

"Rupert! Stop being so mysterious! It's very aggravating."

"As Gwendolen says in *The Importance of Being Earnest*, 'The suspense is terrible. I hope it will last.'"

"Well, I don't! The sooner we can solve the murders, the sooner you can go to wherever you are going!"

"And so, my dear, will Inspector Hunter. Never tell me you want to get rid of *him*."

Chapter Twenty-four

Reminded of Colonel Mellard's philosophy of clearing one's head, Dev had had a good long tramp around the Compton estate. There were no stars in the sky, but he'd discovered the footpath to the village, wandered about the home farm, and stepped in enough sheep shit in his good boots to finally bring him down to earth and watch where he was going.

The day was warm, but not as oppressive as it had been. He'd taken his suit jacket off, rolled up his shirt sleeves, and loosened his tie. This was very pretty country, with rolling hills and valleys, the occasional distant church spires pointing to heaven.

Dev had pulled a tooth or two, and he'd gotten the vicar to recall a little more of his encounter with Mr. McGrath. Mrs. Franklin had been informative, too. Her temporary helper had placed the letter in the wrong cubby, so she'd definitely noted it was going to Scotland when she put it in the mail sack. But not, she thought, to *Mrs.* Robertson.

The handwriting had been awful, but the letter had been addressed to a man. Had she been on duty, she would have made poor Mr. McGrath address a whole new envelope. She was unable to remember the addressee's Christian name, but the last name was indeed Robertson. There must only be hundreds of Robertsons in Scotland, Dev thought with some despair, but perhaps Mr. McGrath's daughter would have an idea to whom the letter was addressed. He'd call her again once he was back at Compton Chase.

He had spent an hour at the gardener's cottage raking through the ashes and peeking under furniture for any other scraps of paper. He'd come up with nothing, save for a greater determination to solve the case and an appreciation of the gardener's tidiness. Mr. McGrath had lived a God-fearing, well-ordered life in his home, and it was disturbing to have it end the way it had.

Dev paused by a stone wall and smartened up his clothing. His injured foot twinged for the first time in a while; maybe he'd taken Mellard's walking business too much to heart. He was no closer to clarity, which boded ill for the inquests. *Person or persons unknown.* It was a general consensus in police work that if the killer was not apprehended within a day or two of a murder, the case might never be solved.

Dev had missing suspects, but his gut told him they were not guilty. For one thing, he had trouble picturing Ernest Shipman climbing the treacherous stairs in the gardener's cottage. The man was soft. Somewhat overweight. The most exercise he probably took was punching a lift button. By the time he huffed and puffed up the narrow stairs, he'd be too exhausted to think of injecting anyone with anything.

His wife, however, was fit and trim. If she had reason to believe her husband was having an affair, she very might well have nipped to the barn and the cottage like a vengeful gazelle while her husband was resting.

Mrs. Shipman claimed no prior knowledge of her husband's unfaithfulness until she found his diary. But she could easily have been lying, enlisting Addie—that is, Lady Adelaide—in her cover-up.

Dev pressed his fingers against his forehead, right where his "third eye" should be. Regrettably, he had been born without one—or perhaps his had a cataract.

The Shipmans

The Hallidays

Colonel Mellard
Sir David Grant
Lady Cecilia Merrill
Lord Lucas Waring
Miss Eloise Waring
Miss Barbara Pryce
Gerald Dumont

No alibis to speak of. Not much in the way of motive, though. But plenty of opportunity.

He heard a car horn behind him and turned. Well, knock him down with a feather. He gave the woman a broad smile.

"Do you want a ride? I presume you're going to Addie's, since you're on her lane."

Oh. With the sun behind her, Dev had thought the driver was Lady Adelaide. Now that he looked more closely, he could see the short golden curls escaping from the blue felt cloche. It was Lady Cecilia Merrill behind the wheel of a bright blue Triumph, sporting a pair of blue-tinted spectacles. Her dress was blue with tiny white flowers—she was completely color-coordinated.

Dev opened the car door and slid onto the seat. "Thank you. No chauffeur for you, Lady Cecilia?"

"I'm not such a bad driver, really. Anyway, Mummy commandeered him. She went to London in the Rolls to buy a new hat for the funeral tomorrow. Not that she needs one—she must have a dozen black hats gathering dust. I was bored and thought I'd drive over, surprise Addie, and cadge some tea. What are you doing here? Have you seen Sir David?"

He recognized the anxiety in her voice. "No. I had other people to talk to."

"How is the investigation going?" She swerved to avoid a rabbit, and Dev hit his head on the canvas roof.

"Do you want the truth? Not well. Detective work is often a process of elimination, and there are precious few suspects to eliminate."

"What about me?"

"Do you want to be under consideration? You'd hang, you know."

"But probably with a silk rope—ever so chic." She gave him a saucy smile.

Lady Cecilia was in a much better mood than she had been when last Dev met her. While he could imagine her as an avenging angel protecting Sir David Grant, it was harder to see her killing off an elderly gardener. She was very young, much too young for Grant, who was almost twice her age. For his part, Dev didn't see the man's appeal at all. Perhaps Lady Cecilia liked to collect helpless and wounded things. She'd be better off with the rabbit who'd crossed their path and barely lived to tell the tale.

The gatehouse came into view and Lady Cecilia rolled to a stop. This time the gates were shut, and Dev got out and opened them. There were numerous ways to get onto the estate, but he remained convinced that one of the "nappers" had left his or her bed and done the unthinkable twice.

"Are you in the habit of popping over unannounced to your sister's for tea?" Dev asked over the noise of the engine.

"Not really. Usually Mummy invites herself and drags me along. Since my brother-in-law's death, we've tried to be good company and cheer Addie up on a regular basis. I'm not sure it's working."

"Why do you say that?"

"My sister is awfully…quiet. Serious. I wish she'd go away, not just to London. To New York, or even California. Somewhere fun and strange where no one knows her. She needs to let loose and live a little."

She'd tried to "live" the other night. Dev kept the two bottles of wine to himself. "She has company already, actually. Miss Pryce and her fiancé are coming for a few days. They must have arrived by now."

"Oh! Barbara's such fun!" Then Lady Cecilia looked stricken. "At least she used to be. But maybe that was because of the pills she took. What she needs is a healthy diet. I wish I'd known she was going to be here. I would have brought my Vegetarian Society pamphlets."

"Another time," Dev said mildly.

"Yes! I can bring them to the funeral. Well, here we are. Should I drop you at the service entrance?"

"Actually, I'm a guest too. Your sister summoned me."

A golden brow lifted. "Really? How very interesting."

"Not especially. She had some additional information related to the case. She's saved me the trouble of going back and forth from London all week."

"Or staying at the Compton Arms, which is a perfectly respectable inn." It was obvious to Dev that Lady Cecilia thought that's where he belonged.

"Yes. Sergeant Wells and I enjoyed our last stay. Excellent food. But all the rooms are booked. I believe the press got wind of the funeral arrangements somehow." Dev knew this to be a fact after he stopped in to see the publican. While happy for the business, Dev got the impression the man preferred a different sort of clientele than the brash newsmen. Even the lowly police were more welcome.

"Damned vultures! They'd better not bother Addie again. When Rupert had his accident—well, nevermind. The colonel dealt with them then, but I suppose it would be expecting too much for him to do so now, poor man."

"You know about his relationship with Lady Grant?"

"Addie told me, but I haven't breathed a word. Honestly."

When Dev heard "honestly," "to be frank," or "believe me," he always looked for the lie; it was a nearly automatic flag. Lady Cecilia seemed truthful, however. He had requested some extra officers from Cirencester to prevent the church funeral from turning into a circus, and more were to be stationed around Holly Hill for the reception.

Forbes opened the door before they had a chance to pull the bell.

"Thank God you're here."

"Gracious, Forbes! What's the matter?"

"Not you, Lady Cee. Inspector, you must come at once."

Chapter Twenty-five

"*Please*, Babs." Addie had said a variation of those words for the past five minutes, and was becoming increasingly alarmed. While Forbes had a key to the bedroom door, the key to the adjoining bathroom had somehow disappeared from his ring. The fact that Forbes had keys for every other guest bathroom did them no good at all—they were not compatible with this particular lock. "Gerald, do something."

He raked a hand through his matinee-idol hair. "I—I don't think we're getting married after all. She won't listen to me anymore."

"Try, for God's sake! Say something, anything."

"Barbara. Darling. Please come out." The "darling" was definitely an afterthought.

Useless.

"Fraulein? You try!"

The nurse shouted in German and pounded on the door with her little fist. Addie found the words terrifying and she had no idea what they meant, but Barbara would. She'd had a redoubtable German governess for years, had spent winters skiing in the Tyrol before the war, and was fluent enough to have been hired and then fired as a translator by the War Department after she missed too many days of work.

She had never known when to say when, war or no war.

"Leave. Me. Alone."

Addie released a breath. Barbara hadn't slit her wrists yet or swallowed the contents of a whole bottle of aspirin that was kept in the medicine closet for tipsy guests.

"What's all this?"

"Oh! Inspector Hunter!" Another wave of relief. "Can you talk some sense into Miss Pryce? She's locked herself in the bathroom."

"I've sent a footman for some tools. We can remove the door, Lady Adelaide," Forbes said from behind him. And behind the butler was Cee!

"Cee, what are you doing here?" Addie loved her sister to bits, but this was not a good time for entertaining her.

"I came for tea, but this is much more exciting." Cee's eyes were sparkling and her cheeks flushed.

Bloodthirsty little wench. "Don't be such a savage! This is serious, not a game." Poor Barbara. Addie had anticipated some unrest, but nothing like this. The screaming that had precipitated Barbara locking herself in was still ringing in Addie's ears.

"Forbes, I don't think tools will be necessary." Mr. Hunter reached into a pocket and pulled out a metal pick.

"But you're a policeman!" Addie said, shocked. The words law and order had probably been invented just for him.

"And I've been taught by the best criminals in London. Very anxious they are to show off their skills before they get sent away and lose dexterity. Step aside, Miss."

Fraulein Schober blinked. "*Polizei?*"

Mr. Hunter dropped to his knees and peered into the lock. "Good afternoon, Miss Pryce. How are you?"

"How *am* I? I'm going mad! I cannot get a minute to myself. And *you* are here. I don't want to talk to you."

"I hear that a lot. Nearly every day, in fact. My feelings aren't hurt."

"I don't care about your feelings!" There was a muffled thud of something falling.

"No. Why should you? I imagine you have enough of your own worries."

Addie thought he was being remarkably patient. Rather soothing, actually.

"You're not going to trick me by being kind. I know what you're after."

"Do you? Then you know more than I at the moment. Your friends have asked me to unlock the door. Is that all right with you?"

"What difference does it make? You're going to do it anyway."

"I won't if you come out on your own." He turned to the little crowd behind him. "Why don't you all go downstairs and have a cup of tea? I'll take care of Miss Pryce."

"You don't even know me," Barbara objected from behind the painted oak door.

"That might be to your benefit. I have no preconceived notions. No long-standing friendship. No emotional entanglement."

Gerald cleared his throat. "I think you should ask her about Saturday afternoon the day Kathleen Grant died."

"Oh?"

"Gerald, you little weasel!" The door sprang open, and Barbara emerged, her face tear- and mascara-streaked. She wore only a camisole and knickers, and Mr. Hunter averted his eyes from his kneeling position on the floor. He was getting much more of Babs than he bargained for.

"Give me back my ring!"

The man pulled the ruby and gold pinkie ring from his finger and put it in her outstretched hand. "I'm sorry, Babs. I tried my best."

"Your best was never good enough! All right, Inspector, you might as well get up on your feet and arrest me, unless you're proposing, too. Gerald thinks I killed Kathleen. Lock me up for real. It doesn't make any difference."

"I never said that!" Gerald sputtered. "Only that you'd be better off telling the truth. The truth always sets one free."

"Lady Cecilia," Forbes interrupted, "I think we should go and leave Mr. Hunter to sort this out."

"Spoilsport. Why do the rest of them get to stay?" Cee pouted.

"Fraulein Schober might be needed in case of a medical emergency. Your sister is here to support her friend. Mr. Dumont has what might be evidence in a murder case."

"I think that covers it," Mr. Hunter said smoothly. "Thank you, Forbes." Cee stuck her tongue out, but was shepherded out the bedroom door, which Forbes closed firmly behind him.

"Lady Adelaide, can you find a robe for Miss Pryce? Let's all sit down and try to get comfortable."

Barbara snorted, ducked behind the door, grabbed a Japanese kimono covered in cherry blossoms, and covered herself. "There. Modesty prevails."

Glaring at no one in particular, she plopped down on the center of the bed. Gerald took a chair by the window, looking very much as if he'd like to jump out of it. Fraulein Schober sat on the blanket chest at the foot of the bed, and Addie took the dressing table chair. Inspector Hunter remained standing, hands in his pockets.

"Mr. Dumont, let's begin with you. Do you want to add anything to the statement you gave me last week?"

Gosh. Only a *week* had passed. Addie felt as if she'd aged five years, maybe more after this afternoon.

"Yes. I perjured myself. Only I didn't know it at the time."

"I don't understand."

"You asked me where I was at the time of the murders. I was here, in this very room, asleep. I thought that Barbara was with me the whole time and told you so. But I was wrong."

"She left you?"

"Yes. I only found out—" He loosened his collar with his forefinger. "You won't believe me. But I saw her in one of my visions. She was in the barn with Kathleen Grant."

"In one of your visions." Mr. Hunter kept his tone neutral. Lord, Addie thought, he must think he's stumbled into a scene from *Alice's Adventures in Wonderland*.

"Inadmissible in court," Barbara snapped.

"Herr Dumont is a medium," Fraulein Schobert offered helpfully.

"He's famous in France," Addie added. Soon they would all be locked up and Mr. Hunter would throw away the key.

"It doesn't make it any less true. I don't know if Barbara killed her or not. I hope not. I love—I loved her, despite everything. But Barbara doesn't love herself. She makes it hard for people to help her."

"I don't want your bloody help! This is ridiculous. I want to go home. Addie, when does the next train leave?"

"Not quite yet," Mr. Hunter said. "Miss Pryce, did you leave this room and go to the tithe barn?"

Barbara stared at her hands, then removed her own ruby ring. "I don't have to say. Not without a lawyer present."

"Shall we call yours?"

"You'd take *his* word over mine?" she asked, nodding toward Gerald. "He's nothing but a fraud!"

"I'm only trying to find out what happened, Miss Pryce. Everyone's words are important. Two people are dead."

"Do you think I don't care? I do care! More than I should!" Barbara burst into tears.

Fraulein Schober took a handkerchief that had been tucked under her belt and passed it over. "Try to be calm, *liebling*."

"How can I? Kath is dead and some people think I killed her. Why would I do that? I loved her!"

Chapter Twenty-six

Addie pressed her lips together so she wouldn't cry out. As Alice herself might say, "Curiouser and curiouser."

"Were you having an affair with her?" Mr. Hunter asked softly.

"Yes. What of it?"

"Nothing, except that you must know she was not faithful. To anyone. That might have…upset you."

"And made me kill her? I wouldn't have, even if she had a hundred affairs." Barbara sighed. "That was Kath. She didn't want to miss a thing. Always looking for the next experience. She'd had a very strict upbringing, you know. Her older brother died when she was practically a baby and her parents kept her in cotton wool to keep her safe. They barely let her out of their sight. Really, I can't believe they were even on the *Lusitania* without her." She blew her nose into Fraulein's handkerchief.

"Did you know she'd be here at Compton Chase?"

She nodded. "We agreed to meet around four o'clock. But she was dead when I got there, I swear."

"You saw her body?"

Barbara shut her eyes and nodded again.

"Please describe it to me, if it isn't too painful."

"She was on her back. Naked. Twisted. I—I touched her to make sure…anyway, I couldn't leave her as she was. I straightened her limbs. I don't know why I did what I did next. I was out of my mind, as if I was watching myself in a film. I made her a bouquet out of the straw and covered her up as best I could."

Like an effigy.

"What did you think happened to her?"

"Drugs," Barbara spat. "You may think it's funny coming from me, but she was getting careless. Nothing was ever enough lately. She'd moved on from snorting cocaine to injecting it. She couldn't be reasoned with. I was worried."

"Do you know who else she was seeing?"

"You mean sleeping with?"

"Yes."

"She wouldn't tell me. But she did say she was thinking of getting married again. Told me we should have a double wedding."

Poor Gerald looked green. Apparently his visions hadn't included that detail.

"What did you do after you left her?"

"I went back to the house. The front door was wide open, and no one saw me. I got myself upstairs somehow and took a few pills. Someone came with a tea tray while I was in the bathroom washing up. I took my clothes off and slipped back into bed. I even fell asleep."

"Why didn't you tell me this before?"

"Would you have believed me?"

Addie wasn't sure she believed Barbara now. Her oldest friend was leading a double life and she'd never suspected. All that arch talk about how attractive Mr. Hunter was, when her female lover lay dead in the morgue. Barbara was a superb actress.

She could be acting right this minute.

This was one more example of how guileless Addie was. She never would have guessed that Barbara was a lesbian, certainly not after five fiancés. What kind of friend was she that she'd missed such an important fact? Of course, the five men might have thrown her off a bit. If at first you don't succeed, try, try, try, try, try again.

Mr. Hunter pulled out his notebook. "I'd like some time alone with Miss Pryce now, so if you don't mind leaving?"

"I shall stay," Fraulein Schober insisted.

"Am I correct in that your connection with Miss Pryce is very recent?"

"Yes, her parents have hired me to be her private nurse. I shall hold anything you or she says in complete confidence."

Mr. Hunter looked unconvinced. "Do you want her to stay, Miss Pryce? It's very unusual."

Barbara gave a bleak laugh. "So am I, Inspector. I don't much care one way or the other."

Addie took that as her cue to leave. She was accompanied by poor Gerald, who didn't appear to be famous in France or anywhere at the moment. Shoulders slumped, he wore an air of defeat.

"Did you know she preferred women?" Addie whispered once they were out in the hall.

"It's almost a relief. I thought there might be something wrong with *me*. She was very keen to get engaged, though—she can be very persuasive. I admit to being swept off my feet."

And wear the matching ruby ring, which Barbara had undoubtedly paid for as well as her own.

They moved along the corridor and down the stairs. When they got to the landing, Addie paused beneath the stained-glass window. Bright patches of color lit the sisal runner. The stairway was magical at this time of day, but it failed to make anything clearer.

"Your, um, insights gave you no warning?"

"You don't have to believe, Lady Adelaide, but we all possess 'insights,' as you say. One must just open oneself up to them. In my case, my enthusiasm for Barbara—and, I'll be honest, her financial status—overrode any warning signs. I thought I could handle the drug business and help her, wean her off them, but I was wrong there, too." He traced the leaded glass with a finger. "This will ruin me."

"What do you mean?"

"If my clients get wind of this mess, I might as well join a traveling carnival and read some ruddy tarot cards to drunken punters. Who will trust me when I can't even keep my own life in order?"

"Like the shoemaker who has no shoes? Inspector Hunter would say you're too close to the situation to see clearly. And that you're only human. He was very helpful when I doubted myself."

"Huh. Not much gets by him, does it? He's got a very strong aura."

Addie had no idea what that meant but was sure it was true. She linked her arm in Gerald's. "Let's see if my awful little sister has left us anything to eat."

They found Cee in the Great Hall, where a lavish spread had been set out in hopes that tea would cure all, and everyone's sanity would be restored. Compton Chase had had too much excitement over the past ten days, and everyone was frazzled. Even Addie's staff was showing signs of stress—some of the biscuits were burnt. Mr. McGrath hadn't mingled much, but his presence had been comforting and his handiwork admirable. He had been the oldest worker on the estate, someone who remembered "how things should be." Addie knew Compton Chase would never be restored to its glory days—for that matter, neither would she. She'd pulled a silver hair from the gold just this morning.

Another thing to blame on Rupert.

"Cee, you remember Mr. Dumont."

"May I pour you a cup of tea?"

"Quite frankly, I'd prefer something stronger. It isn't every day I get unengaged," he said with a crooked smile, which must have worked its charm on Barbara at one time.

Addie pointed to the drinks cart in the far corner. "Please help yourself."

Gerald returned with a full glass of unadulterated whiskey and took the plate Cee had made up for him. After a long swallow, he said, "I think I should leave tonight, if possible, Lady Adelaide. There's no point in me staying. I certainly don't want to go to the funeral now, not that I ever did."

"You'd better check with Inspector Hunter. He may want you to formally amend your statement." Addie signed something declaring her own ignorance of the events, and she assumed everyone had.

"Will you tell me what happened upstairs? I feel like a child who was sent to bed early," Cee said.

Gerald's expression was pained. Addie jumped in. "Maybe later, Cee. It's Mr. Dumont's story to tell, and I don't think he wants to yet."

"Oh, all right. So tell me this at least—why is Mr. Hunter here? Apart from his convenient ability to break in and enter. He told me he'll be here all week."

"I thought it would be easier for him. There were some new discoveries, here on the estate and in the village."

"Do you know the press has taken over the Compton Arms?" Addie's heart sank. "No!"

"Well, all three rooms. There hasn't been much in the papers so far, only the worst ones." The ones Cee liked to read, Addie imagined. "Nothing about you at all, if that will make you feel any better."

The Metropolitan Police were probably doing all they could to quash the story. With so many high-profile people involved, Addie realized the potential for a very juicy scandal.

What if someone besides Rupert popped out of the bushes? She'd best be prepared.

Chapter Twenty-seven

Tuesday

Last evening had been just as awkward as expected. The only bright spots: Cee had driven home, her junior bloodhound instincts thwarted, dropping Gerald Dumont at the train station on the way. Barbara and her nurse had requested dinner upstairs after the ordeal of so many confessions, thus Addie was left alone with Inspector Hunter.

Instead of the formal dining room, they ate, punctuated by long silences, in the cozy morning room. Small talk became even more minute as each course was served. Addie failed her duties as a hostess. It wasn't because she was six months out of practice—she couldn't manage to escape the embarrassment she felt about those bottles of wine, and conspicuously drank only water with her lamb cutlets. Mr. Hunter had excused himself early, claiming he had paperwork to do, and Addie had gone straight to bed, only to lie awake most of the night.

She looked like she was the one who belonged in a coffin this morning. Beckett tutted and did the best she could with makeup, including a swipe of mascara. Addie expected to remain dry-eyed, although Kathleen was coming into focus at long last. She wasn't just a husband-stealer, but a free spirit who broke the rules every chance she got. There was something admirable about it, in a way, and it cast Rupert in a different light as well.

"Now now now. Don't forgive me. I don't deserve it. Yet." Rupert appeared out of thin air in one of the wingchairs in front of the empty fireplace. Addie almost didn't recognize him, but who else would be popping in for a spectral chat?

"Your mustache is missing!"

He patted his pockets down in a great show of searching. "I've come up empty. Yes. It was time for a change. It's one thing to wear this bloody tie day after day, but I got sick of—what did you once call it? A moth-eaten caterpillar? Which makes absolutely no sense, my dear, and is cannibalistic to boot."

"It tickled," Addie said, blushing and remembering.

"As it was meant to. Imagine our grandfathers with those great bushy beards and mutton chops pleasuring their ladies—"

"Rupert, that's quite enough. Are you coming to the funeral?"

He shuddered. "My own was enough, thank you very much. I may drift over to the reception, though. Keep an eye out. It's too bad that Dumont fellow escaped. He could have been useful."

Addie fastened a single strand of pearls over her collar. "What do you mean?"

"He might have received some dark energy from the murderer. Really, you missed your chance—you could have had a séance last evening and solved the whole thing!"

"I can't see Inspector Hunter agreeing to that." Not that the thought hadn't actually crossed her mind for a few fleeting seconds. Which showed she was still losing it.

"No, the man is all about regulations and procedures, isn't he? By the book. Do you know he keeps his notes in a secret code? It's very irritating."

"You shouldn't snoop, Rupert!"

"What's the fun of being a ghost if I can't? You'd be very surprised at what people hide. In their Wellington boots."

Addie was not going to rise to his needling. "I've got to go." She picked up the deceptively plain black straw garden hat—a misnomer, since one would never garden in such an expensive headgear—and pinned it to her hair. The brim was wide enough so that she might hide if necessary.

"You look very elegant."

"Thank you."

"Don't let that rotter get his hand up your skirts."

"Which one?"

"Waring, of course. Bounder. Rotter. *Boy scout.*" He made the last sound the worst.

Addie had not heard from Lucas and wondered if he was still in London. Probably not. He'd consider it his duty to support a neighbor in his time of need, although he and Sir David were not close.

She picked up her gloves. "I think I know why Babs turned you down."

Rupert snapped his fingers. "Old news."

"It was new news to me. I'm beginning to think I don't understand a thing."

"Just you wait until you're dead."

"It will become clear?"

"Ha. If only. I'm more confused now than ever. Well, have fun. Don't forget a handkerchief." He disappeared up the chimney like a reverse Father Christmas.

There was no room in Addie's enameled vanity case for a handkerchief—Beckett had packed it with important things like powder and a lipstick—so she stuffed one up her sleeve and went downstairs, not that she had any intention of crying over Kathleen Grant. Barbara and Fraulein Schober were waiting for her in the drawing room, head to toe black. Barbara wore a heavy veil concealing her face, like some devout Italian widow. Addie had not seen them at breakfast, and wondered if they too would decide to go back to London after the funeral was over.

"Ready?"

"Where is Inspector Hunter?" Barbara asked.

"I believe he intended to leave early and coordinate with the other policemen. He's got men stationed around the church perimeter." Edward Rivers would not like that much.

Eloise had told her on the phone this morning that Rivers was officiating at the service today under some duress—he hadn't known Kathleen and was horrified by the nature of her death, especially the naked part. However, as the vicar of the parish church of the deceased's remaining family, he felt under an obligation. Addie wondered what platitudes would tumble out of his mouth from the pulpit.

Would the boys come? They were awfully young and didn't sit still in the best of circumstances. When she'd been in London, Addie had ordered a box of books for them as a kind of sympathy present, though most likely they were going to tear the pages out to make paper airplanes rather than read them.

They took the Daimler, her young chauffeur driving the half-mile to the church. A small clot of people stood outside the lych-gate, and Addie tried to figure out which of them were reporters. A uniformed policeman stood at each church door, barring the way until names could be checked off a list. There was at first some trouble over Fraulein Schober, but Mr. Hunter appeared and smoothed that over.

Compton St. Cuthbert's thick old stone walls kept the building arctic even on the hottest summer day. This is where Addie should have come to cool off, if one hadn't been trying to avoid Mr. Rivers at all costs. Sir David Grant was already seated in the first pew, with Eloise Waring at his side. There was no sign of the children.

The coffin was covered with informal sprays of roses and ivy from gardens in Sir David's village, arranged by Eloise. She'd done the altar flowers too. The simple arrangements gave a homey touch to the occasion.

The church wasn't near to being full, but there were enough friends and neighbors showing their support. Addie waved to her mother, Cee, and Lucas. She and her party slid into seats toward the rear of the church and listened to the somber organ music. Barbara sat rigid beside her, Fraulein Schober patting a black-gloved hand now and then. By the time Mr. Rivers showed up with his altar boys, Addie was longing for one of her fur coats—her teeth were about to chatter. But then she felt a hand on her shoulder.

She turned, and just stopped herself in time from crying out.

"I convinced Ernest to come. He got back last night. He'll meet with Inspector Hunter right after the funeral. Could you be present? For me? I want to know what's going on. *He* won't tell me."

Angela Shipman was the epitome of chic in a lighter-weight black windowpane Chanel suit, perfectly made-up, quite a contrast from the last time Addie had seen her.

"I'll try, but Mr. Hunter might not like it," Addie whispered back. Nor would Ernest.

"Nonsense. The man values your opinion. He told me so. Anyway, I asked if you could be there when he questions Ernest. He didn't say no."

Addie was ridiculously pleased, but tried not to show it. "Where *is* Ernest?"

"Waiting in the car, the coward. Just as well. We weren't on the list, but Mr. Hunter waved me through. I do hope no one got a photograph." Her smile and her charming hat said otherwise. It was plain she wanted Ernest to suffer, to be publicly humiliated, which Addie understood completely.

"They're taking pictures?"

"They were before they were warned off."

On the whole, Addie was in favor of reporters, as long as they got their facts straight. But in Kathleen's case, the facts were so lurid no one really needed to know. Someday her sons would be old enough to read about their mother's abysmal end. Addie didn't envy Sir David one bit trying to explain.

The funeral was as boring as only Edward Rivers could make

it. The vicar went out of his way to create a bloodless, lifeless, cardboard Kathleen, who'd never stepped—no, leaped—over the line in her life. After his innocuous descriptions, Addie wasn't sure the right body was in the coffin in the front of the church.

The handkerchief came in handy after all. Addie passed it to a vulnerable Babs, whose rigidity had dissolved some time ago. She'd already drenched her own and Fraulein Schober's. Gone was the wise-cracking, hard-drinking flapper. Addie had a feeling Fraulein Schober would have her hands full of tonic tonight.

Lucas was one of the pallbearers; that must have been Eloise's doing. The interment in the graveyard was to be immediately after the service, but Mr. Hunter stopped Addie from leaving the church. He was wearing his nice dark pinstriped suit and a black silk tie, looking as if he stepped out of the pages of a glossy magazine.

"Good morning again," he smiled. "I have an odd request."

"Does it have to do with Ernest Shipman? Angela told me what she asked of you. You don't have to do it, you know. Ernest won't like it—me being there."

"I'm not especially interested in what Shipman likes or dislikes, Lady Adelaide. I'd like a neutral observer at the interview. He's already tried to bribe me at least once. He tried to be more subtle the second time, so I can't be sure."

Somehow Addie wasn't surprised. "Why not ask one of the men from Cirencester?"

"They're not *my* men. You may be aware, the entire police force in this country has been subject to allegations of corruption from top to bottom. If Bob were here—well, he's not. I trust him, and I trust you."

Addie's cheeks warmed. "Thank you."

"I'll drag Shipman out of his car. Meet me in the sacristy. Don't worry, I've cleared it with Rivers."

"Tell Miss Pryce and Fraulein Schober to go on to the reception without me. They'd better take Angela with them too. You'll drive me to Holly Hill later, won't you?"

"With the greatest pleasure."

Addie settled herself in the sacristy's only chair and waited. A ride in the country with a handsome man. So what if it was a journey of less than two miles? She would take what she could get.

Chapter Twenty-eight

Dev had found two spindly folding metal chairs in the parish hall next door, so they were all sitting in uncomfortable propinquity in Compton St. Cuthbert's sacristy. The small leaded-glass window was open, but he could still smell Lady Adelaide's Chanel No 5. He'd splurged and given his mother a bottle of it last Christmas, but she saved it for special occasions only. Dev figured Lady Adelaide splashed it on about every day.

"All right. I'm here," Shipman grumbled. "It was most inconvenient to get back early. Canceling my appointments. Changing all the tickets. I went to considerable expense and effort. But Angela said you were insistent."

Angela probably said a few other things too.

"Thank you, Mr. Shipman." Dev let the silence stretch.

"So, get on with it! I've answered everything to the best of my knowledge. Yet you keep asking me more questions."

"And you avoid answering them. Or lie," Dev reminded him.

Shipman didn't dispute this. He kept his eyes on his expensive shoes, waiting for the axe to fall.

Dev dropped it. "Tell me about meeting Lady Grant at three o'clock in the afternoon a week ago Saturday."

The banker looked up. "How do you know I did? No one saw me there, did they? You have nothing. I told you I was in my room, ill."

Dev removed the diary from his jacket pocket, flipped it open, and began to read each date that a "K" appeared.

Shipman raised a hand. "All right, all right. But I could deny that those entries are mine. Perhaps my wife wrote them."

Dev had actually thought of that, but dismissed the idea. The handwriting was consistent throughout.

Unless Angela Shipman was a master forger.

"Are you denying the K stands for Kathleen? The number in the back matches her telephone number."

"She was a client of the bank."

"Are you still sticking to that? You were very…attentive to her, considering how small an investment you claim she made."

Shipman shrugged. If he thought he could wait it out, he was mistaken.

"Are you denying you saw her?"

"Fine. I met her for a few minutes. But she was very much alive when I left her."

Dev glanced at Lady Adelaide and soldiered on. "Did you have sexual relations with her?"

Shipman's face turned crimson. "Why is *she* here? Is nothing sacred?"

Not his marriage vows, that was for sure. "Lady Adelaide is acting as a witness in the absence of my sergeant. Would you rather I conduct this interview at Scotland Yard?"

"No! You're out to wreck my life, aren't you?"

Shipman was on his way to wrecking his life all by himself. One would think with his age and experience, he would know better than to mix himself up with a woman like Kathleen Grant. "Not at all. If you are truthful, I see no reason why your name has to be revealed publicly. Sir David is anxious that his ex-wife's name is not further compromised."

Considering the salacious nature of the death, it had been a miracle that the newspapers had not got hold of the whole story. Mr. McGrath had not been mentioned at all, which irked Lady Adelaide.

"We—we didn't do the usual thing. There wasn't time."

Dev stopped himself from asking why Kathleen Grant had removed her clothes. Perhaps she was a naturist. It was none of his business in the end, but Shipman's admission did confirm the coroner's report that she hadn't been, as they so quaintly put it, "interfered with."

"Why should I believe you?"

Shipman stood up, knocking the flimsy metal chair against the wall. "I'll have your badge!"

"Sit down, Mr. Shipman. Perhaps you've forgotten—I'm conducting a murder investigation. My superiors have given me their full support, despite your meddling. According to your various stories, you didn't know the victim. Or you were only the victim's banker and barely were acquainted with her. Or you were indeed conducting an affair with her, and may have been the last person to see Lady Grant alive. I want the truth, all of it. It doesn't look good for you right now. If I'm not satisfied, I'm prepared to remand you into custody for the murder of Kathleen Grant and Stuart McGrath."

"I didn't kill anyone! You cannot prove I did!" For all his bravado, Dev could hear the fear in Shipman's voice.

"That remains to be seen. I think any jury would be interested in your diary."

Shipman slumped back into the chair. Dev was reminded of a balloon that lost its air. "Kath sought my advice about some investments after her divorce. We met every now and again. It wasn't serious. I never planned to leave Angela, and Kath knew it. She didn't mind—she had quite a few irons in the fire."

More than Shipman probably knew of. "Were you aware she used cocaine?"

"She dabbled. Morphia. Cannabis. Chloral hydrate. Whatever was handy. Lately, though, yes. Cocaine was her preferred method of escape. That Saturday—" He closed his eyes. "She had some vials with her in her handbag. She kept them in a little leather case." The case had been found in her handbag, its contents missing. No convenient fingerprints, of course. "She offered to share as soon as I got there sometime before three, but I declined."

"Were you in the habit of indulging?"

The banker's face reddened. "No! No, not at all. Oh, perhaps once or twice. Sometimes Kath thought I needed cheering up—a boost. Running Shipman's takes all my energy. She worried that I worked myself too hard."

While she played too hard. "Go on, sir."

"She unrolled her stocking and injected the stuff between her toes. Then she laughed and took everything else off before I could stop her." He paused, obviously reliving the scene.

"I was very nervous. Afraid we'd be discovered. We were under everyone's noses—the barn door was open. But she got on her knees—" Shipman gave a desperate look at Lady Adelaide, who was studying her black-gloved hands as if she'd never seen them before.

"I understand," Dev said hurriedly. "Tell me how you left her."

"There was an old blanket on a sawhorse. She took it down and lay on top of it and said some things I don't want to repeat in front of Lady Adelaide. About what we'd do the next time. She—she touched herself. I was tempted, but I had to go. I was honest when I told you I wasn't feeling all that well. I rushed back to the house and was sick."

Out of guilt? Dev wouldn't bother asking.

"When you left, were the drugs still in her handbag?"

"Yes. I wouldn't have touched them. Wouldn't know what to do with them by myself. She was the expert."

"How much time elapsed between the injection and you leaving?"

"No more than five or ten minutes, if that. I really wasn't there long."

Long enough for his own quick, selfish pleasure, however.

"And she was lucid?"

"Yes. Brazen." Shipman's mouth twisted. "Happy. Euphoric."

"Did she say if she was meeting anyone else?"

"No. Really, you might not believe me, but we barely spoke that afternoon. I assumed she was in the area to see her children. She knew we were coming down, and thought it was a lark to meet me when Angela was right across the lawn." He gave a ragged sigh. "I've been a fool, Inspector. I'll admit to that. But I swear I did not have anything to do with her death. I liked her. She was one-of-a-kind."

"She never threatened to tell your wife of the affair?" Dev asked.

"Of course not! Why would she?"

"Blackmail, Mr. Shipman."

The man chuckled. "You've got Kath all wrong. She wasn't like that. Not a mean bone in her body."

Not according to her ex-husband. Dev was beginning to think Kathleen Grant had had as many colorful pieces as the inside of a kaleidoscope. Each viewer saw something different—bright, quicksilver, impermanent. How much was a result of the drugs or her own personality was impossible to determine.

She'd led a severely sheltered childhood. Married young and took on motherhood too soon. Once unshackled, she pushed every limit. Who she was at heart would now never be known.

After Shipman left, with a warning, Dev turned to Lady Adelaide. "Well? What do you think?"

"Do you think he was telling the truth?"

He considered for a moment. "He's lied religiously. The diary is damning. I could have arrested him."

"But you didn't."

"No. I think he finally told the truth."

"I think so too. Gosh, am I the only person who doesn't use drugs? *Ernest Shipman?* I wonder if Angela knows all that he's been up to."

Dev smiled. "It's impossible to know what goes on behind the façade of respectability."

"I should know that. I *do* know that." She shook her head, the ribbon on her straw hat fluttering. "I feel like I'm finally waking up. And I'm not sure I want to."

"I hope you don't become jaded. I shouldn't have involved you. Police work can bring you into contact with too much reality." Which was one reason he spent so much time reading philosophy. He may not have a university degree, but Dev felt he could go toe-to-toe with some of the dubiously graduated gentlemen he'd encountered.

"What are you going to do?"

"Keep plodding along. Hope to hear from the Hallidays."

She placed a finger against her chin. "I wonder…"

Her instincts had been good so far. "What?"

"What if George *did* know Kathleen was his long-lost cousin? He might have gone to Yorkshire to see his grandfather."

He'd talked to the Yorkshire solicitors a week ago, but they might not be aware the Hallidays had arrived. "That could explain why I can't find them in London."

Lady Adelaide frowned. "I just can't see George—or Pansy, for that matter—doing something so heinous, even if they need the money. George is so…average. And the old man might live on forever. Unless," she said with grisly enthusiasm, "George has gone to Yorkshire to murder *him*!"

"We don't need any more murders, Lady Adelaide. Two is quite enough. And one of the deaths…I wonder. Could Lady Grant have miscalculated and overdosed? Maybe she wasn't killed deliberately after all, and I've been barking up all the wrong trees. Now that we know of Miss Pryce's participation in positioning the body, I've got to consider that."

"But how did my gardener die? Unless you think *he* took Kathleen's drugs from her handbag!"

"I admit that's unlikely. Ready to go? Let's see who looks guilty over the funeral meats."

Chapter Twenty-nine

Holly Hill was looking its best on this sunny afternoon. A modest Georgian manor house, it had been home to the Grant family for two hundred years and had been cared for lovingly. Fading pink brick, sharp white trim, and, of course, masses of holly bushes made for a pretty picture. Sir David was an avid gardener, although Addie ventured that most of his garden and glasshouse had been stripped to decorate the church and Kathleen's coffin. A few cars were parked at the bottom of the steep drive, and Mr. Hunter pulled up behind the last of them. Two uniformed police officers stood as sentries.

He looked at Addie's black pumps. "I've been up this hill a few times. Do you want me to drop you at the door?"

"I've been here a few times myself. I'm not so decrepit I can't climb." Even though she'd yanked yet another gray hair out just this morning.

"This hill must be a treat in the winter."

"It is, actually. For the boys. They slide down on their sleds." Last winter, Rupert was among them. He'd been good with the Grant children, acting like a child himself.

"I resent that."

Addie stumbled and turned. Rupert was behind her, hands in his pockets. He winked.

Well, he had warned her he might attend the gathering. Mr. Hunter put a hand under her elbow. "All right?"

"Yes, of course. There was a pebble in my shoe." A large one named Rupert.

They were greeted by Moss, Sir David's butler, and escorted onto the back terrace. A marquee had been set up on the lawn, and if it wasn't for the plethora of black clothing, one would think one was at a garden party. Addie recognized most of the guests, and headed straight for Sir David to give him a hug.

He looked rested, less careworn than he had at Compton Chase. Sudden death must agree with him, she thought, a little unkindly.

"Lady Adelaide, thank you for coming."

"Don't you think we should be David and Addie after all that's happened?"

"You're right. I want to thank you for everything—the books for the boys especially." At Addie's direction, Cook had sent meals over to Holly Hill as well.

Addie heard a shriek from behind a hedge. "How are they doing?"

"Pretty well, considering. Eloise has them in hand, for the most part. She's a remarkable woman, isn't she?" He spotted her across the grass and waved. Eloise waved back, a serene smile on her face. Somehow she looked much less like a spinster today than she had the weekend before last.

Oh dear. Poor Cee.

"Yes, she is. She's had a lot of heartbreak. It would be nice if she found happiness." Unless she was a murderess...no. Eloise was the type of woman who caught moths inside and released them unharmed to go munch on someone else's woolens. She, like Lucas, was simply too good.

"I agree. Inspector, any news?"

"Some. Nothing conclusive, though. Thank you for allowing me to come."

"Whatever will help bring this nightmare to an end. You saw the press outside?"

"Only at the church. They seem to have been scared off by the men on your driveway."

"Good. Nothing to see here anyhow. Help yourselves to lunch. I'm going to check on the boys." David ambled off in the direction of a blood-curdling yelp.

"And *I'm* going to walk the garden perimeter, see if anyone's trying to vault over the wall. That will give you a chance to talk to your family and friends."

Addie's mother was sitting under the shade of the tent wearing the very becoming new hat that she hadn't needed. Cee was with her, looking droopy and holding an empty champagne glass. Champagne seemed an odd choice for a funeral reception, but perhaps David was celebrating his ultimate freedom.

Mr. Hunter hadn't arrested Shipman, or Barbara either, despite them providing false information—and in Barbara's case, tampering with evidence as well. The trouble with this detecting business—no one, even those who had been proven liars, seemed capable of murder. Addie supposed anyone could take a life if they were sufficiently provoked. She hoped she'd never be in the position to find out.

"Too late to try to kill me now anyway," Rupert said from his perch on the terrace railing. "You had your chance."

She lowered her head so the brim would cover her face. "Stop talking to me in public."

He hopped down. "All right. I'll go circulate and see if I hear anything incriminating. That Eloise is a dark horse, isn't she? Moving right in to save the day. I hear wedding bells."

"I wonder why Babs dislikes her so."

"Oh, that's easy. I overheard Babs explaining all to the pretty little fraulein last night when I couldn't find a place to sleep."

"You sleep?" She pictured him hanging upside-down like a bat on a branch.

"Sleep is not really the word we use for it, but yes. One must recharge one's batteries for the challenges ahead. Anyway, Eloise came upon Kath and Babs having lunch in London. Let's just say they were both under the influence of their respective vices and a little too obvious. Eloise was shocked, to put it mildly, and expressed that shock in no uncertain terms. She's a traditionalist. Conventional with an upper case C. Very little imagination. David won't be having any trouble with *her*."

The same could be said about Addie. All in all, these past ten days had been eye-opening. How had she managed to stay so clueless for so long? She was a thirty-one-year-old woman. Had lived through a dreadful war and its aftermath. Was widowed in the most embarrassing way. She felt like a thoroughbred that had been blinkered all its life.

Enough. She wandered over to the marquee, where a lovely compilation of sandwiches and sweets was laid out. Filling a plate, she joined her mother and sister at a small round table.

"Pretty hat, Mama."

"Thank you, dear. I hear there was some excitement yesterday at Compton Chase. Do I need to call Barbara's mother?"

Addie stuck her tongue out at Cee, who stuck hers right back. "I don't think that will be necessary. Babs seems better today."

"Her parents are worried sick. All they want for her is to marry and settle down. Cee tells me this latest fellow is gone."

"I think it's for the best," Addie said without explaining. Babs' parents would have a long wait if they were hoping to buy a tulle veil and bridal bouquet for their only daughter.

Or would Babs betray her own inclinations and go for fiancé number six? Addie supposed, with her new knowledge, that one could be receptive to male *and* female offers, as Kathleen Grant had been.

Her mother sighed. "Another scandal. Thank heavens the Pryces didn't put an announcement in *The Times*. I understand from Hetty that he was unsuitable anyway. He had no people to speak of."

Living people, at any rate. Who wouldn't want a medium in the family? He might be useful in all sorts of domestic crises.

Unless *he* was the murderer.

Addie's limited imagination was running away with her. She looked around. There was no sign of Angela—her husband must have picked her up and sped back to London. That was a car ride Addie was happy to miss. Mr. Hunter had stopped to chat with Babs and her nurse, and caught a balsa wood airplane in one hand as it flew his way. A band of tow-headed boys barreled out of the bushes after it, and were treated to a mild lecture from the policeman. Turning the toy over to the oldest, he moved next to Lucas and Eloise.

It was hard for Addie not to compare the two men. Of similar height and build, Mr. Hunter was as dark as Lucas was fair. The inspector was a few years older, most definitely a serious adult, while Lucas still had plenty of boyish charm. Lucas, like David Grant, had been based in London during the war and had been little touched by its hardships, either personally or financially. Addie had observed Mr. Hunter limping on occasion, and wondered if he'd been wounded.

She shouldn't be wondering about Devenand Hunter at all.

"Penny for them," Cee said.

"Oh, I was admiring Eloise. That dress looks well on her. It has more style than her usual frocks."

"I'm off for more champagne," Cee said abruptly, leaving for the bar, where Moss was now presiding over a drinks table.

Addie's mother leaned forward. "I saw her at Fenwick on Bond Street yesterday. She was carrying a dress box. I asked her if she wanted to come home with me instead of on the train, but she stayed *here* last night." She pursed her lips in disapproval.

"For heaven's sake, Mama, Eloise is not some twenty-five-year-old girl like Cee. If she can get David Grant up to scratch, bully for her."

"I suppose you're right. Part of me is delighted, of course. With Eloise in the picture, Cee might finally look elsewhere. But she's my daughter, and I can't bear to see her hurt by that foolish man. I do want her to be happy, whoever her choice might be."

"Don't press her and try to matchmake. She'll hate it. And it's not as if potential husbands grow on trees now, either. Give her time." So many young men that managed to stay alive in war were uninterested in settling down in peace. London nightlife was burgeoning with subscription night clubs, jazz hangouts, and wild supper parties. Police raids were common. The Prince of Wales just missed being swept up in one at the private nightclub, the Embassy.

"Time! I'd like to be a grandmother one day." Her mother blushed. "I'm sorry—that was tactless of me. I know you and Rupert tried."

At this point, Addie was glad she didn't have children, when their mother could so easily be declared insane. Although—both Gerald Dumont and Reverend Rivers didn't think ghosts were out of the question. She could take some comfort in that.

"How's the vegetarianism going?" Addie asked, changing the subject.

"She tried to enlist poor Barbara to the cause in the churchyard. That German nurse put a stop to that. There was firm talk about vitamins and protein necessary for Barbara's full recovery. She seems very capable, despite looking like she should be on the cover of a candy box."

Even in a simple black sack dress and plain cloche, the nurse stood out. "She is very pretty. I wonder what her story is."

"*I* know that. Her father was one of the Kaiser's doctors. Hetty was very impressed with her credentials."

"I hope she can help Babs."

"Perhaps Kathleen Grant's death will be a wake-up call. Drugs bring nothing but death. The woman could have accidentally killed herself, don't you think?"

Now that Addie had some of the facts of that fatal afternoon, she supposed it was possible. Even Mr. Hunter had mentioned something like it. But that still didn't explain why Mr. McGrath had been murdered.

She was coming to feel more charitably toward Kathleen. She'd certainly left a positive impression on those who were close to her, with the exception of her ex-husband. And, as Mr. Hunter said, who really knew what went on behind closed doors? The most proper of people might be petty tyrants or perverts. Maybe David Grant had faults Addie hadn't seen yet.

Maybe he murdered his ex-wife.

Oh, bother. She couldn't accuse everyone.

"I don't know, Mama. Mr. Hunter is working hard trying to figure it all out."

"He's staying with you as well?" Her mother's tone was light, but Addie heard her reservation.

"Yes." Never complain, never explain. If it was good enough for Disraeli, it was good enough for her.

"Oh, look who's come! There's Pansy and her husband. I didn't realize she was so friendly with the Grants."

Addie turned around. Well, Mr. Hunter would be pleased he wouldn't have to go all the way to Yorkshire.

Chapter Thirty

Pansy looked plump and pretty, her dark hair curling under the brim of a very fashionable hat. George was also well-turned out, wearing an expensive-looking new suit. They must have come into a windfall from somewhere.

Addie excused herself and met them on the terrace. "What are you doing here?"

"We came to pay our respects. Unfortunately, we missed the funeral. George had a punctured tire."

They had a new car too? Interesting.

Pansy took Addie's hand. "I have something to tell you."

Several somethings. Addie was glad she was still wearing her gloves. "Mr. Hunter has been looking for you for a week." He was coming toward them right now.

Pansy made a face. "I know. But we can explain. It was a sort of emergency."

"I hope so. He could charge you for obstruction or...or something." She was not conversant with legal terminology or consequences, but would like to toss Pansy in a dank dark cell for old times' sake.

"Hunter!" George stuck out his hand as the detective mounted the terrace steps. "Awfully glad to run into you here. They said you were in the country. Scotland Yard, that is. Phoned your office yesterday."

"Mr. Halliday. Mrs. Halliday. I do have some questions for you, but I'm not sure this is the time or place. Please accept my condolences on the death of your cousin."

George cleared his throat nervously. "About that. I only found out recently. Just a few weeks ago. Something Kathleen said at a dinner party about her mother reminded me of something *my* mother told me. Almost word for word, all the bells ringing. I went home and looked in the family Bible and, sure enough, there she was, though my mother had scratched out most of the names and it was devilish tricky to read. Could have knocked my socks off. There was an ancient family feud, you know. The two sisters and my grandfather didn't get along." He took a breath. "I would have told Kathleen but didn't get the chance to. Odd that all these years of running into her at various places I never guessed we were related."

"You didn't think to tell me at our interview?"

"I know it looks bad. But I've read the books—'who stands to benefit from the death of so-and-so?' Finger points right to me and Pansy, doesn't it? Look, I want to get all this off my chest. Where can we talk?" He paused. "Though I really should go see Sir David first."

Addie knew what she should do, and did it. "Come to Compton Chase after the reception. If you need to, you can spend the night." She hoped they'd drive off into the sunset before it came to that.

"That's very generous of you, Lady Adelaide," Mr. Hunter said. "Will that suit?"

"Yes. See you later then." George took Pansy's elbow to steer her down the steps.

"Hmm."

Mr. Hunter laughed. "I totally agree. I wonder where they've been."

"I'll bet with the old grandfather, and it looks like he's given them some money. I hope they didn't take advantage of his infirmity."

"Are they the sort of people who would fleece a vulnerable old man?"

"I wouldn't have thought so once. But what do I know? Gosh, I sound bitter. I used to be more cheerful."

"And I'm sure you'll be cheerful again, once all this is over. It's been a great strain on you, hasn't it?" Mr. Hunter was being kind, which almost made everything worse.

"Look, I know what you must think. I'm just a spoiled little rich girl. One hiccup in the road and I fall apart."

"I'd hardly call two murders in your own backyard a hiccup. Don't be so hard on yourself. If it means anything, you have my, um, full admiration." He looked very serious.

"Oh." Addie was flustered. "Gosh. Thanks. You really haven't seen me at my best. I haven't been at my best in ages." The talking to ghosts, the drinking—golly, she was kind of a mess, wasn't she?

"I understand time cures everything. Maybe when this is over, you should think about going away somewhere to recuperate. Get a fresh perspective. Your sister thinks so, at any rate."

"Does she? I might have to bring her with me. She's about to have her heart broken." David was now talking animatedly to the Hallidays, Eloise at his side.

Mr. Hunter followed her gaze. "Oh, you mean about Sir David and Miss Waring?"

"You see it too, don't you?"

"I *am* a detective. They seem quite chummy. Do they deserve a happy ending?"

"Only if you decide David couldn't have murdered Kathleen. And Mr. McGrath." Now *she* was forgetting him!

He shook his head. "I can't rule him out. That heat spell kept everyone apart. No one saw anything, but that doesn't mean that someone didn't do something."

"Are all your cases so annoying?"

"Not usually. In ordinary circumstances, there are far fewer suspects. A jealous husband. A betrayed business partner. A thief where the robbery's gone wrong. Your friends are much more complicated."

"Yes, I'm finding that out. Do you ever find you can't solve the crime?"

"Frequently. It's not something we brag about, and you mustn't tell anyone I told you." He'd gone from serious to playful. Addie liked playful better. It was more…relaxing.

"Did you always want to be a policeman?"

"Not really. I wanted to be a fireman. Doesn't every little boy? Bells ringing. So much excitement. But my father was in the Military Mounted Police in India. When he left the army and came home, he joined the Metropolitan Police Force. One might say it's in the blood, but if I'm honest, he pushed me a bit. He thought his contacts there would provide more opportunity for me."

Addie simply couldn't see Inspector Hunter being forced into anything. "You didn't rebel?"

"The joke was on me. I discovered after not too long I loved police work—even starting out on foot patrol—and was good at it. My mixed background has been both a help and a hindrance, but I'm fairly certain that would be the case anywhere."

Addie supposed Britain, in its way, had every bit as much of a caste system as India. As a marquess' daughter, she'd always known what her parents and society expected of her, and done her best to toe the line. It was true the world over—parents wanted the best for their children, and would do whatever they could to ensure it. Right now her mother was worried about Cee. Maybe they could all go away, have a family vacation in some pretty, secluded spot.

Preferably without Rupert.

"You must meet a lot of strange people."

"That would be an understatement." He covered his eyes against the sun. "Your colonel isn't here."

"Oh? Was he at the church?" Addie had been so preoccupied with Barbara she hadn't noticed.

"I don't recall seeing him there either. He was on the guest list."

"Sir David knows about them now? Their engagement, I mean?" She wondered if he'd been at all jealous that Kathleen had found someone new. Well, several new someones.

Probably not.

"Yes. I gauged his reaction last week before I left the area. I can't say he was terribly shocked—he expected his ex-wife to land on her feet."

Like a cat with nine lives, except Kathleen's chances had been truncated. "Coming here may have been too much for Colonel Mellard. He's put on a good show—stiff upper lip and all that—but he must be devastated. He's never been married, you know. To reach his age and finally get so close to happiness—" Addie broke off. How happy could one be with Kathleen Grant, whose morals were…flexible, to say the very least? "I should invite him to tea tomorrow."

"Would you mind if I joined you?" Mr. Hunter asked.

"Not at all. I assumed you'd be there. Did you want to see the colonel again for any particular reason?"

"Just a few follow-up questions. I thought he'd be here."

"You're stuck with me instead."

"I wouldn't say stuck. But I should circulate. Your mother is giving me the evil eye."

Addie could feel herself blush. "She isn't!" She squinted across the lawn. "Oh, my goodness, she is! Please pay no mind to her. She's in a very overprotective mood concerning Cee and me. I'm sure she means nothing personal."

Mr. Hunter raised a dark eyebrow but said nothing.

"I can speak to anyone I like! I'm not a child. I'm a grown woman. A *widow*."

"You go and tell him, my dear. Although methinks the lady doth protest too much. Have I got that quotation right? No one ever does."

Oh, God. Rupert, again when he was least wanted.

"'The lady doth protest too much, methinks,'" Mr. Hunter said as if he'd actually heard Rupert bungle it. "Anyhow, I'll see you later on. I'll be meeting briefly after this with the Cirencester force to compare notes, and then it's on to the Hallidays." He gave her a finger salute and stepped down onto the lawn.

Addie turned her back to the people milling about on the grass. "Did you find out anything?"

"What a boring lot. Except there has to be a killer out there somewhere. For the life of me—ah, that's a misnomer, isn't it?—I find it impossible to pin the dirty deed on anyone. It's quite a puzzle. Uh oh. Here comes Eloise, ever the good hostess. Thinks you've been abandoned. Taking pity on you."

"Taking pity on *me*? Why—?" Addie shut up before Eloise could hear her talking to herself.

"Addie, we haven't had a chance to speak all afternoon. How are you holding up?" Eloise said with genuine concern. Eloise was always genuine. Always concerned. For an instant, Addie could see why Babs disliked her so.

Murder did not bring the best out in Lady Adelaide Compton.

"I'm holding up perfectly well. Why wouldn't I? I wasn't really close to Kathleen."

"No, of course not. Two women could not be more different. I just meant since she was discovered on your property, it must be awfully awkward. And your poor gardener. I know you valued his service. You're such a good steward of Compton Chase. They're lucky to have you."

"Th-thank you." Oh, Addie wasn't going to cry, was she? She'd given away her damned handkerchief.

Chapter Thirty-one

Dev was becoming uncomfortably comfortable at Compton Chase. He knew he should not be enjoying its amenities so much—the attentive and respectful service from the staff, the glorious architecture, the soft feather bed, the excellent food. And its lovely mistress could not be altogether ignored, though God knows, he was trying to do just that.

Lady Adelaide had made herself scarce for his interview with the Hallidays, but had supplied them all a tray with sandwiches and tea in the Great Hall. The Hallidays were bright enough to know not to relax in the deep leather chairs. Dev flipped his notebook open.

"Tell me where you went after you left Compton Chase a week ago Monday."

George Halliday looked at his wife. "You mean when we were thrown out."

"George," Pandora Halliday murmured.

"Well, she threw us out, Addie did. Reneged on her offer. It was very inconvenient. We were having a spot of bad luck with our flat—a misunderstanding with the landlady about redecorating, but it's all been smoothed over."

"Are you home at the same address now where I can reach you?" Dev asked.

"Yes."

Someone must have paid the back rent then.

"Anyway, after we learned about Kathleen's death, it was Pansy's idea to break the news to my grandfather. We've never been close—in fact, I barely know him, but it seemed the right thing to do. We were going to write to the old fellow, but once we were at loose ends, we decided to go to Yorkshire in person. Earn some points. Soften the blow."

"We stopped first to see our son at school," his wife added.

Dev hadn't realized they had a child, and chided himself for overlooking the possibility. "I spoke with your grandfather's solicitor. He made no mention of your visit."

"I expect he didn't know when you called. Yes, Inspector, I knew you were on the lookout for us. I asked Arkwright—that's my grandfather's solicitor, and now mine—to give us a chance to explain when we got back to London."

Did he, indeed? And the bloody solicitor went along with it? Subverting the course of justice was a serious offense. There must be more money involved than he'd originally thought to make it worthwhile. Dev bit his tongue and waited.

"Anyhow, when I spoke with my grandfather about Kathleen's death and our, um, circumstances, he agreed to advance us some of my inheritance. Very decent of him; he wants to make up for lost time. I suppose he's got regrets about all the family fighting in the past, and now it's down to the two of us. He doesn't want for anything—he's very comfortably situated in a genteel care home. Receiving first-rate services."

"I was under the impression your grandfather was showing signs of dementia."

"Who told you such a thing?" Halliday sputtered. "He's as sharp as a tack most of the time. Certainly he has periods of forgetfulness at his great age, but then we all do, don't we? If you're implying I've taken advantage—*hoodwinked* an elderly man—your superiors will hear of it."

Dev leveled a gaze at him, wishing Lady Adelaide was here

as a witness. "I've implied no such thing. But I could easily charge you for not cooperating in a murder investigation. You were ordered to make yourself available, and you chose instead to flee London and conceal your whereabouts for over a week."

"You wouldn't!" Pandora Halliday was pale under the rouge on her cheeks. Good.

"Pay no attention to him, darling, he's just trying to rattle us. Look, we had nothing to do with my cousin's death. As we've told you, we were having a lie-down in our rooms after that bloody stupid tennis match when she died. I had no idea she was even on the property—why would I? We were hardly great friends or in regular communication. And if you think I knocked off Kathleen Grant so I could get my hands on the whole of my grandfather's estate, that's ridiculous. He might live on for years yet, or at least that's what his doctor says. His ticker is as strong as mine."

Unfortunately, Dev agreed with everything Halliday said. From the first, he'd doubted the Hallidays were involved. It still irked him, however, that they'd ignored his orders. He spent the next five minutes attempting to put the fear of God into the couple with little success. Lady Adelaide might have called George Halliday "average," but he had more than his fair share of pugnaciousness, especially now that his financial pinch had been eased.

It was more difficult to read his wife. She'd smartened up considerably since their first meeting, but it was hard for Dev to see her appeal. Why would Rupert Compton pay her any attention at all when he was engaged to Lady Adelaide?

There was no accounting for taste.

He left the Hallidays to their sandwiches and went in search of his hostess. He found her outside, walking slowly along the lavender border, plucking florets as she went and tucking them in a muslin bag.

"I'm done. And done in." Being on his best behavior all day had consequences, and he really was knackered.

"Did you learn anything interesting?"

"They went to visit their son, and then the grandfather. You were right once again."

Lady Adelaide smiled. "But they didn't kill him."

"No. There was no need. The old man gave them money. I didn't ask how much, but apparently it was enough to settle the dispute with their landlady. Perhaps the flat will get painted after all."

"*And* to buy a car. New clothes. Pansy has a decent haircut now too." She paused mid-pluck. "I should be happy for them."

"But you're not."

"I should rise to the occasion. It's what I do. But not, I think, today." She put her palm to her nose. "Oh! This smells so luscious."

Dev was in a haze of lavender and Lady Adelaide's own unique scent. He shook his head to clear it, narrowly averting a passing bee. "I think they're expecting to speak to you before they leave."

"They can expect away. Would you mind very much going back to the house to tell them I'm indisposed? You don't mind fibbing for a good cause, do you?"

"My mother wouldn't like it, but she's not here."

"Oh, I think our mothers are always here," Lady Adelaide said, somewhat wistful. "That well-meaning little voice in your head never goes away, no matter how old you are. I tend to know what my mother thinks, even if she never opens her mouth."

Dev laughed. "We have something in common then." His mother was an opinionated woman herself.

"What would your mother think of me?"

Oh, dangerous ground here. He decided to be honest. "She would like you, I think. You are, um, very likable. But she'd warn me to keep you at least one arm's length, preferably ten."

Lady Adelaide's hazel eyes widened. "Am I a danger to you? I'm not used to being dangerous."

"Let's just say you have that potential for any red-blooded

man. In spades." He remembered, as he did several times a day, carrying her to her bed on Mount Street. Soft, warm, tempting woman. If he'd possessed a shred less honor—

"Are we...are we flirting?" She looked pleased.

"I believe we are. And I must not." He really did know bet-ter—he hadn't advanced in his career by being stupid. His father's influence only went so far.

"Oh. I'm afraid I'm out of practice. It's been a long while."

"What about Lord Waring?" Dev wanted to kick himself for asking.

"Lucas? One doesn't flirt with Lucas, he's too...I don't know. We've known each other since we were children."

"So he's like a brother."

Lady Adelaide blushed. "I wouldn't say that exactly. I know he...likes me."

"And how do you feel?" He was digging himself deeper by the word.

"It's too soon to feel anything. My husband has only been dead six months, and we have—had a very complicated relationship. If I had a brain in my head, I'd swear off men completely until the end of time."

"That would be a loss." Dev stopped himself from saying more. It was none of his business how she chose to live her life. He'd leave after the inquests and this interlude, lovely and confusing as it had been, would be over.

Lady Adelaide looked over his shoulder and frowned. "Here comes Forbes, in the nick of time, as usual, before I say or do anything stupid. I wonder who that is with him?"

Chapter Thirty-two

The young man was limping several yards behind her butler, leaning heavily on a cane. He was wearing an obviously new suit—it was a day for them—a black armband, and a serious expression.

"Lady Adelaide, Inspector Hunter, I thought I should bring Mr. Robertson out here at once. He is Mr. McGrath's grandson."

Addie felt a fresh wave of guilt. She stepped forward and held out her hand. "I am so very sorry, Mr. Robertson."

He gripped hers, his hands callused. "Please call me Jack. Death comes to us all, my lady. My grandfather lived a good life, and was ready to meet his Maker."

His words were simple and reassuring. "Let's sit down," Addie said. The pergola wasn't far.

When they were seated on the teak benches—with Forbes dispatched to send the Hallidays off and bring out more sandwiches, and ale this time—Addie immediately invited Jack to spend the night.

"I was counting on that. I thought I might stay in Granddad's cottage."

Addie bit a lip, seeing the stripped beds, gathering dust, and personal possessions heaped on the table. "You'd be more comfortable in the main house."

"You'll be thinking of those stairs, I'll wager. I visited here years ago when I was a wee lad and had two legs. They were an obstacle even then. It's a wonder the old man didn't break his neck—that would have been even worse for you, aye?"

Addie really needed to do something about those cottages before she was swamped in guilt. What had suited previous generations wouldn't do in the twentieth century at all. "It's bad enough, believe me. I was awfully fond of your grandfather."

"So was I. I didn't see him that often, but I know he was proud of me. I'll take you up on that offer to spend the night. In the servants' wing, mind. I don't want to get ahead of myself."

"You were injured in the Great War?" Inspector Hunter had been quiet until now.

Jack nodded. "I was too young to go. My mother had a fit and wouldn't sign the papers. My dad had died over there early on, you see, and she thought that was enough. So I lied a little, and got in right before the end. In time to get my leg blown off. She says it serves me right for being a pig-headed fool, but her bark is worse than her bite. It's taken a while for me to get my bearings and a properly fitting prosthesis, but I'm back to earning a living."

"What do you do, Jack?"

"Why, a bit of this and a bit of that. Mostly, I garden, My Lady, when I can find the work." He reached into the pocket of his jacket. "My grandfather sent this right before he died. It finally came yesterday. My mother told me you were looking for it and I came straight down." He passed a neatly folded letter to her.

Addie's hands shook. "Here, Mr. Hunter. You read it."

"'Dear Jack, How are you? Your mam says you get around better day by day. Wish I could say same. My lumbago is bad tho I do not complain to Lady A. who is a saint poor thing if she knew what her friends got up to she would not call them friends. I think she would hire you if I asked her to, and you and I could trade places. I have been here too long

seen too much. A woman and a man here fooling around in my barn, she as bare as a babe tho not as innocent if you get my drift. To my shame, I watched too surprised to move really and the colonel came up from behind me almost gave me a heart attack and told me to go away. I am too old for such carryings on. Don't tell your mam she would worry more than she already does. She offers to take me in in every letter. Now I know what you are thinking, but I believe you could do the job if she can spare you. There are a few boys in the village to help. Let me know and I will talk to Lady A. Your loving grandfather, Stuart McGrath'"

Mr. Hunter looked up and met her eyes. "The colonel?"

Oh, my God. "He couldn't have—it doesn't make any sense. He just…wouldn't."

No. It was impossible to believe the kind man who'd been such a lifesaver when Rupert died committed a crime. Two crimes. Perhaps when he'd seen Kathleen with Ernest Shipman, he left, too upset to confront her. Of course he'd lie about it to save face. One didn't want to be proved an old fool.

Jack Robertson scowled. "Are you saying this colonel fellow killed my grandfather?"

"Let's not jump to conclusions, Mr. Robertson. But I am most grateful you took the trouble to bring us this letter so quickly. I realize it's the last bit you have from your grandfather, but I'm going to have to take it as evidence. We'll return the original to you as soon as possible." He tucked the letter into his ever-present notebook.

"And of course you can have the job!" Addie said quickly. "If you want it, that is. I certainly need a gardener, and here you are. We could fix up your grandfather's cottage, put a bed downstairs. If it was his last wish—" Addie felt the tears form and struggled to keep her voice strong—"I'm under a moral obligation to hire you, aren't I? It's not out of pity, either. Your grandfather had confidence in your abilities."

Jack gave her a crooked grin. "Well, he *was* my granddad. He might have been a little prejudiced. For all you know, I don't have green fingers but a brown thumb."

"I doubt that. You come from a long line of gardeners, don't you? Your great-great grandfather worked here too. It's a family tradition! And if I must, I'll ask for references from your current employer."

Jack produced more papers from another pocket. "I came prepared."

Addie skimmed through them, hardly registering the words. Her mind was a jumble, and her heart raced.

Colonel Mellard had lied. Why?

The obvious answer—he'd been ashamed to admit he was wrong about Kathleen's fidelity. They may have made a bargain, but apparently she'd been up to her old tricks, with Ernest Shipman *and* Barbara. Were there even more partners? It boggled Addie's mind. What if one called out the wrong name in the throes of passion? Addie could only dimly remember what that kind of passion felt like—hers had curdled once she'd discovered Rupert's penchant for other women.

According to Shipman, Kathleen had been alive when he'd left shortly after three. By four o'clock, Barbara found her dead. Mr. McGrath had gone back to his cottage, written his letter, mailed it before four, taking Fitz with him, and then met his own end a few hours after.

Somewhere in the middle of all that was Colonel Mellard. And Fitz, who hadn't barked a useful word.

A footman came out into the garden with a tray and set it on the round table in the center of the pergola. After telling him to ask Mrs. Drum to ready a room for Jack, Addie poured ale for both Mr. Hunter and her new gardener, then listened as they exchanged what she presumed were much-edited battle stories. Jack had a healthy appetite, and wolfed down the platter of sandwiches almost single-handedly. He'd left Scotland near midnight, switching trains and traveling all day. She couldn't be more grateful that he'd come, confirming her sense that Mr. McGrath held the key to the investigation. Maybe Gerald Dumont was right about everyone having access to the spirit world.

But... *Colonel Mellard.* She shut her eyes against an impending headache.

Mr. Hunter noticed. "Lady Adelaide, it's been a long day, and we must be boring you. If you'd like to rest before dinner, don't worry about leaving us to our own devices."

"Thank you. I think I will. If you need anything at all, please see Mrs. Drum." She picked up her bag of lavender and walked back on the grass path. Would Barbara and Fraulein Schober join them for dinner tonight? Addie wasn't sure she was up to it. Maybe she'd have a tray in her room. Keep herself safe from the chaos around her.

It was not to be. As soon as Addie opened the French door to the drawing room, she encountered Forbes and Lucas Waring.

"I was just on my way to fetch you, Lady Adelaide. Shall I bring in tea and sandwiches?"

If Addie saw another neat triangle today, it would be too soon. But it was officially teatime, even if she would much prefer a large whiskey and soda.

"Lucas, what's your pleasure?"

"That's fine, Forbes." Lucas settled into a wingchair overlooking the lake, and Addie sat opposite. "Thought I'd swing by and see how you were, while I was so close, before I drove home. I got so busy talking at Sir David's that I hardly ate a thing, and never did manage to get on your side of the garden. Quite a nice funeral and reception, don't you think? All that was proper."

"Yes. Eloise did a lovely job."

"Didn't she just? It paid off for her too."

Addie debated removing her shoes but thought the better of it. "What do you mean?"

"Cat's almost out of the bag, so I don't think they'd mind me telling you. She and Grant are going to get married once a decent interval has passed. Good for both of them—he needs someone dependable, and Lord knows, that's Eloise's middle name. And she'll have her own household. A built-in family. All's well that ends well, eh? If Kathleen Grant hadn't been bumped off, they might never have been more than passing acquaintances at one of your dinner parties."

"I suspected as much. Congratulations to them both." She said the words, but her heart wasn't in it. It seemed somewhat brutal to build a life on Kathleen's grave.

But Kathleen would have undoubtedly done the same thing, given the chance. She'd never let a shred of happiness pass her by, no matter which direction it came from.

"They've inspired me, Addie," Lucas said. "I know it's too soon, and I don't expect you to answer me today, but will you marry me? After our own decent interval has passed, of course. We've known each other forever. No surprises."

Chapter Thirty-three

You're joking!
  This is so sudden.
  Are you saying you love me?
  I'm very flattered, but…
  I'm never marrying again.

All these responses and several more vied with each other, but in the end, Addie chose to slip off her chair and pretend to faint. She followed her mother's rules, her hem a safe distance from her knickers, her legs together. It seemed as good a plan as any, and really, she deserved to pass out after all this bother, or at least go to sleep for about two weeks. She was exhausted, and Rupert was not here to call her bluff and tell her to buck up. Or at least he hadn't manifested yet from behind the sofa. For all she knew, he was still at Holly Hill eavesdropping.

She pretended not to hear Lucas' startled oath. The new carpet was amazingly comfortable, its thick pile cushioning her from the ancient parquet flooring. It did her back a world of good; she'd been coiled as tensely as a spring all day, her shoulders venturing right up to her ears, her neck crackling.

She'd felt that way—tight, mostly miserable—for days. Since well before her dinner party, when she had wanted everything to go smoothly.

Ha. Her wish hadn't been granted there.

Addie could sense Lucas hovering over her. If he put a hand on her, she wasn't absolutely sure which course to take. Ignore his touch? Scream? Play possum indefinitely? How long was it realistic to remain unconscious when one fainted? Surely her mother should have apprised her of such a strategy when she was instructing Addie on gracefulness and knicker-concealment.

She heard rapid footfalls in the direction of the doors and cracked an eye open. Lucas had deserted her, which was a relief. She wiggled her bottom deeper into the rug and exhaled. Then she admired the plasterwork on the ceiling. Compton Chase had many splendid architectural details which she tried not to take for granted. The house was much too large for one person, and sometimes she felt guilty living alone in such grandeur. However, at the moment she had far too many people under her roof who were not at all restful to her health.

The French door handle clicked open, and Addie shut her eyes.

"Lady Adelaide! My God!"

She was immediately pulled up in Inspector Hunter's arms and then across his lap, a warm hand lightly tapping her cheek. Addie imagined his concerned expression, his sober, soulful dark eyes—it was a pity she couldn't see for herself. She attempted to remain limp and refrain from snuggling up against the man.

It was a challenge.

"Hunter! Get your filthy hands off her!"

Oh, dear. Lucas was back. A bellicose Lucas. Most unlike him. And Forbes, too, if the rattle of the tea tray as he set it down in haste was any indication.

Hunter's tone was freezing. "I beg your pardon. I found Lady Adelaide on the floor, and am only attempting to rouse her." He kept his filthy hands on her, thank goodness. Addie found them very reassuring as he brushed her cheek with the faintest pressure.

"I'll call Dr. Bergman," Forbes said.

"Nonsense. She's only fainted. Women faint all the time."

Lucas was disappointingly dismissive. Maybe he wasn't as

nice as she thought him to be. Still, he couldn't be a murderer; she was fairly sure of that.

She had yet to make a decision about Colonel Mellard's aptitude in that direction. How she'd like to discuss it in private with Inspector Hunter, but that didn't seem practical at the moment when she was supposed to be mute and unresponsive.

"Please do call him, Forbes. She fainted the other day, too, when Mr. McGrath's body was discovered. There might be something wrong. Has she eaten anything today?"

Addie would have answered Mr. Hunter if it didn't mean blowing her cover. She'd had coffee, scrambled eggs, and a piece of toast with butter and marmalade for breakfast, hardly anything from her plate at Holly Hill once Pansy had shown up, and nothing at all in the pergola. She was hungry. Not hungry enough to faint, but hungry enough to produce the loud and embarrassing gurgle in her stomach that all three men couldn't overlook.

"Just as I thought. Forbes, in lieu of smelling salts, a jigger of brandy, please. Lady Adelaide, do wake up."

Addie heard activity at the drinks cabinet. Before she had a chance to flutter her lashes, a glass of brandy was held under her nose, then pressed to her lips. She didn't really want it, but was polite enough to take a sip and sputter.

"There you go. Does anything hurt from your fall?"

"N-no. I'm fine." Addie gazed up into Mr. Hunter's handsome face and felt no shame at all in her ruse. Those eyes were as soulful as she'd imagined, and she gave him a tentative smile.

Lucas dropped to his knees. "Eloise said you wept this afternoon. You're overwrought, my dear." He pressed a clean handkerchief in her hand as if he expected her to cry on cue.

"And in need of some sustenance." In a feat of strength and agility, Mr. Hunter lifted her up off the floor and placed her back in the chair. How did he do it without dropping her? Addie was no lightweight. Although the fashions of the day emphasized a boyish figure, there were plenty of curves beneath her dropped-waist dress, and he hadn't even tipped her sideways.

Forbes fussed making up a plate for her. "Shall I call the doctor, My Lady?"

"No, please don't disturb Dr. Bergman—he *is* retired and deserves some peace. It's been another long day," Addie said with honesty. She bit into a cucumber sandwich and chewed, a little uncomfortable to be the focus of attention of three pairs of eyes. Another sandwich and two biscuits followed in quick succession, and then she didn't care who watched her.

"Where is Jack Robertson?" she asked, once she'd swallowed.

"He wanted to take a peek at his grandfather's cottage, then make himself known in the servants' hall. He seems a capable young lad."

"Who?" Lucas asked.

"Jack is my new gardener. Mr. McGrath's grandson. He came down from Scotland to—" Addie caught the slight shake of the inspector's head—"get his grandfather's belongings."

"And you hired him on the spot? That doesn't seem wise. He could be anybody, come to rob you blind."

Addie wanted to argue with Lucas, but it was only too true that her judgment regarding people was faulty.

"We'll have to see then, won't we? If he cleans out the silver, Forbes will have less polishing to do."

"Heaven forfend. Is there anything else I can get for you, My Lady?"

"I don't think so. Are Miss Pryce and Fraulein Schober home yet?"

"They are resting upstairs. Which, if I may be so bold, you should be doing yourself."

As had been her intention when she left the garden. Until Lucas' visit and unexpected proposal. Should she act as if she didn't remember it? That might buy her some time.

Maybe he'd come to regret his impetuosity already. He wouldn't want to shackle himself to someone sickly, would he? She'd have to look languid and vague, which really wasn't a problem lately, as she was in the process of losing her mind.

She couldn't marry anyone for at least six months. Her mother might even want her to wait longer for propriety's sake. And what about Addie's vow to swear off men? Husbands frequently broke their wives' hearts. While Lucas and Rupert had little in common, one never knew what the future might bring. From the frying pan into the fire. She wasn't sure she could try to domesticate another man—her attempt with Rupert had been a failure.

True, that was more on him than her. He'd admitted as much just the other day. If only he'd said the same while he was still alive, Addie might be more confident in her choices.

"Let me help you to your room," Inspector Hunter offered.

"I'll take her. I know the way," Lucas said.

Which was true, but the implication was unfortunate. Addie looked at Mr. Hunter, who suddenly found his shirt cuff fascinating.

Oh dear.

"He doesn't mean it like that."

Lucas' face darkened. "Addie, you are forgetting yourself."

Was she? To Addie, it was as if she was remembering herself for the first time in ages.

She felt a gentle chilly squeeze on her shoulder and shivered. She knew that squeeze. Why did he always turn up at such fraught times? Maybe that was part of his alleged mission.

Or her delusions.

"Faux fainting again? I'm disappointed in your lack of creativity. You really need to expand your arsenal of tricks. 'Variety's the very spice of life.' Cowper, I believe."

Rupert.

She resolutely ignored him. "I have my reputation to defend, Lucas, if you won't do it," Addie said tartly.

"I never meant to impugn your honor! You know I think the world of you! I never would have asked—"

"Let's change the subject," Addie said quickly.

Rupert sniffed. "Coward. Are you going to accept him? You could do much better. Isn't there an eligible duke out there? Someone with most of his own teeth and hair? Not too many mangy wolfhounds. You'd make a grand duchess. Think of the tiaras and ermine stoles."

"I think I'll walk to the village before dinner," Mr. Hunter said. "Then you two can finish your conversation."

Oh, damn. Oops, she'd said it out loud.

Chapter Thirty-four

Dev had decided to wander into the village earlier just on a hunch. The mention of Colonel Mellard in McGrath's letter was significant. Lady Adelaide had been aghast at the inference that he could be involved in Kathleen Grant's death. Dev questioned that himself, remembering how Mellard had choked up during his first interview. The man's reputation was spotless—he was a national hero, for God's sake.

But heroes could have feet of clay.

He'd found Mellard late in the afternoon in his picture-perfect front garden cutting back day lily stalks. Dev made the encounter appear to be an accident—which it was, basically—and had no intention of questioning the man about the contents of the letter quite yet.

"Good afternoon, Colonel Mellard."

The clippers stilled. "How was it, Inspector?"

"How was what, sir?"

"The funeral, of course." Mellard wiped a bead of sweat from his forehead. "I couldn't make myself go. The thought of Kathleen, so full of life, in an airless cramped box—no, I couldn't do it."

"Understandable. Everything went off without a hitch, with a very creditable turnout. Miss Waring organized everything. I think you would have been pleased." Dev had attended many such affairs in his line of work. Apart from Barbara Pryce's gloomy presence, Kathleen Grant's reception stood out more as an occasion for celebrating than mourning. Even her raucous children were untouched by the tragedy, but perhaps they were too young to understand.

"I couldn't face anyone."

"If it's any consolation, I don't believe word has gotten out about your relationship with Lady Grant. Your absence wasn't noticed." *Except by me.*

"Thank God for that. I wouldn't want any pity."

"No, certainly not. I'm following your advice, walking and thinking. I'll let you get back to your garden."

"You're at Addie's?"

It must be common knowledge in the village by now. Dev hoped *he* wasn't the one impugning her honor. Places like Compton-Under-Wood were hotbeds of gossip. Residents of "the big house" always fell under exceptional scrutiny. It must have been hell for Lady Adelaide when her husband was roving all over the county with other women.

And it was a wonder that Colonel Mellard was able to keep his engagement a secret. He was still a new arrival, and would be under suspicion from the village tabbies until he was buried in Compton St. Cuthbert's graveyard himself.

"Yes. Until after the inquests. I know she's worried about you, amongst other things. She told me she wanted to invite you to tea tomorrow. I'm not sure she's had the opportunity to ring you up. It's been a very busy day."

"Tell her I'm fine. Hell, I'll tell her myself. I'll come. Life goes on, what?"

"See you then."

And so Dev had ambled away, no more informed than he had been before the encounter.

His patience had been put to the test on his return to Compton Chase. That pompous ass Waring had been invited to stay for dinner, after claiming he had difficulty starting his car. Dev suspected he'd removed a pertinent part, but it was true—the bloody thing would not move from the drive, even after the chauffeur and two elderly grooms-turned-mechanics fiddled with it. Dev himself had a hand to no avail. The car had been towed to the garage in the village. Addie had offered the use of one of her late husband's cars, but Waring said he'd be too tired later to start for home after the day he'd had.

They'd all had the same damned day. Dev, for one, was anxious that it end at a reasonable hour.

So Waring was invited to spend the night as well. Lady Adelaide was a gracious hostess despite everything. Dev worried about her. Perhaps it was presumptuous—he hadn't known her before the murders, so her somewhat erratic behavior might be what passed for normal in her rarefied world. Talking to oneself was a sign of genius, wasn't it? He did it from time to time when trying to work out a vexing puzzle.

He'd rather talk to Lady Adelaide alone tonight without the distractions of her other guests, though.

And now he sat across from Lord Lucas Waring in Lady Adelaide's wood-paneled dining room, the viscount's resentment of Dev's presence wafting over the table like a black cloud. It was clear Waring thought he was much too good to break bread with a mere policeman, an Anglo-Indian at that.

Dev had faced worse, and kept his conversation with Barbara Pryce and her nurse light and inoffensive, using the right knives and forks in a rebuke of Waring's expectations. The man had clearly never met Chandani Hunter, who prided herself on her adaptation to British customs.

Miss Pryce had decided a week in the country was not in order after all, and they were going to leave tomorrow. There was talk of Paris, and Dev wondered if her sobriety would be put to an unfair test. However, Fraulein Schober, despite her fluffy looks, appeared to have a will of iron and a good influence on her charge, so perhaps all would be well.

Drugs had infiltrated all levels of society, and the Bright Young People were definitely not immune. Alcohol-fueled hijinks were the talk of all the gossip rags, too. Treasure hunts—one involving the Prince of Wales just this July!—scavenger hunts and the like had made headlines. It was Dev's opinion that rich people should find something more useful to do than wander around London's dark streets in evening wear looking for obscure clues and stealing bobbies' hats.

Miss Pryce was a little too old for such nonsense, he hoped.

Addie folded her napkin and rose. "Forbes, we'd all like coffee in the drawing room. We've already relaxed the rules." A good thing, since Dev did not own, and Lucas Waring did not bring, evening clothes. "I presume you gentlemen won't mind joining the ladies and skipping the port."

That was a relief to Dev—he had nothing much to say in private to Lord Waring without a gallon of port for inspiration.

His first impression of the viscount had soured somewhat. Gone was the genial clubman who was anxious to cooperate with the police, although he had little useful information. If Dev wasn't mistaken, Waring was *jealous* of him. Territorial.

Which was almost flattering, if it wasn't so foolish.

Filthy hands, indeed. Not that Dev was likely to get another chance to touch Lady Adelaide's smooth cheek ever again.

Dev followed the women and Waring down the hall, feeling less oppressed with every step when they entered the modernized drawing room. Dark wooden paneling gave way to light striped wallpaper and sheer gold drapes, with modern art instead of dyspeptic Compton ancestors on the walls.

He realized he'd neglected to inform Lady Adelaide that he'd invited Colonel Mellard to tea—there really had been no opportunity—so he slid next to her on the sofa and did so, effectively cutting out Lord Waring.

Now who was being foolish?

"Oh! I did mean to telephone him, but the day got away

from me, didn't it?" She lowered her voice. "Will you ask him about the letter?"

Dev nodded. "I have to. He'll be more relaxed if he thinks it's just a social visit. I hope I haven't overstepped my bounds, involving you in this."

"No. It's all right. I want to help. Get all this over with." She took a quick look around the room as if she wished them all to disappear.

"If my presence is in any way a burden—"

She put a hand on his arm. "No, no! I'm glad you're here. I feel safer."

Would any man do, or was he specific to her confidence? He couldn't ask. And truly, what did she need a man around for? She was financially secure, attractive, intelligent, surrounded by a conscientious staff and a supportive family. Some men, like her late husband, were more trouble than they were worth.

"Addie, what about some music?" Barbara Pryce said unexpectedly. "Something to cheer us up after the Day from Hell."

"Music?" Her surprise was evident.

"Something jolly we can all dance to in memory of the jolliest girl there ever was. Inspector, you do dance, don't you?"

Dev's twisted foot was rather weary, if he were to be honest. "It's not part of my job description, Miss Pryce. I have to admit, I've never been asked before while I'm on a case."

"Pretend you're not on duty, and that we're all old friends. Lucas, be a darling and crank the Victrola up. You still have Rupert's record collection, don't you, Addie?"

"Y-yes."

"Wonderful!" Miss Pryce kicked off her shoes, and after a minute, so did Lady Adelaide. That left Fraulein Schober, who smiled in resignation. "I shall sit this one out, unless we can get your so-proper butler to participate."

Lucas went to the handsome walnut cabinet, opened the storage door and sifted through the records. "This will do, I guess." He placed the record on the turntable, set the needle in the track and turned the handle for all it was worth.

Strains of clarinets echoed through the room. It was *Farewell Blues*, the Georgians' version, popular last year. Not exactly jolly, but rousing in spots.

Miss Pryce spun toward him. "A fox trot, Mr. Hunter. Shall we?"

If Dev was disappointed in his partner, he knew better than to show it.

Chapter Thirty-five

Addie's silk pajamas felt like heaven against her flushed skin. It had been forever since she'd danced—in fact, she couldn't even remember the last time. How odd it was to bounce about with unseemly abandon on the day Kathleen Grant was buried. But if Babs—practically a grieving widow, if not Italian—thought it was fine, who was Addie to argue? She wanted Babs to be happy, or as happy as she could be under the circumstances. It would be awful to have her fall back into her old habits. She'd even given up overindulging in drink, if this evening was anything to go by.

Addie had partnered with both Lucas and Inspector Hunter, and even Fraulein Schober. Rupert's jazz records got quite a workout. Since his death, the Victrola cabinet and its contents had gathered dust, or would have if her parlor maids were any less efficient.

Addie slipped between the sheets, folding her spectacles on the bedside table. What a day. After longing for quiet and privacy, even after a scented hot bath, she was now too stimulated to fall asleep. Despite the late hour and unaccustomed exercise, she was as restless as if *she'd* taken some kind of drug. She picked up and put down the new Agatha Christie she'd started, the words not penetrating her overtaxed brain. And if she brushed her hair any more, her arm would fall off.

It was one-thirty. Compton Chase's clocks began to chime

throughout the house within seconds of each other, and over them came the shrill ring of the telephone. Fitz gave a muffled yip and rolled over on his back, paws in the air, ever hopeful in his sleepy state for a tummy rub.

Addie froze. Late-night calls were never good news. She threw on her robe and went out into the hall. When she picked up the receiver, she heard poor Forbes on the line, explaining why he couldn't possibly disturb her at this late hour. He must have been asleep himself when the phone rang, since she'd told him over two hours ago to go to bed.

"It's an emergency." The male voice was familiar, but Addie couldn't place it.

"It's all right, Forbes, I'm on the line." She heard the respectful click. "Yes? Who is this?"

"Thank God you're all right."

"Of course I'm all right." Addie kept her voice low so as not to wake the guests down the corridor. "Who is calling?"

"Gerald Dumont. I know you think I'm a crackpot, but you are in grave danger, Lady Adelaide."

Grave danger of not getting enough beauty sleep. If she'd looked horrid this morning, tomorrow was bound to be twice as bad.

"Did you want to speak to Barbara?"

"No! Didn't you hear me? It's you I'm worried about."

Addie sat down on the chair next to the console table. "Why are you worried, Mr. Dumont?"

"I had one of my visions. Please don't laugh."

The last thing Addie felt like doing was laughing. She was so irritated she was tempted to hang up. *Famous in France*, she reminded herself.

"Go on."

"There is a man in your life. One you've trusted implicitly. Admired. He's been like family to you. An—an older brother, perhaps. I don't know any more than that. I can't see his features, or anything distinctive about him, but he means you harm."

"That's it?"

"I'm sorry it's not clearer." To Dumont's credit, he did sound sorry.

"I thought you couldn't see into the future."

"Generally, I can't. But this vision was so strong it woke me out of a deep sleep. A message from the other side is often confused. Sometimes we get the right answer to the wrong question, and vice versa. Perhaps this man has already hurt you in some way."

Was Lucas' proposal harmful? She'd lose the autonomy she had if she accepted—he was an old-fashioned, traditional sort of man. Addie's days of doing mostly as she pleased would come to a screeching halt. She'd have to plan menus around Lucas' favorites, and he liked deviled kidneys for breakfast. Ugh. Buy modest clothes he liked, no doubt with longer skirts. Move to Waring Hall and organize hunts and house parties for his bluff and hearty friends.

Share a bed with someone other than Fitz.

"Maybe it was just a regular dream, Mr. Dumont. I have crazy dreams all the time."

"I considered not calling you, especially at this hour. But it's my sworn duty to warn you. Please, please be careful."

Did he take some kind of Medium's Oath? Was it like honor among thieves? Addie wished he hadn't decided to scare her so earnestly with his conscientiousness. "Mr. Hunter is still here. I'm sure he'll look out for me."

There was silence on the other end. "I can hear you're placating me. Trying to be kind. You're a kind woman, and that's part of the problem, I think. You never want to hurt anyone's feelings. If I can't convince you—" He sighed. "At least I tried. I'd be happy to come down and hold a séance once Barbara has gone. There would be no charge, of course."

Oh, joy. "I'm sure that won't be necessary, Mr. Dumont. We'll muddle along here, like we always do. You haven't, by any chance, any opinion on who killed my gardener, have you?"

"I'm sorry. Nothing's come to me. I can't force it, you know. The spirits have minds of their own."

"That's a pity. Your skills could be useful to the authorities if they could be properly harnessed."

"I doubt the police would believe me any more than you do. Well, good night then. Remember what I said."

She wasn't apt to forget.

Addie put the phone down and rubbed her eyes. Did she believe Mr. Dumont? It was clear he believed in his gift. Rupert had said the man was legitimate, a real medium as opposed to the charlatans Mr. Rivers warned her against. Where was Rupert anyway? She could use some advice.

She nearly jumped off the chair when she felt the hand on her shoulder. It was a warm hand, not a cold one though, and she relaxed a fraction.

"Who on earth called you at this hour?"

Lucas stood over her in one of Rupert's old dressing gowns. It was very disconcerting to see something so familiar on someone so familiar and have it be so unfamiliar, but he didn't look *dangerous*.

Addie really should give all of Rupert's clothes away—it was ridiculous to have turned his room into a sort of shrine.

Maybe Rupert might like to pick out another tie for eternity before she did.

"Gracious, you startled me. What are you doing up?"

"I couldn't sleep. We never finished our conversation."

Addie glanced around the hall and all its shut doors, which were blurry without her glasses. "Not here, Lucas. Can't it wait until tomorrow?"

"I'll have to leave at the very crack to get to Waring Hall to pick up my things, then go to the Morrises for the rest of the week. Their grouse shoot, you know. Thanks for the loan of the car, by the way."

Lord knows, she had too many cars in the converted stables.

It was probably time to give them away too. Or sell them and give the money to charity.

"Over my dead body. Oops. There's a phrase I can't use again."

Rupert.

"Not now, please," Addie begged.

"Just give me five minutes, Addie. Please don't faint again. I realize I bungled things this afternoon and took you by surprise."

"I'll say," said Rupert. "Where were the flowers? The yearning looks? The heartfelt compliments? He never even got down on one knee, and he's supposed to be such a great sportsman. Agile and what-not. The man promised you *no surprises.* You might as well shoot yourself now. I wouldn't wish for such a tedious existence on my worst enemy. The grouse will have it better—there's a chance for escape."

Addie ignored Rupert as best she could. "All right. Come into the sewing room where we won't bother anyone. But no more than five minutes. We all have to get up early." She had to see Babs and Fraulein Schober off, and consult with the inspector as how to best coax the colonel into admitting the truth without offending him.

"Tut. You're making a huge mistake. You can't invite a man into a sewing room without giving him ideas, Addie. Undoing buttons. Ripping seams. Unlacing laces. Ideas I won't sully your innocent ears with."

Addie rolled her eyes. That was the problem. Everyone thought she was so innocent. So sweet. So good. So *kind,* according to Gerald Dumont. Why, she'd like to prove them all wrong, starting tonight.

"Scram," she whispered to Rupert, pushing him away and closing the door, once again, in his face. It was very satisfying.

The little room smelled of starch and lavender. Addie switched on the light before they stumbled over the ironing board and caused a commotion. The last thing she needed was Inspector Hunter springing into action and finding her in a compromising position with Lucas.

Addie sat down in the worn slip-covered chair where Mrs. Drum did her sewing, leaving Lucas to stand. "Five minutes," she reminded him, admiring the glass jars of sorted buttons lining the windowsill.

Lucas looked remarkably right at home in his borrowed night-clothes and bare feet. His curly fair hair was boyishly disarranged, his blue eyes bright in the lamplight. Contrary to Mr. Dumont's admonitions, Addie could not imagine anyone less threatening.

She would hear him out, and then—

She'd have to throw him out. In the kindest way possible, of course.

Chapter Thirty-six

"How long have we known each other?"

Addie didn't have to think. "Your father inherited the viscountcy when you were six. So, twenty-five years." When Lucas had moved into Waring Hall, Addie had been living a dispiriting life as a big sister to an uninteresting pink lump called Cecilia, who cried twenty-four hours of every day. How thrilled she'd been to have a playmate right next door who could talk and run and count to twenty in French, even if he was a boy.

"I thought Waring Hall was intimidating at the time. You know my father hadn't expected to inherit. But Broughton Park—why, it might as well have been Buckingham Palace. You were like a fairytale princess come to rule the world. You certainly ruled me." He gave her a winsome smile.

Addie thought this was a little better than his earlier declaration, but still said nothing. She *had* bossed Lucas around when they were children. But that stopped about the time he'd grown whiskers and an outsize sense of male superiority.

"We've been there for each other through thick and thin all those years, haven't we? The abject misery of boarding school. Our first spots. Dance classes with that silly Mr. Brazledean, who was far more determined to hold on to me than you. I must tell you—all along, I wanted to express my warmer feelings. But we were both so young. I figured we had plenty of time. And then came the war. And Rupert Compton. One couldn't compete with him. Or at least *I* couldn't."

"Damn straight."

Rupert was now sifting through a pile of linens in a wicker basket that were waiting to be mended. How did he get in? "I shut the door," Addie muttered to herself.

"Yes, I saw you. I don't think anyone will bother us at this time of night, but if it will make you feel safer, I'll get up and lock it," Lucas offered. "Then we cannot be disturbed."

Would that give him leave to bludgeon her to death with the iron, or stab her with scissors, then climb down the vines outside the window? Dead bodies were always discovered inside locked rooms in the books she read.

"No, it's all right. You were saying?"

"It doesn't matter what he was saying—it's all a load of twaddle. You're like brother and sister, Addie. There's no chemistry between you. I know about such things."

Rupert certainly did. He'd had enough chemistry with women to blow up several university science laboratories. "Shh!"

Lucas leaned forward. "I'm being as quiet as I can, my dear. I don't want any of your guests to get the wrong impression if they overhear us. I was thoughtless before with that police detective. Not that you should feel the need to impress him—he's only a—a foreigner—"

Something about Addie's look must have gotten through to him.

"A stranger," Lucas amended. "Whereas, we know each other so well. Why, I bet I know what you're thinking right this minute."

Addie very much doubted it. She stole a glance at Rupert, who was crossing his eyes and waggling his tongue like he did when she was talking to Mr. Hunter the other day. What she was thinking was that Rupert should go to Hell or some other suitable environ and grow up. If he was to continue haunting her forever, at least he could do it in a dignified fashion. For heaven's sake, he was wearing a frayed embroidered napkin on his head now.

Lord Lucas Waring was telling her things she wished he'd said over a decade ago. She'd had a tremendous crush on him for years before he went away to university. Observing her moping, her parents had encouraged her to branch out a little. So she had, becoming friendly with a select group of young men in her social circle. There had been parties and picnics and some very tepid adventures, but when the war began, those young men disappeared to do their patriotic duty.

Most of them were no longer alive, sad to say.

"Anyway, I know it's far too soon to talk of marriage, as much as I'd like to kidnap you and go to Gretna Green like they used to do. Get married over the anvil by a burly blacksmith, what? But your mother would not condone such an action, and I don't want to get on the wrong side of her. And you are still mourning Rupert, though frankly I don't know why. He was never good enough for you."

"Can't fault him there—for once we agree," Rupert said ruefully. "Sorry, pet. I really was a disgrace."

"But I'm willing to wait until you're ready, Addie. Six months. Even a year. I'm sure we can make a go of it. Please say you'll consider my proposal. I'll get down on one knee if I have to, though I'm not sure I trust the pajamas to stay where they belong."

Addie had a brief flash of a naked Lucas. She'd already seen him in his swimming costume numerous times, and just erased the fabric in her mind where it counted. And once half-naked. When he was about eight, he'd fallen into the lively stream that divided Waring Hall from Broughton Park and his trousers fell down. She was sure he was larger now. The water had been freezing.

Her heart beat a little faster. Wasn't this what she had wanted for years? Handsome, broad-shouldered, tanned Lucas, his body fit and lean from riding and cricket and shooting and fishing.

Did one get fit from fishing? One would acquire a tolerance for the cold and wet at least, which would come in handy living in Britain.

She opened her mouth, hoping to dislodge the family of frogs in her throat.

"Don't say anything you don't mean. But I don't want to be let down gently just yet, either. You know what? Think about it for now. I won't pressure you. It's been a hellish two weeks for everyone. Damn Kathleen Grant—I'd like to kill her all over again for upsetting you. I'll go and try to fall sleep. But before I do, may I kiss you good-night? A proper kiss, not a peck on the cheek." He pulled her up gently from the old chair.

"Oh, God, deliver me." Rupert had covered his eyes with the napkin, but Addie could see he was peeking around the edges.

She'd kissed Lucas dozens of times, even "properly" on more than one occasion. Champagne and youthful indiscretion might have been involved, but tonight Addie was stone-cold sober and feeling very much older. And she was out of practice in the kissing department. Fitz's slobbery licks definitely did not count.

"I—I—"

Lucas brought her close. "Don't be afraid. I've been dreaming about this for weeks. Years." His lips slanted over hers, and Addie shut her eyes.

"I'm going to be sick. Perhaps even retch. Is there a bowl about for just that purpose? I'll take a dented washbucket, if I must."

Addie's stomach was doing somersaults too, but she wished Rupert would keep his annoying feelings to himself. She tried to lose the tension running like a wire from the base of her skull to her waist, and took a breath.

Lucas took advantage of her opened mouth and swept in so gently she wasn't really sure he was there at first. Addie felt like a delicate porcelain doll, possibly shattering at his touch. But then he became more forceful, just enough so as not to frighten her too much. Imagine being frightened by a kiss! But she was, and trembled a little.

His lips were firm and warm and, she realized suddenly, rather expert. He hadn't wasted all those years mooning over her and what was not to be. But he'd been discreet. Addie had no idea who he'd been kissing.

Damn Kathleen Grant—I'd like to kill her all over again for upsetting you.

Addie stumbled backward. Oh, my God. He didn't mean it quite like that, did he?

You are in grave danger. Mr. Dumont's words came back to spook her, and she gave Lucas a tiny push. He broke the kiss immediately.

"Forgive me, darling. I lost my head there for a minute. Too much too soon. I promise to take things more slowly in the future." He tucked her hair behind her ears and kissed her on the forehead.

Addie's blood rushed about wildly, but not precisely from lust. She looked up into Lucas' smiling face. He was a little flushed, a lot handsome, but he may as well have been a complete stranger.

Addie covered her mouth to stop her lips from tingling, and also from saying anything. Her imagination was running away with her again. A quick check showed her that Rupert had mercifully disappeared in disgust, so the situation was not as mortifying as it could have been. She *had* to talk to Dr. Bergman.

"I'll leave you. Sweet dreams, my dear." Lucas tightened the belt of the robe, and Addie could not fail to see that he was aroused.

That meant he wouldn't try to kill her, didn't it? Maybe not. Why were crimes of passion committed, after all? Because of thwarted desire, that's why.

She waited until he was back in his room, then raced to her own and splashed cold water on her face. If only she could wash away ghosts and mediums with a sponge and bubbles of Pears Soap.

Addie faced herself in the mirror, assessing the damage. She resembled someone who'd been punched in both eyes, and her bottom lip was swollen from Lucas' masterful kissing.

She'd never fall asleep now. Had she been kissed by a murderer? Did she want to be kissed by him again?

Chapter Thirty-seven

Wednesday

It was three o'clock before Addie pulled herself together to go downstairs. She had finally fallen asleep an hour or so before dawn (after finishing her book!), and was dimly aware of early morning movement in the household as her guests left her one by one. Beckett had been banned after holding a mirror under her nose to see if Addie was still alive around eleven, but summoned at one to bring a pot of hot, strong coffee and a roll.

After a long, lazy bath, a longer stint at the dressing table while Beckett tried to improve her looks with powder and paint, Addie put on her best black tea gown for the colonel's visit. She was already feeling guilty for luring him here under false pretenses. And she needed to talk to Mr. Hunter about what Lucas had said.

Damn Kathleen Grant—I'd like to kill her all over again for upsetting you.

A confession or a figure of speech? That would be up to Devenand Hunter to sort out.

Beckett informed her that the inspector had left the house to go on one of his walks. He was getting to be a regular country gentleman, wasn't he? Addie wondered if the villagers were comforted by his presence or up in arms that a stranger was wandering around invading their little paradise.

That was what two deaths would do, cause unwelcome attention to the darkest corners.

Jack Robertson waved to her through the drawing room window as he watered the dying plants on the terrace. He was making himself useful already.

By three-twenty-five, a footman had rolled in the tea trolley. At three-thirty, the doorbell rang, and both Mr. Hunter and Colonel Mellard were ushered in by Forbes.

"We met on the lane," Mr. Hunter said. "It's been a lovely afternoon for a walk. Clears the head, as you say, Colonel."

"Glad I can give a young fellow some advice and actually have it followed. I was afraid I was losing my touch since I've been put out to pasture. Thank you for inviting me, Addie. It's been a rough few days."

"I know, and I'm so sorry. Mr. Rivers did a good job with the eulogy." As long as one was unacquainted with the deceased. Addie busied herself pouring three cups of tea and passing plates.

"Couldn't bear it. So, Inspector, are there any new leads?"

"Not leads, per se, but we have a better understanding of the timeline. You might be able to help us with that."

The colonel raised a gray eyebrow. "I? I've told you everything I know, I'm afraid. I wish I'd gone back to the barn once I returned from the village. I might have stopped the bastard."

"Didn't you?"

"Didn't I what?"

"Go back to the barn. A witness has placed you there around three o'clock."

Colonel Mellard set his cup down with a splash. "Rubbish! Who is this witness?"

"Mr. McGrath."

"Who? Oh, the gardener. He's dead, isn't he? Don't tell me his ghost came back like Banquo to slander me. I've never heard anything so ridiculous!"

Mr. Hunter pulled the letter from an inside pocket. "Libel, perhaps. If you would be so kind to read it?"

The colonel held Mr. McGrath's letter out a distance, his face growing darker by the word. "I left my reading glasses at home. I don't understand the half of it. The handwriting—it's indecipherable, isn't it?"

"Allow me." Inspector Hunter took the letter back and began to read aloud. Addie could imagine the burr of Mr. McGrath's gravelly voice in every simple line. He finished, and the room was uncomfortably quiet.

Mr. Hunter took out his notebook. "He states you found him watching two people in the barn, uh, fornicating. Is this true?"

"Of course not! I told you I met Kathleen that afternoon after lunch, but nothing, *nothing* like that happened."

"Why would he write such a thing?"

"How should I know? Maybe the old fellow had a fit or something and hallucinated. Got into the dandelion wine or ate a bad mushroom," the colonel said with agitation.

"Maybe," said Addie, "he saw Kathleen and Ernest Shipman. We know she met him."

"What? Preposterous! She would never."

"Shipman has finally admitted it, Colonel Mellard, but swears she was alive when he left her. Suppose you tell us what really happened."

"I've already told you! I can make up a story of whole cloth if you wish." The colonel braced his arms on the chair and rose. "I've had about enough, Addie. Of all people, I would think you'd understand. You lost someone close to you. Like you, I'm grieving, and I thought you invited me for tea to be kind."

Kind again. "I did. There's your cup." Addie wished there was a truth serum in it, so they could put this matter to rest.

"I know you're tempted." Rupert appeared out of thin air, leaning on the mantel in relaxed fashion. "But don't throw a scone at him. Or at me," he said after a pause.

It only needed this.

"Go away now," she said without thinking.

Inspector Hunter frowned at her. "No, no, Colonel Mellard, please sit down. It will go easier on all of us if you tell the truth. The whole of it."

The colonel let out a sigh of defeat. "Fine. I wondered when—I suppose it was inevitable. At least I've had a few days to get my affairs in order." He sat, took a sip of tea and made a face. In her nervousness, Addie had added too much sugar.

And after his words, she became even more nervous.

"When I came back from the village, I went to the tithe barn to tell Kathleen the coast was clear, and she could use the footpath to take the shortcut to my house. I thought she'd be reading the book she'd brought with her to kill the time on the train—some Agatha Christie murder mystery. Ironic, isn't it?" He gave an approximation of a smile, a ghastly rictus thing that made Addie flinch. "And then I came upon that gardener and your dog standing at the open barn door."

The colonel's left eye began to twitch. "An open door, where anyone could, and did, see her—can you imagine? But that was Kathleen all over—she didn't care what people said."

Or the drugs made her so high, she'd lost all sense of decency, Addie thought.

"Anyway, I shooed the fellow away. That damned fat banker was inside buttoning up his trousers, and Kathleen was just lying there on a blanket naked watching him, a…a dreamy smile on her face. I knew at once she was not herself, that she was under the influence, but I was angry. I had a right to be. We'd agreed that sort of behavior must stop. She'd promised." Mellard took a handkerchief and blotted the perspiration from behind his neck and continued.

"I ducked behind some bushes and Shipman hustled back to the house, whistling a merry tune as if…as if there was not a thing wrong in the world. Smug bastard. It set my teeth on edge, it did. Then I went in. I only meant to talk to her, to remind her that she was to cut back on the cocaine, and, of course, stop having her meaningless affairs. But she got angry."

"What did she say?" Inspector Hunter asked.

"It wasn't only what she said. It was what she did. She grabbed her purse. There was a fistful of ampules in it, more than enough to kill all three of us sitting here. And her syringe. She never went anywhere without her kit lately, even though I'd begged her. Offered her more money. Whatever she wanted, really. But it was never enough."

Addie felt a wave of sympathy. Colonel Mellard was completely unused to being disobeyed. He'd placed his confidence—and his heart—with the wrong person.

"Addiction, Colonel. You could not change it with money or love. What happened next?"

"I—I don't know why I couldn't move. I watched her sit cross-legged and inject that poison between her toes, a horrible, defiant smile on her face. She was already impaired. The extra dose was too much. She fell back like a rag doll." His voice broke.

"Take your time, sir," Mr. Hunter said gently.

"There was no time to dress her—I couldn't have if I'd tried, I was shaking so. Imagine, someone like me, who has killed with very little thought—I fell apart completely. But I had the sense to take the drugs and the needle with me. I didn't want people to know what she'd done. How very careless she'd been.

"I couldn't think straight. I knew I should tell someone, but it was all so sordid. She did this to herself, Inspector. No one murdered her. It was an accident. You must believe that."

"What about Mr. McGrath?" Addie asked.

Mellard looked down at his brown, capable hands. "I am sorry. I truly am. But I didn't want him ruining Kathleen's reputation any further."

It took her a few seconds to realize what he'd said. "She had no reputation left to ruin, you stupid man!"

"Be quiet, Addie! Mellard has quite a temper when he lets himself go. All of us who served under him knew it," Rupert said. "I wouldn't put it past him to have given Kathleen that overdose to teach her a lesson. He's probably sorry, but it's too late now."

"Lady Adelaide," Inspector Hunter said, "why don't you leave us for a few minutes?"

"He murdered my gardener! Am I just supposed to smile graciously and pass him a biscuit? And, no, I will not be quiet!"

Suddenly Addie found herself staring into the barrel of the colonel's pistol.

Oops.

"Told you," Rupert said softly. "Please don't move. I like you just as you are, with no unnecessary holes to spoil your beauty. Just the usual nostrils, mouth, etcetera. Speaking of which, close yours now, that's a love."

"Colonel Mellard, give me the gun, please." Inspector Hunter sounded calm and in control, when he must be anything but. As for Addie, she was forgetting how to breathe, especially now that she'd shut her mouth per Rupert's instructions.

Tiny black dots were swirling in front of her. This was no time to faint for real, although if she was unconscious, she wouldn't know she'd been shot dead, would she? Then she and Rupert could haunt someone together, bickering throughout eternity.

That did not sound promising at all.

"I have nothing to lose, Inspector. My retirement is not going to plan. When Rupert—that was Lady Adelaide's husband—encouraged me to buy a house in the village three years ago, I thought I'd find some peace for a change. Congenial neighbors, a bit of hunting, pottering around in the garden, that sort of thing. I looked upon him as the son I never had—did you know that, Addie? He reminded me a bit of myself when I was a younger, dashing fellow, although I never had his way with women. In fact, Rupert introduced me to Kath last year, thought we'd hit it off. We did. She brightened my life, but then the drugs took hold. Such a waste, when she had so much to live for."

The gun remained pointed at her, the colonel's hand steady. Addie was afraid to look away. To think she'd once hoped her mother would marry this man.

Some stepfather.

"She loved those boys, she did, even if they were little hellions. I shouldn't wonder if their behavior contributed to her problems. She was delicate. Had lost her parents. Been bullied by Grant. Needed someone to take care of her and show her the way."

"And you were the best man for the job," Inspector Hunter said, his expression sympathetic. Unless Addie was mistaken, she sensed him moving a tiny fraction forward.

"I thought so. Shipman wasn't—he never would have left his wife. She wears the pants in that family, no matter what he thinks. Kath would tease me about him sometimes to make me jealous. But I knew I was the one to settle her down."

If a gun wasn't pointed at her heart, Addie might have felt sorry again for the colonel, who was obviously delusional. Crazy. And she'd been worried about her own mind. Addie didn't hold a patch on the colonel.

"Steady on. You're doing beautifully, Addie. No one would know you have a care in the world," Rupert said soothingly. "I'm going to do something in a minute or two, not sure what. Let's see if your inspector is smart enough to take advantage of it. No guarantees. This is all new territory for me and I haven't really practiced."

That didn't sound promising either.

"You must have a good solicitor, Colonel Mellard. You are a distinguished war hero. I'm sure we can work something out."

"Don't give me that guff, boy. I know when I'm finished. And what's one more life to take? No one will miss the prim and proper Lady Adelaide, nose in the air, always judging. Always perfect. Butter wouldn't melt in her mouth, would it? Ungrateful little bitch. Couldn't keep her husband satisfied—"

Rupert pitched himself across the tea trolley, knocking it and plates and cups to the floor, and tossed the silver pot of hot tea directly into the colonel's lap. The sound the man made was ungodly but satisfying just the same. Inspector Hunter grabbed the pistol that had dropped to the floor, then clipped the colonel smartly on the head with it. The man fell onto the broken crockery and did not move.

"Are you all right, Lady Adelaide?" The inspector's voice was somewhat ragged, just like her startled brain at the moment. He was every bit as pale as she must be.

"Qu-quite."

"How did you tip the trolley? I never saw you move."

"I don't know. It j-just happened. Maybe there was an earthquake."

Rupert brushed the crumbs from his jacket and grinned in an annoyingly superior fashion. "That was ripping! I wasn't sure I could pull it off. That business with the molecules, you know. Tricky. Well, I'll leave you two to clean up the mess. This has got to earn me some points, what?" He dissolved, the trace of his smile lingering just like the Cheshire cat's.

Inspector Hunter handcuffed the colonel where he lay, then emptied the chamber of the pistol. "I should have checked to see if he was armed. I'm so sorry, Lady Adelaide. I know it's small comfort that today has taught me a lesson I'll never forget. I'll know better than to expect people to be civilized when faced with their downfall. I deeply regret asking for your help. The colonel had me fooled. I thought he was an honorable man."

He had been. Once. Addie's throat was exceptionally dry. She wondered if she needed to lie down for a while. Or call for a pitcher of martinis—Beckett was getting expert at fixing them. Olives or a lemon twist? She didn't care.

"Th-that's all right. All's well that ends well," she managed, standing up on shaky legs.

"But it almost didn't. And *you* could have been ended." The inspector touched her shoulder, and she felt a pleasant zing through the silk shantung of her tea gown.

Addie looked up. Goodness, his eyes were dark, and he had eyelashes most women would kill for. His nose might have been a touch too prominent, but it saved him from being beautiful.

Good Lord. Could Rupert be right? Was she ready for a "bit of fun?" What about Lucas? Apparently, he hadn't murdered anyone at all. She shifted out from under the inspector's warm hand. "You'll want to get your men here, won't you? I believe I need to get a breath of fresh air."

Addie didn't wait for Hunter's response. She stepped out of the French door to the terrace and shut her eyes briefly against the brilliant late afternoon sun. The potted geraniums were reviving already, thanks to Jack's care. She was comforted by the fact that he had employment now, stepping into his grandfather's boots. Well, boot. So many wounded, so few opportunities. If anything good had come out of all of this, it was hiring Jack.

"Rupert," she whispered, "where are you?"

Addie waited. Waited until the police van had gone. Waited until Inspector Hunter bid her a shy farewell and went off to stay at the Compton Arms. Waited until the sun slipped behind the Cotswold Hills and the shadows lengthened.

Beckett crept up on her without her even noticing. "Lady A., don't you think it's time to come in? You've had a shock. I'll run a nice hot bath for you. Set you up with a strong G and T, more G than T. Slice of lime or slice of lemon? You choose. I'm sure Cook has both—she's got everything, don't she? Then maybe some clear soup on a tray in bed? Or do you think it's still too hot for soup? The temperature has dropped some while you've been out here, but summer ain't over yet."

What if Rupert was "over" after his ghostly heroics today? Addie should be relieved.

But somehow, she wasn't.

The trip had been arranged hastily to cheer Cee up and give Addie time to consider Lucas' proposal without undue influence. He'd taken to sending flowers and bad poetry, which was disconcerting. When they returned, her mourning period would be over, and normal life could resume.

Of course, normal was a relative term. Addie had been encouraged that her headaches had stopped—thanks to wearing her glasses regularly, she presumed. And since Rupert had tossed that teapot, there had been no sign of her other headache anywhere on the Compton Chase estate. Addie found herself talking to him anyway when she was alone. She was still trying to work out where their marriage had gone wrong, but didn't feel as responsible as she had.

"Yes, Lady Adelaide. But won't you miss Fitz?" Despite there being kennels on the ship, Fitz was spending the winter at home. Snoozing on the chaise, he opened one eye at the sound of his name, found nothing of interest, and promptly closed it.

"Well, yes, though I have every confidence in Forbes that he won't get too lonely. Jack likes to have him romp about the garden, too."

Folding a dress in tissue paper, Beckett turned scarlet.

Ah. Why had Addie not seen it before? But if a romance was meant to be, it could survive five months and an ocean. And so she'd told Lucas.

Though she never told him she'd suspected him of killing two people on her property. That was all Mr. Dumont's and his inconsiderate spirits' fault anyway.

"I'll leave you to it. Have I told you lately how pleased I am with your service, Beckett? I think you're due for a raise."

The little maid dropped Addie's favorite black silk crepe dress. "A raise! That's very good of you, Lady Adelaide. I'm sure I don't deserve it."

"Nonsense. You'll want to save for your future, I imagine. I do hope you don't decide to leave me, though."

"Oh, no, My Lady. I like it here."

Epilogue

Compton Chase, Compton-Under-Wood, Gloucestershire,
a morning in late September 1924

"I think that's all." Addie's clothes were piled on the bed like a convention of crows—a murder of crows was the correct terminology, but she was done with murder and all things relating to it. She'd even tossed her mysteries away—well, given them to Mrs. Franklin's little lending library corner in the shop. Someone with better brains than she could puzzle out the endings.

"Very good, Lady Adelaide. I'll get right to packing." Two enormous Louis Vuitton steamer trunks stood open on the carpet, and more cases were stacked in the corner.

Addie stared hard at Beckett. For the past month, her maid had turned over a brand new leaf of subdued deference and diligence.

It was all wrong somehow.

"You do want to go, don't you?" she asked her maid. "It's New York! Broadway! All the movie theaters you could ask for. We'll see the very first Macy's Thanksgiving Day parade! Everyone loves a parade." The day after tomorrow Addie, her mother, her sister, and their maids were booked on the *Aquitania* for a crossing from Southampton, to be followed by five months' accommodation in a Park Avenue duplex belonging to one of Lady Broughton's friends.

Addie could see why—Jack Robertson was a charmer. And hard-working, too. She should really order those cottages knocked down and rebuilt before the weather turned. Jack's and Beckett's could be all on one level. She'd talk to her estate manager tomorrow.

She practically skipped downstairs, filled with goodwill. She was going on an adventure! She'd never been in a boat bigger than an English Channel ferry, had never seen a skyscraper, had never visited a speak-easy, which was first on her to-do list.

If she got arrested, could she drop Inspector Hunter's name? Probably not. He'd have no jurisdiction in the United States, and would be far too far away to help. Addie had received a letter from his superior, Deputy Commissioner Olive, thanking her for her part in capturing Colonel Mellard. She would miss his trial, which suited her to the ground. The whole affair had been a lesson to her—trust no one.

Gosh, that sounded cynical. But it was time she looked out and stood up for herself. If she decided to marry again, at least she could have a few memorable flings before another diamond ring was put on her finger. Nothing serious. *Carpe diem.* After all, look what had happened to Rupert and Kathleen, cut down in their prime.

Oh, who was she kidding? Addie was a serious person. And her mother would take her chaperone duties seriously as well. What Addie needed was a diversion for the woman—some nice New York millionaire who wasn't scared of an English marchioness.

Maybe two more nice New York millionaires who weren't scared of an English marchioness' daughters would be available as well. Millionaires for everyone!

But money wasn't everything. Character counted.

And when Addie thought of character, she thought of Devenand Hunter, whom she would never see again. Unless she could lure him back here without producing a dead body.

She'd have to give it some consideration. She had five months to think, after all.

To see more Poisoned Pen Press titles:

Visit our website:
poisonedpenpress.com
Request a digital catalog:
info@poisonedpenpress.com

Robinson, Maggie

Nobody's Sweetheart now

DATE DUE			
JAN 0 1 2019			
JAN 2 8 2019			

PROSPECT LIBRARY

Prospect Free Library

0001500142078